DACOBRA

DACOBRA

or

The White Priests of Ahriman

BY

HARRIS BURLAND

AUTHOR OF "THE UNSPEAKABLE THING, ETC.

WILDSIDE PRESS

Published by:

Wildside Press
P.O. Box 301
Holicong, PA 18928-0301
www.wildsidepress.com

To
Lillah

CONTENTS

DACOBRA

OR

THE WHITE PRIESTS OF AHRIMAN

CHAPTER I

A LEGEND OF PERSIA

I SET forth this plain tale of my own experiences at
Ardrachan, in the county of Stormshire, on the west
coast of Scotland, knowing, as I write, that I can
hurt the feelings of no man, for the last survivor of
a strange tragedy is dead. I can only hope that
the personal shortcomings of the narrator will not
entirely destroy such interest as might be felt in a
story of unusual facts and circumstances.

For myself, if you care to have a description of
me at the time of these events, I was forty years of
age, tall and thin, with a face that did not pretend
to be anything but gaunt and ill-favoured, a skin
burnt dark brown with a year's travel in the East,
and scarred from lip to forehead with a dull red

A *

gash, strong teeth, a hearty appetite, and a vigorous
constitution, which has stood more strains and
privations than I trust it is ever likely to meet with
again.

I am a sculptor by profession, and I came to
Ardrachan in January, 1895, to design and execute
what I hoped would prove the great work of my life.
I had so far been fortunate enough to make a
considerable name for myself by perpetuating the
features of uninteresting people in marble, and had
made no small amount of money. But on my return
from a long holiday in the East I resolved to cut
myself free from London and its continual shower
of commissions, and to devote myself in quiet and
solitude to something more worthy of my art.

The idea that I had in my mind was a representa-
tion of Ormuzd and Ahriman, the two deities of the
Zoroastrian religion, fighting for the control of the
life of man. I had roughly sketched out Ahriman
as a squat figure, muscular to the point of deformity,
with an evil but handsome face. Ormuzd I had
depicted as fair and tall, with splendid limbs. The
combat was to be rather suggested than represented.
Between them lay the body of a beautiful woman
with closed eyes. By her side crouched Ahriman,
the Prince of Darkness, his evil eyes fixed on her
face, and one of her hands clasped in his vigorous
fingers. Ormuzd, the splendid God of Light, knelt
at her head with one hand upon her brow, and his
own eyes turned with scorn and loathing toward his
opponent. On the ground lay the pieces of two

broken swords, suggesting that the physical combat was over, and that the battle had resolved itself into one of will and intellect.

This somewhat strange and unusual subject had been suggested to me by the following circumstances.

Like most men, I have a hobby outside my profession. I am an earnest student of biology, and take almost as much interest in this relaxation of my leisure hours as in the work which brings me in my daily bread.

I think the imaginative side of the science attracted me to what may seem a rather dull pursuit. It fascinated me to let my mind play about the border-land which lies between life and death, and I pursued the subject into many bye-paths that would seem ridiculous and even puerile to the professional scientist. I ransacked all literature and many places, not indeed for scientific " facts," which often in a hundred years are relegated to the dust heap of " exploded ideas," but for some explanation of those tales and traditions of centuries which form the foundation of most of the religions of the world—the stories of the dead raised to life ; the dark superstitions of savage races ; the legends of China and Hindustan; the weird narrative of the Arabian Nights, and even the fairy tales of all lands, now thought only fit for the minds of children. All these exercised a peculiar fascination over me. Scientists had no explanation for them beyond the statement that they had their origin in the imaginations of simple savages, and that the original facts had been so overlaid with poetical imagery as to be nothing more than incredible fiction, acceptable to the ignorant, but ludicrous to men of learning and discrimination. But it pleased me to think otherwise, and to believe that there was a solid substratum of fact in some of these traditions, and certainly in many cases I had reason to think that science did not provide the best explanation of the problems of life.

Now at the beginning of the year 1894 there fell into my hands a profoundly interesting book. I discovered the volume on an old book-stall in Paris. It was entitled "The White Priests of Ahriman," and printed in the Persian tongue, and I was induced to buy it—though at that time I did not understand the language—by the fact of its being offered for a few centimes, and the somewhat quaint character of the binding. A friend of mine, who is a Persian scholar, and who has published a book on his travels in Kurdistan, saw it one day in my rooms, and was kind enough to translate the title and one or two paragraphs for me. I was so interested in these fragments that I paid for a complete translation, and was well rewarded for the expenditure of the money.

Ahriman, as most people know, is the Zoroastrian God of Evil, and scarcely inferior to Ormuzd himself. The book told how in the far past this "Prince of Darkness" had fought with the "Prince of Light" for the possession of the gift of life. At one time the contest was so fierce and so equal that Ormuzd, fearful of his supremacy, suggested a truce and the possibility of an equitable arrangement.

Ahriman asked for power over one hundred lives as a guarantee of good faith, so to speak. This was granted, but before negotiations proceeded much further, the "Prince of Light" rose in renewed strength, routed his enemy, and refused to make further parley.

These hundred lives, so the book went on, were known as the White Priests of Ahriman, and were driven forth from their fellow-men to the eternal darkness of some gorge in the Kohrud Mountains, and condemned to live forever; but—and this was the special point of interest to me—it was alleged that not only had these men the gift of eternal life, but they had the power to take any life voluntarily offered to them and keep it bound in some form or other on the earth for ever.

The author of the book went on to discuss this legend calmly and scientifically, not in the words of a simple believer, nor yet quite like an ordinary scientist, but with the voice of one who discusses not the probability of a legend, but the explanation of a fact. He, moreover, definitely asserted that to this day the White Priests were known to be living in the Kohrud Mountains.

I am not ashamed to say that I was profoundly impressed with the story. I was at the time greatly in need of a holiday, having worked unceasingly for five years in the noise and bustle of London, and my brain was tired with the hard struggle for fame and fortune. I thought that a change would do me good. My imagination had been stimulated by the story I had read, and I resolved to go to Persia.

I drew five hundred pounds from the bank, and through the good offices of my friend, the explorer, managed to get myself attached to a scientific expedition which was starting to the snow-bound fastnesses of those very mountains in which the White Priests were still said to live. Some of the party were in search of flowers and insects; some in search of birds and animals; one, at least, had come out to study mankind; and another to study the language and religion of the country. There were several geologists, and it was hoped that disputes as to the rock formation of the Kohrud Mountains would be finally settled. Everyone had his work mapped out. I alone was the free lance of the party.

And, personally, I was not much interested in the substance of the ground we traversed, nor in the insects which crawled over it. I was more engrossed in the wild magnificence of the mountains; and, indeed, I do not think that I had ever seen more striking grandeur of scenery in any part of the world. The vast craggy ravines from whose depths the clouds drifted like smoke, now gray, now white, now golden and rose as the sun caught them; the long rolling slopes of snow; the far-off peaks of range upon range of hills, belted with mist and crowned with fire; the black precipices falling away beneath our feet, often to the depth of half a mile;

the fearful snow-storms sweeping all unprotected life before them into one white grave; the gorgeous sunsets and the long indigo shadows on the plains; the ghostly desolation and silence which hung over everything, all combined to produce a profound impression on my mind. Here, indeed, was a land in which anything might happen and anything exist. It was ridiculous that men should collect insects in a place where they themselves seemed so small and insignificant.

The expedition was full of interest, but I found no confirmation of the story beyond certain vague legends in some of the most remote villages in the mountains. They agreed in some particulars, but were so overlaid by the speaker's fancy that it was difficult to connect the different accounts.

There were, of course, dark caves inhabited by devils, mysterious disappearances from the villages, men who went out hunting and came back raving madmen, with wild words on their lips, strange sounds in the gorges at night, a bottomless precipice, where a man could push over a ton of stone and never hear it fall, and similar tales that are usually current with imaginative races whose lives are passed in the remote and scarcely explored regions of the earth. But I neither saw nor heard anything myself, though I followed up every clue; and anyone who knows the almost impassable nature of some of that mountain country will realise that I did not waste my time. The expedition was in other ways a complete success. Several absolutely new specimens of flora and fauna were discovered; the geological formation of the Kohrud Mountains was mapped out for a considerable portion of their area, and an exhaustive account of modern Zoroastrianism, which still survives and flourishes in the provinces of Yezd and Kirman, was written by the Rev. Dr. Lindsay. And not the least interesting discovery was made by Professor Tiernay, who found the complete skeletons of two small monkeys in one of the deep gorges. Now there are no monkeys in Persia, and he looked in vain for any living specimens, though one old man told him that about fifty years ago he had seen something like the picture that Tiernay drew of one; but Tiernay was not an artist, and the man might have been mistaken. When he got home, it was suggested by a rival scientist that the carcases had been carried in from India by eagles.

For my part I brought back no information at all on the subject of my inquiries, but I returned with fresh life and vigour in both brain and body, and with the half-formed idea of a work which I hoped might keep my name alive for many years after my death.

CHAPTER II

IT was to accomplish this work that I came to Ardrachan, and took the house on a yearly tenancy. The place had been the home of a rich but unsuccessful sculptor, and possessed a fine studio. It also contained what it would have been hard to find elsewhere, a magnificent block of Carrara marble, which the former owner had purchased and placed in his studio at enormous expense a month before his death.

The place stood about three miles from the sea, in a deep valley, sheltered from the north and west winds. I often stood in the wooded grounds of the estate and watched the leaves scarcely rustle on the trees, though I could hear the gales go shrieking and roaring overhead, and see the clouds of mist whirled past like the smoke of a furnace.

The house itself was not more than fifty years old, and built with a square solidity that aimed rather at practical comfort than any architectural pretensions. The grounds were about twenty-eight acres in extent, and were laid out with all the care and skill that an eminent Scotch gardener could bestow upon them.

The lawns were green, soft, and perfectly kept, and even in the month of February the garden was gay with crocus and snowdrops, and a few hardy flowers of early spring.

I 'could scarcely have found a quieter or more suitable place for a work which would demand the whole of my thoughts and energies. The solitude was splendid. The nearest town of any importance was ten miles away, and the village of Ardrachan itself contained but twenty houses.

Seven miles along the coast there was a larger village of some five hundred inhabitants ; it was called Balath, and was chiefly famous for its castle, which had frowned across the sea for seven hundred years. There was no other house within six miles, and the rocky monotony of the shore was only broken by a few fishermen's huts, scattered at long intervals in little gaps and inlets, where some mountain torrent had cut its path down to the sea.

Six months passed away quickly and uneventfully in this quiet and remote place. At the end of that time I had conceived and modelled every detail of the work, and had nearly completed two of the figures in the marble itself.

During the whole period I never stirred outside the grounds, and saw no living soul except my servants, and the one or two models which I obtained with some difficulty from the countryside. A few people called on me, but a brief letter of apology explained that I was grateful for their kindness, and that the results of a severe illness alone prevented me from returning their courtesy. I do not approve of social lies, and only stoop to them in extreme cases, but I felt that if my mind was to be concentrated on my work, and if I was to make it something out of the common, I must be absolutely undisturbed by engagements of any kind whatever. When the ice of solitude is once broken, it is easy to fall straight into the deep waters of dinner and garden parties. Even my hobby was now laid aside; I had no time for playing with the mysteries of science. I was working at concert pitch, with one idea in my mind, and striking one string till the whole of my existence vibrated to that note. All else was forgotten, laid aside, thrust clean out of my mind.

Nothing occurred to break this monotony of solitude and hard work until the night of August 5th—I remember the date well—when an event happened, which, in spite of its trivial character, was the precursor of many strange circumstances, and which at the time filled me with a wholly unreasonable sense of fear.

It was, I remember, a very hot night, and the valley was as close and stifling as the stoke-hole of a liner. I went to bed at eleven o'clock, leaving both windows and the door of my room open, in order to get as much air as possible. But I was quite unable to get to sleep, and lay awake listening to the clock in the hall striking quarter after quarter until it was half-past one. I was in that uneasy state of mind which precludes all possibility of rational thought, although it does not allow the brain to rest. Ridiculous and fantastic ideas in connection with my work floated before my eyes, and circled aimlessly round and round in an endless procession, only broken by the periodical chiming of the clock.

Then at last I fell asleep, and the same ideas continued to course through my dreams, until some noise suddenly woke me with a start, and I sat up in bed and listened, trying to make out what had roused me.

I could not have been asleep long, for it was still dark, and the windows only appeared as faint patches of iron-grey against an inky background. I listened attentively, but could hear nothing except the ticking of my watch by the bedside.

Then suddenly my Irish terrier, who always sleeps on a cushion in the corner of my room, gave a short sharp bark, and began to growl ominously. I guessed then that he had roused me from my sleep. I struck a match, but could see nothing at all likely to make him bark, and coming to the conclusion that he was chasing rats in his dreams, I threw a slipper at him, and called him up on to the bed. He came at once, but continued to growl. I struck another match, and saw that his eyes were fixed on one of the windows. I could see nothing there, and cuffed him sharply across the head, but without effect. He yelped, and then went on snarling. I could see in the dim light that his teeth were bared, and that the hair on his back was ruffled with rage.

I got out of bed, lit the lamp, and made a

thorough examination of the place. While I did
so, the dog stood with his paws on the window sill
and barked furiously. I looked out, but there was
nothing to be seen.

Then I began to get angry with him ; it was bad
enough to have a restless night, but perfectly
maddening to be roused out of one's only short
period of sleep by a dog barking at nothing. I led
him by the scruff of the neck to the door, and gave
him a kick which sent him half-way down the stairs;
then I shut the door, put out the lamp, and went
back to bed.

I was just dozing off to sleep again, when I heard
a faint scratching sound. I could not tell from what
part of the room it came, but thinking that it was the
dog asking to be let in, I told him to lie down, and
threw a boot at the door to emphasise my command.

For a minute there was silence ; then the scratching began again, and the door came unlatched with a
faint click. I heard no sound of the handle being
turned, and I thought that I had only half-closed it,
and that the dog had pushed it open.

This idea was confirmed when I heard the patter
of claws across the oil-cloth, and felt something jump
up on my bed.

I called out to him, and there came a responsive
bark from the hall. I am not ashamed to confess
that a faint shiver passed over me. It was not the
dog on the bed after all. I reached out for the match
box, but could not find it ; then I remembered that
I had moved it when I lit the lamp.

I laughed, for the idea struck me that it was only a cat after all, and reaching down to the bottom of the bed, I aimed a sharp blow at the place where the animal was. My hand encountered soft fur, and the thing sprang off the bed, squeaking and chattering. It was certainly not a cat. I whistled for Rags, who was still barking in the hall, and he came rushing up the stairs and into the room. Then he appeared to stop short, and began to growl and whine.

"Cats!" I cried. "Good dog! Cats!"

There was a sudden dash, a yelp and a squeak, and for a single moment I saw against the faint outline of the open window a small dark object like a cat sitting up on its hind legs. Then it vanished.

I sprang out of bed and lit the lamp. The dog was trying to get on to the window sill, and was furious with excitement. I held the light outside the window, and saw something small and white at the bottom of the rain-pipe, twenty feet below. Before I could get hold of anything to throw at it, it had hopped quickly across the grass and disappeared into the shrubbery.

A sensible man would doubtless have gone back to bed, and tried to snatch an hour or two's sleep; but my curiosity was now aroused, and I made up my mind to investigate the matter. I hurriedly slipped on a pair of flannels and a Norfolk jacket, thrust my feet into some socks and boots, and went downstairs, followed by the dog.

I took a stick from the rack, and opened the hall-door quietly. Rags dashed round the corner of the house, eager with all the excitement of the chase, and barking furiously. A window opened at the top of the house, and a tousled head was thrust out. It was the footman, with waking visions of burglars. He called out, inspired with a faint hope of being answered.

" All right, John," I replied ; " I am only taking a stroll."

He recognised my voice, and closed the window with a bang. I followed the dog to the lawn underneath my window.

There was absolute silence, save for the chirping of a cricket and the rustling of leaves as the dog searched about the shrubbery. I crossed the lawn and called to him. He came running towards me, wagged his tail, and darted off again among the bushes. I followed him, and grasping my stick firmly, plunged into the dense mass of laurels and rhododendrons, which were nearly ten feet high, and shut out every glimmer of light from my eyes.

I groped my way as best I could, following the sound of the dog's movements. It was impossible to see anything, but he appeared to be on the track of some animal, as I could hear him sniffing among the dead leaves.

Then suddenly a faint light filtered through the dense branches overhead, and looking up, I saw that the moon was shining. At first I thought that I was dreaming, for it was an absolutely moonless night. I rubbed my eyes and looked again ; it was undoubtedly moonlight, and I could distinguish the full white circle

in the west.   A spray of laurestinus was silhouetted
against it, as though it had been cut out of ebony.

At the same moment the dog began to howl, and
came running back to my feet.   A patch of light fell
on him, and I saw that his tail was tucked down
tight between his legs.   I pushed forward, and
noticed that there was a broad open space of light
ahead.   Now the shrubbery here is nearly seven
acres in extent, and though I had often explored
it, I did not remember a single opening of this
sort in all its mass of bushes.   I concluded that I
had gone farther than I had thought, and come out
to the far side of it.

I moved towards the open space, and as I did so
the air seemed to grow more close and sultry, and it
was filled with the perfume of flowers, though I could
not recognise the scent of any particular one that I
knew.

Then I suddenly passed out from the semi-darkness
into the light, and at the same moment I stepped
back with a cry of surprise.   I was standing on the
brink of a precipice, and before me lay not the
smooth field and wooded hill of my estate, but a
long vista of moonlit cloud, and rugged gorge, and
towering mountains.

I clung to one of the bushes with my left hand.
There was a faint mist over the whole picture, which
only intensified the grandeur of the scenery, and the
awful depths which fell away beneath my feet.   I
stared as if in a trance.   Then something moved on
my right, and I seemed to be brought back to earth

again ; it was something small and white, and it was sitting on the very edge of the precipice. I raised my stick and struck at it, and as I did so, the whole scene faded into darkness, and moving a step forward I ran my head into a dense clump of rhododendrons.

I passed my hand across my eyes and stared into the darkness, then slowly retraced my steps towards the lawn. The chase of animals appealed no more to me that night ; but the scene I had just looked upon was imprinted deeply on my brain, and as I forced my way through the shrubbery it seemed to me that it was not entirely unfamiliar.

I re-entered the house, locked the hall-door, and went to bed. But I slept no more that night. For some reason or other I was afraid. I tried to laugh my fears away, and persuade myself that there was nothing to be frightened of ; but for all that I kept the lamp burning until the room was flooded with sunlight.

CHAPTER III

WHAT I FOUND ON THE ROCKS

AFTER this occurrence I had good reason to think that my nerves had been affected by overwork, and that it would be good for me to slow down the engines. One is but a machine after all, and the spirit has to accommodate itself to the strength of the machinery and the amount of fuel at its disposal. So the following morning I left the grounds for the first time, and walked along the cliffs towards Balath.

It was a glorious summer day, and the white haze hung over the sea like a shroud. The water was calm as a lake, and no ship broke the monotony of its surface. There was complete silence, save for the gentle splash of the waves rippling on the shore, and the incessant, weird calls of the sea-gulls that circled round the cliffs and floated between their summits and the sea six hundred feet below.

At this point there was no possibility of descending to the beach, but when I had walked two or three miles along the cliffs, the shore suddenly curved round in a little bay, and the cliffs ran down in grassy slopes to the sea. I descended here to the shingle.

The grass on the slopes was short and springy to the feet, and covered so thickly with flowers that it was impossible to set one's foot down without crushing them, while the air was so bright with the wings of butterflies that it seemed as if all insect life had gathered to this sheltered spot.

I ran down the slope, feeling fresh life in my veins with every step and every breath of the soft air from the sea. The studio was forgotten, and the very stones of the shingle seemed a pleasant change from the smooth green lawns that I saw every day. Even the science of biology seemed nothing to me now. Here was the blue sea, and here the freedom of life and all the quiet of Nature, which does not trouble whence it came, nor why.

I walked along the beach, and, crossing the bay, made my way under the cliffs. The tide was coming in, but there was still a strip of shingle fifty feet wide to walk upon, and I thought I could easily go for some distance along the coast and return if there were no other break in the cliffs. But progression was difficult; the stones were just the wrong size— too small to tread firmly from one to the other, and too large to crush comfortably under foot. At the end of an hour's walking I had barely progressed two miles, and was already ·beginning to feel tired. I sat down on a large boulder, and, pulling out my pipe, settled myself comfortably for a few minutes' rest. The cliffs here were seven hundred feet in height, not absolutely sheer, but sloping back about ten degrees from the perpendicular, and the surface

was broken up into ledges and patches of grass. It
would have been possible for an active man to have
climbed them, if it had been a matter of life and
death to do so, but he would have required nerves of
steel and the sure foot of a chamois. Far up the
slopes I saw some mountain sheep grazing ; they
were about half-way down the cliff, and looked like
fat white flies ; they moved about with absolute
freedom and unconcern from one patch of grass to
another, and seemed to pass along little cracks in the
sheer face of the cliff as easily as though it were a
high-road.

I watched them with interest until one of them
dislodged a stone of about a pound or two in weight,
which fell with terrific force on a boulder not two
yards from where I was sitting, and ricochetted like
a cannon ball into the sea. Then I rose, and,
retreating to the water's edge, looked at them from
a less dangerous place.

As I did so, there was a sudden stir among them,
and they all began to move and turn in one direction
towards the summit, not, as before, proceeding
leisurely, and stopping to graze on the way, but
scurrying quickly and eagerly, as though something
had frightened them. I thought at first that I had
caused the alarm, and that perhaps they had heard
the crunching of the pebbles under my feet. But I
saw on reflection that this was absurd, as I had made
just as much noise before, when I had approached
them along the beach, and they had taken not the
slightest notice of me.

In two or three minutes· they had all reached the top and disappeared out of sight.

But there was still left a single white patch on the grass about fifty yards to the right of where they had been. I had noticed this before, and was not quite certain if it were a sheep or merely a large white stone. It was barely a third of the size of the others, and had not moved since I had first looked at it. I thought it might be a lamb having its first lesson in mountaineering and too frightened to move, but I recollected that lambs were larger than this in August.

I watched the white spot with interest, and began to realize that it was neither a lamb nor a white stone, but some other living creature which had frightened the sheep. I had not seen it move, but of course it might have done so while I was not looking; in fact, I had not noticed it particularly until the sheep began to stir, and then it caught my eye by the fact of its not hurrying away with the rest. I picked up a stone and threw it as far as I could up the cliff. I can throw a cricket ball a hundred yards, but throwing a stone almost straight up into the air is a different matter. It struck the cliff about fifty feet below the patch of grass. The noise was sufficient to alarm the thing, whatever it was, and it began to move more quickly than any sheep could have done, running swiftly across the grass with a curious hopping motion, and swinging itself easily from ledge to ledge. I recalled the events of the previous night, for the animal's movements reminded me of the little creature that had hopped across the grass into the shrubbery. Now in the daylight it reminded me very much of a monkey, but one does not expect to see monkeys running at large on the west coast of Scotland. An Englishman's love of killing anything unusual, and having it stuffed, rose within me. It is this love of sport that is wiping out all rare animals in every land. But it is ineradicable. If I had had a rifle with me I should have tried to bring the animal down, and might have succeeded at that distance. As it was, I had only a stone, and I prayed that the creature might be foolish enough to descend within range. However, it declined to gratify my prayer, and moved along the side of the cliff towards Balath.

The excitement of the chase was now strong enough to induce me to trudge a little farther along the beach up to the next point, which ran some way out into the sea, and which looked low enough at its base for a man to climb over to the other side. It did not take me ten minutes to reach it, and I saw that it could easily be surmounted. It was composed of large masses of rock, which had evidently fallen at some time or other from the face of the cliff and were now piled up to a height of about thirty feet from the shingle. The masses of granite were still rugged and broken, and I was not long in getting to the top.

Here I saw for the first time the towers of Balath Castle, famed in Scottish song and history as the home of the Black Knight of Balath. The cliffs beyond the point on which I stood swept back in a sharp curve, and, gradually sloping down to a height of not more than two hundred feet, ran out in another point into the sea a mile farther on. The castle stood at the extreme end of this point. A large part of the building was in ruins, and the broken ivy-covered walls stretched along the cliff for at least one hundred yards, but the keep and one wing of the building had been restored, and I could see the sunlight on the windows and the new patches of stonework.

I had gathered from my valet that the place had been bought by a Dr. Rawlins, who lived there with his daughter. At first I thought it was a little strange that he alone of all the people within a radius of fifteen miles had not called on me, as Balath was the nearest house of any importance to my own. But I understood from the servants' gossip that he and his daughter held no intercourse with anyone; that they were rarely seen even in their own village; and that he was, in my servant's own phraseology, "a scientific gentleman who kept himself to himself"; from which I gathered that he was probably like myself, a man engaged in some work which demanded all his time, and unwilling to be interrupted by any social duties or observances. At the same time I felt sorry for the girl, who would scarcely be so interested in scientific research as in the display of a new hat at an occasional garden party. I looked at the building across the bay with some curiosity for a minute or two, and then turned to see what had become of the white animal on the cliffs. Whatever it was, it had disappeared entirely. I examined the face of the rock carefully for some sign of a white patch or for the movement of any living thing, but I could discover nothing. My walk had made me hungry, and looking at my watch, I saw that I had just time to get home to dinner, so I began to descend the rock again to the shingle.

Just at that moment, however, I heard the bark of a dog, apparently close to my feet, and I looked back towards the castle. I could not see the animal, but it continued to bark furiously. The pile of broken rock upon which I was standing was about thirty feet in width, and I remembered that I had not been right across it. The dog was evidently barking at something, and I thought that probably the animal I was in search of was there. I crossed the ledge quickly, and, as I did so, I heard a howl and the scratching and scrambling of claws on the rocks, and then a thud on the beach, as though something were trying to scale the rock and had fallen backwards. I looked over the ledge and saw a black and tan collie, with its paws dug forward into the shingle and its head thrown back, barking apparently at nothing. When he saw me he ran to the foot of the rocks and tried to scramble up again. There was evidently nothing there or he would have been looking under the ledge instead of trying to get up to me.

Then I noticed that the great boulders on this side had fallen in such a manner that the topmost ones overhung the beach, and consequently I could not see into the hollow underneath. So I risked being bitten by the dog and climbed down on the chance of finding something. To my surprise, as I descended to the ground, I caught sight of a foot sticking out from under the ledge, and, on drawing closer, I saw the body of a woman.

I hesitated for a moment, as I saw she was absolutely still, and that the dog had begun to whine and lick her foot. It almost looked as if she had been drowned, and cast up by the tide. Then I walked quickly up to her, half afraid of what I might see.

It was a young and beautiful girl ; her face was a dead white, her eyes closed, and her black hair had come partly uncoiled and lay in dark masses round her head. I could see at once that she had not been drowned, and stooping down, I laid my hand on her pulse. It beat very feebly, but she was certainly alive. She had evidently fainted. I rose to my feet, and going down to the sea, filled my cap with water, and dashed it over her face. This I repeated two or three times until her hair was soaked, and little streams began to run down her neck. I wondered whether she would be grateful to me for making her in such a mess. Then she shivered, and opening her eyes, gave a little moan of pain.

" Oh ! " she said, sitting up sharply, and rubbing her knuckles into her eyes.

" Excuse me," I replied, " I had to do it. Can I help you ? "

She ran one hand through her damp hair, and a

faint colour came to her cheek. Then she tried to do up the wet coils, but the effort appeared too much for her ; her face grew white as a sheet, and, biting her lips with pain, she sank back on the shingle and moaned pitifully.

"My ankle!" she gasped. "It is awful."

"May I see to it for you?" I said, looking at her little feet.

"Yes, please ; it's the left one."

I stooped down and touched it gently. It was swollen to about twice its natural size. It was evidently a bad sprain. I had little or no surgical knowledge, save that which comes to a man who has often had to shift for himself, but I thought I could not go far wrong if I bandaged it. So I dipped my handkerchief in the sea, and bound it round the swollen part as tightly as I could. She winced with pain as I touched her, but she was a brave little thing, and said nothing until I had finished. Then she smiled.

"Thank you so much," she said. "You must think me very silly, but I twisted my foot on a stone. It seems such a little thing, but it hurts a good deal."

"I must carry you home," I said. "Where shall I take you?"

"I live at Balath."

"Miss Rawlins?" I queried.

She nodded.

I took off my cap and bowed.

"My name is Lionel Maxwell," I said. "I live at

Ardrachan. I can easily carry you if you will let me."

" I am eight stone," she replied, and began to look about in the pebbles with a troubled expression.

" You have lost something ; can I find it for you ? "

" I can't see any of them," she answered, with a forlorn expression on her face.

" What have you lost ? "

" Hairpins," she said wistfully. " I cannot move until I find them."

I went on my knees and searched carefully until I had found three. If they had been sovereigns she could not have looked more pleased. She put them in her mouth, and, deftly coiling up her damp hair, pinned it together with three sharp stabs.

" Now," she said with a smile, " I am ready."

I picked her up as gently as possible, but I could see the tears of pain come into her eyes. At first she felt light as a feather, but it was a good mile and a half to Balath Castle, and I had to put her down two or three times on the way and rest. It is not easy to carry eight stone over rocks and shingle for a mile, where one has to look at the next spot to step on, or else to wade along ankle deep in small pebbles. I am not ashamed to say that, though I am fairly strong and muscular, I am not one of those heroes of romance who carry rescued damsels in one hand, while with the other they scale impregnable fortresses. If these intervals for rest served no other purpose, they gave opportunities for conversation.

" It was lucky I came across you," I said to her,

while we both sat on a boulder about half a mile from our destination. " I might not have heard your dog bark."

" Good old Sam !" she cried, patting the dog on the head. " I think he was frightened."

" I thought he was barking at something else," I replied.

"Yes," she continued, in a low voice ; "it was fortunate you came across me. I could not move. The tide would have been up in less than two hours, and they might not have come to look for me by then, though this is my only walk."

" Your only walk ? " I asked, with surprise.

" Yes. Father won't let me go inland, nor in the villages, nor on the top of the cliffs. Why do you laugh ? He wishes me to have as much sea air as possible, and the cliffs are dangerous. I am not strong ; you can see that. Do you think I should have fainted at such a little sprain if I had been strong ? But I was very ill two years ago."

" I am awfully sorry. You do not look strong," I said, "and I am sorry I laughed ; but it seems so odd for you not to be allowed anywhere ; quite like a little child."

She gave a slight pout, and looked at me with a quaint expression of amusement.

" I am only a little child," she said, looking at me with serious eyes. " You can't guess how young I am."

" I never guess a lady's age," I replied solemnly. " It is dangerous."

"No, guess; really. I shall not be cross with you."

"All right." I answered, "but you must take the consequences. Let me look at you closely."

She turned her face towards me with a look of mock solemnity and a comical little smile; but I could see at the same time, from the expression of her eyes and the occasional quiver of her lips, that she was suffering intense pain. "Here is a brave little woman," I said to myself, "that can make fun while she suffers agony. She must have known a great deal of pain in her life, or she could not bear it so well." I looked at her intently for about a minute. It was a beautiful face, mobile and sensitive to a degree, and almost piquant at times, though it was not the face of a girl with either a light heart or an empty head. I could see that much in the large grey eyes; there were shadows in those eyes, and not the mere shadows of temporary pain. They were the eyes of a woman with a fine soul, and of a woman who had thought, and had suffered. She flushed as I looked at her. I think she felt that I was trying to read her character rather than her age.

"Well," she said petulantly, "have you done? or would you like to see my teeth?"

I woke up from my study. Her personality interested me, if her age did not. I made a random guess.

"You are twenty," I said. Twenty is a safe age. Whether a woman is fifteen or fifty, she is not likely to be offended.

"You are wrong," she replied; "I am only *two*. Quite a child, you see."

She spoke with perfect gravity; there was not even a twinkle in her eyes.

"You look astonished," she continued, "but I am really only two years old—not bodily, of course, but mentally."

"Please explain!" I said humbly. "I must confess you are beyond my depth."

"The tide is coming in," she said. "May I talk to you as you carry me? You need not speak, as I know you want all your breath."

I picked her up again, and as we continued our journey she proceeded to explain.

"Two years ago," she said, "I had a severe illness. I remember nothing whatever of my life before that illness; in fact, it has cut my existence into two parts, and if you come to think of it, I am really two people. One of them (the one before my illness) is dead for all practical purposes. That Miss Rawlins has no connection with the present Miss Rawlins, for the link is absolutely broken. The memory of all that passed before that day has vanished so completely that I speak the truth when I say I am a little child, and scarcely more than two years of age. I had to learn even to read and write."

"What an extraordinary experience!" I said. I was beginning to be interested in this girl. I knew from the first that there was something uncommon about her.

"Yes," she replied; "it is not very pleasant to learn to read and write when one has grown up. Of course I learnt very quickly. In a way it came back to me almost mechanically, because I suppose these sort of things only require an effort of memory, and the mere suggestion is sufficient to set the machinery working again. But all events, and people, and everything I had ever seen, done, or heard, were completely forgotten."

"Of course," I said, "you have been supplied with an artificial memory; your father has filled in the blank; he has described the scenes, events, and people of these years very minutely to you. If he has placed everything chronologically and in order before you, so that you could grasp the whole course of years, and what has happened in them, you would then possess a sort of memory, defective in vividness, of course, but better than nothing."

"You must not talk so much," she said, as I gasped out this rather strong string of sentences; "and I don't think I ought to have said so much to a stranger, but I wished to amuse you; besides, you have been so kind that you are not really a stranger."

"Of course not," I replied, and with some truth, for one cannot carry a girl in one's arms for over a mile without feeling a sort of physical intimacy, at any rate.

"I am afraid I talk too much," she continued; "but a child of two will prattle. I rarely see any-one to speak to; besides, you must remember that I am now an infant in arms."

"How does your artificial memory work?" I said.

She was silent.

"Is it of no use at all?" I queried.

"I have no artificial memory," she replied, in a low voice. "My life begins from March the 15th, 1893. Of my life before that date I know absolutely nothing, for I have been told nothing. But why do you ask me about myself? It does not interest you, and I ought not to speak. If my father knew, he would be very angry; I am a chatterer."

I said nothing in reply. I only thought what a curious man her father must be, and the sense of something unusual and mysterious began to grow strong upon me. We were now almost under the walls of Balath, and I wondered how we were going to get up from the beach. There did not appear to be any steps cut in the rock, as I had expected, and the cliffs here, though much lower than I had seen in any other part of the coast, were over a hundred feet in height.

"How do we get up?" I said, looking about for some possible means of ascent.

The girl did not answer, and I saw that her eyes were closed. She had fainted again, and lay limply, like a dead body, in my arms. She had been suffering acute pain, poor little thing, all the time she had been chattering. I walked along the beach under the castle wall, and examined the rock; at the same time I gave a loud call to attract the inhabitants. There was no reply but the echo, and no one appeared at the windows or walls. The sun was setting now, and it would soon be dark; my dinner had become an impossibility. I felt tired and hungry, and laying the girl gently on the stones (the water was within five feet of the cliff) I shouted at the top of my voice. Then I ran along to the extreme end of the point, where the last flanking tower of the castle stood in ruins. The water was washing the cliff a few yards farther on. Here I caught sight of a door let into the rock. It was made of iron and painted the same colour as the cliff, so that it was impossible to distinguish it at a few yards' distance. I picked up a large stone and beat on it so vigorously that the sounds must have been audible half a mile away. In a minute or two I heard the faint sound of footsteps, and the door swung open. A gigantic Hindoo in native costume stepped under the narrow archway and confronted me.

"Miss Rawlins has had an accident," I said sharply, "and we are likely to be drowned if you do not hurry up. I have been here twenty minutes."

He bowed solemnly, but did not speak.

"She is here," I continued, and led the way to where I had laid her on the shingle. The waves had already wet the soles of her feet.

The servant showed no surprise and said nothing, but he picked her up carefully in his arms, and walked back to the entrance. When he had carried his burden inside, he began to close the door. I was astonished, and placed my foot in the opening.

"Are you going to let me drown here, you black scoundrel?" I said.

He opened the door again, and looked at me without emotion. Then it seemed to strike him that it was not a proper thing to do, and he beckoned to me to follow him.

"It is against the rules, Sahib," he said, in perfect English; "but the Sahib has rescued the little one, and my lord will forgive; moreover, the Sahib ought not to drown."

"I should think not," I cried angrily. "Take me to your master, and I will soon tell him what I think of his servants."

"The master cannot be seen," he replied, and motioned me to enter.

I stepped in, and he closed the door with a crash. There was absolute darkness.

"The Sahib will be careful," he said, and walked on in front of me, never stumbling nor hesitating in the darkness.

I followed, groping with my hands, and feeling my way so carefully with my feet that I was soon some distance behind him.

When we had ascended about a hundred steps I heard the man open a door, and saw a light. When I came up to the entrance and had passed through, I found myself in a small vaulted chamber, and as I entered, a door closed on the other side, and I heard the key turn in the lock. I was alone.

CHAPTER IV

THE MASTER OF BALATH

SUCH was the hospitality of Balath Castle.

At first I could not believe my senses. I walked to the door and shook the handle angrily, cursing Miss Rawlins and all her belongings. Then I realised the situation, and turned to go back the way I came, but I remembered that the tide was now up to the cliffs, and that I was more or less a prisoner. I looked at my watch; it was eight o'clock. My dinner was waiting for me seven miles away. I was tired and hungry with my long walk and exertions; and here I was, cooped up in a room that more resembled a prison cell than any other form of habitation. The only furniture consisted of a square oak table and a couple of massive chairs. The floor was of uncarpeted stone, and the wall was as bare as the outside of the castle. Architecturally, the place was interesting. Some small pillars and arches on one side were undoubtedly Norman, and the piece of herring-bone work in the outer wall was probably built before the Conquest of England.

There was a single small window in this wall, but the masonry was so thick and the opening so narrow that I could see nothing through it but a strip of sea and sky.

I sat down upon one of the straight-backed chairs, lighted a cigarette, and awaited further developments. So unconventional a reception could not fail to be more or less interesting, and if I had not felt so hungry, I might have been almost amused by it. But I had not to wait long. Before my cigarette was half smoked through, the key turned in the door, and the Hindoo servant entered with a white tablecloth over his arm.

" I am obliged to you," I said. " I hope you were not afraid I should steal anything. Can I see your master ? "

The servant bowed and handed me a note. The envelope was addressed in a feminine handwriting. I tore it open, and read the contents :

" Dr. Rawlins presents his compliments to Mr. Maxwell, and sends him most earnest thanks for the services rendered to his daughter. He regrets that he is at present in the middle of a chemical experiment of so delicate a nature that it is impossible for him to leave it for a minute, but he hopes that Mr. Maxwell will excuse him, and partake of such hospitality as Balath can offer him."

And then at the bottom a line in pencil in the same handwriting :

" I am so sorry ; please do not be angry.—E. R."

I was too hungry to give up the chance of a dinner for the sake of mere pride, and the postscript did much to appease me. I told the servant I should be glad to accept Dr. Rawlins' invitation, and requested him to show me the way to the dining-room.

" Dinner will be served in here, Sahib," he replied, unfolding the cloth and placing it on the table.

I shrugged my shoulders and said nothing. It was useless to be annoyed, though few people care to eat their dinner in a stone cell.

He left the room, and in a few minutes re-entered with a lamp, as it was now growing dark. He placed it on the table, and I noticed that it was a most exquisite example of the silversmith's art. Wrought by hand in the form of some grotesque bird, it was evidently of Eastern workmanship, and from its worn appearance and the rough strength of its design, must have been made several centuries ago, for modern Oriental work has degenerated with the power of the race that executed it. He then began to lay the table, and I noticed that all the silver and glass were not only of the very finest quality, but that the various articles were all of such curious and unusual designs that their owner could only have acquired them at an enormous cost and an infinite amount of trouble. The spoons and forks were of seventeenth century silver ; the tumblers and decanters were the most magnificent specimens of old cut glass that I have ever seen ; and the Venetian wine-glasses could scarcely be matched in any museum in Europe. Even flowers were not wanting, and a huge Cloisonné enamel bowl, filled with yellow and white roses, was placed in the centre of the table. The handles of this bowl were of copper gilt, in the form of the Imperial

Dragon of China, and I should say that it had been taken from the loot of the Summer Palace at Pekin.

The whole effect was too bizarre to show the most perfect taste in dinner decoration, but it was artistic, and the productions of the various ages and countries were so arranged and chosen that the whole effect was in perfect harmony. Even the colours of the Cloisonné bowl blended with the masses of roses that filled it. It was obvious to me that the touch of a feminine hand was over the whole arrangement.

When everything was ready, the Hindoo brought in a large Persian rug, about nine feet square, and laying it in the centre of the room, placed the table and one chair on it. Then he motioned me to be seated.

The dinner was not in any way inferior to the manner in which it was served. The dishes were few, but choice and cooked to perfection. The wines —if I am any judge—were superb, and everything was served quickly and silently.

The bare, cold walls of the vaulted room, and the red glow of the lamp falling on the glass and silver and exquisite flowers, made a scene of strange contrast. There was no sound to be heard but the splash of the waves on the rocks below, and the occasional cry of a seagull. The Hindoo stood behind my chair during the meal, and when it was over, he produced a box of excellent cigars. I lit one, and leaned back in my chair, completely content with the world. My anger seemed to have vanished, and even my sense of wonder at the somewhat extraordinary treatment I had met with had simmered down into a vague curiosity. The servant brought in coffee and a choice of several liqueurs, and then left me. The sound of the key turning in the lock broke in harshly on my thoughts, and reminded me that I was still a prisoner, and was not, after all, finishing a superb dinner in the Savoy or Café Royal. I rose and went to the window. By standing on the chair I got a fine view of the moonlit sea, and by raising myself up, I caught sight of one of the flanking towers of the castle rising darkly against the sky. There was no light in this tower, and no sound from any part of the building. I opened the door I had entered by, and looked down the passage. All was as dark and silent as the grave. I closed the door and turned again to the window. The heavy red shade of the lamp kept all the light from the upper part of the room, and I could see some large star or planet twinkling through the narrow slit.

Then, as I looked, a cloud seemed to pass over the lower part of the dark blue sky, and the star vanished. It was evident that something was outside the window. I walked quickly to the table and took the shade off the lamp ; the light fell full upon the embrasure, but there was nothing to be seen except a small white spot on the lower ledge, no bigger than a walnut. It was impossible to say what it was, but it might have been the paw of an animal. I went up to the window, and, as I did so, the spot vanished, and I heard a faint scratching sound on the outside, as though something were descending from crack to crack in the masonry. I gave the matter no further thought, and resuming my seat, began to wonder what sort of people these were that I had come into contact with.

Through the blue smoke of my cigar I conjured up the piquant face of my little friend, and the strange look of perpetual pain in her grey eyes, and I pictured her father to myself as a hard, cold man, who was so wrapped up in his scientific researches that he had not a word or thought of kindness for his daughter, and no more than a formal courtesy for the man who had saved her from death. My reflections were broken by the entrance of the Hindoo.

" My master would feel it an honour," he said, with a bow, "if he could have the opportunity of seeing Mr. Maxwell ; he is now at liberty."

"Present my compliments to your master," I replied, "and tell him I shall be pleased to see him here. I do not wish to intrude upon his privacy, which he has hitherto preserved by locking his doors."

The Hindoo smiled.

" My master is not as other men, Sahib," he said. " He means no unkindness, but he is engaged in a matter of life and death ; he wishes to thank the Sahib for his great services."

" I will come," I said curtly, for my desire to penetrate farther into this somewhat unusual household overcame my natural sense of irritation. I followed him to the door, which opened into a long passage, similar to the one by which I had entered. He held the lamp, which he had taken from the table, over his head, and I saw that there were two

doors at the end of the passage, one on either side.
He unlocked the left-hand one, and, when I had
passed through, locked it again. He then descended
a long flight of stone steps, and about half-way down
I noticed that the masonry of the wall ceased, and
the passage became a mere tunnel cut out of the
solid granite.

We had descended nearly a hundred steps when
my guide opened a door, and a blaze of light burst
in upon us. The room we entered was about thirty
feet square and twelve feet high, excavated apparently from the rock. It was brilliantly lit by several
lamps hanging from the ceiling, and half-a-dozen
tables were scattered about, some covered with
innumerable bottles and crucibles, and others littered
with various mechanical appliances. I recognised a
few of these as electrical instruments, but a great
many I had never seen before. In one corner of the
room a furnace blazed at white heat, and over it
stood a small man with his back turned to us.

He was silhouetted against the fierce light of the
furnace like a black shadow, and he did not move
as we entered, but lifting something white and
sparkling, dipped it two or three times into a bowl
of liquid ; it hissed violently as it touched the fluid,
and the corner of the room was filled with vapour.
Then I heard the door of the furnace close, and the
small figure came out of the mist towards me with
outstretched hands. He was not more than five feet
in height, but was so bowed with age that he might
have been a fairly tall man in his youth. His face

was as brown as that of an Indian, and his features certainly suggested an Eastern or Jewish origin. The aquiline nose, dark flashing eyes and high cheek bones were already familiar to me from my travels, and I could easily have mistaken him for a Persian if his name had not been Rawlins, and his home life and surroundings had not been so obviously English. I traced no resemblance to his daughter. She, indeed, was dark, but it was the darkness of Southern Europe rather than that of the East.

His face at a distance seemed smooth as that of a boy, but when he came closer to me I could see that his skin was crossed and recrossed with thousands of fine wrinkles. It was impossible to guess his age, but he must have been considerably over seventy.

He came towards me slowly, and taking one of my hands in his, bowed over it until his lips almost touched my fingers.

" You have saved my daughter's life, sir," he said, in a quiet and musical voice, " and I wish to thank you from the bottom of my heart. She is the only thing I have to love in the world."

"Except your scientific researches," I replied, drawing away my hand. " I have done nothing that requires thanks, sir, and you have given me an excellent dinner."

" Pardon me," he said quickly ; " you are annoyed, and justly so. Believe me, Mr. Maxwell, I would have come to you at once if it had been possible. But it was impossible. For eight hours I have not moved from the side of that furnace, and for a whole day and a whole night I have not left this room."

"I hope you have been successful, sir," I replied.

"I have failed," he said quietly, "and perhaps you would not understand me when I tell you that ultimate success is a matter of life and death to me."

"Success is the life of every man," I answered, "and failure is often worse than death."

"Ultimate failure," he said, with a keen flash from his dark eyes, "comes only with death. But sit down, Mr. Maxwell; I should like to have a talk with you, if you can spare me a few minutes."

He cleared some papers off a heavy wooden chair, and motioned me towards it with his hand. Then he handed me a cigar, and taking one himself, leaned against the edge of the table. We lit our cigars, and for a few seconds neither of us spoke.

"You are a scientist yourself, Mr. Maxwell?" he said abruptly.

"I am interested in science, but it is not my profession," I replied.

"I read an article of yours in a paper some years ago. It was an explanation of some part of the Bible."

I confess I was a little surprised at this remark. The article in question had been printed in an obscure paper, and he must have read very widely to have remembered all he read, and to have even recollected my name. I did not flatter myself that the contribution was of such unusual merit as to have remained in the mind of an ordinary magazine reader.

"Yes," I replied, "I did write such an article, but

it does not in any way express my present views on
the subject."

" I suppose not," he said, with a smile ; " but I
gather that you like the picturesque and imaginative
side of science."

" I am afraid I am not very fond of uninteresting
facts, if that is what you mean," I answered ; " but as
I said before, science is not my profession."

" All England knows that, Mr. Maxwell," he said,
with a bow, " and is glad."

His manner more and more suggested the Oriental
with every word he spoke. No Englishman would
have said a thing like that except to a lady.

" But it is in connection with your profession that
I want to speak to you. I very much wish to have
a statue of my daughter in marble. I hope that I
shall not offend you if I ask how much you would be
willing to accept for such a work ? "

" You will not offend me in the least, but it is
quite impossible for me to oblige you in the matter.
I left London on purpose to avoid all such commissions, and to devote myself entirely to the execution
of a particular work I have in hand. Until to-day I
have never even left the grounds of my house, and
every hour of daylight has been spent in my studio.
I cannot interrupt my work."

" What would be the ordinary cost of such a work
if you could do it ? "

" About five thousand pounds," I replied, naming a
high price in order to close the conversation.

" I will give you ten thousand pounds," he replied,

"if you can see your way to complete it before January 13th of next year."

I was astounded at the price he named ; I should doubt if any sculptor had ever been offered such princely terms for a mere portrait ; but I had made up my mind on this point, and it usually takes a great deal to move me from my purpose.

"Your offer is magnificent," I said ; "but you, at any rate, can understand me when I say that it is impossible for me to accept it. We both have our work to do, and allow nothing to interfere with it."

"Money is no object to me in this," he replied, watching my face keenly as he spoke.

"Nor to me either," I answered. "I do not work now to earn my living ; if I did, I should not be at Ardrachan. This work of mine, even if it realises my highest ambitions, will not sell for such a price as you have just offered me, and yet the statue of your daughter would not cost me one-tenth of the labour."

"Yet it would be possible for the statue of my daughter to be a great work. She is beautiful, if I may say so, and worthy of your great skill. Such a statue might become as famous as the portraits by Rembrandt and Sir Joshua Reynolds."

"You are persistent, Dr. Rawlins," I said ; "but you know as well as I do that when a man has one idea in his head, there is no room for any other. My whole thoughts are now saturated with one subject, and I can turn to nothing else."

"May I ask the subject of your work ?"

"Well, it is hardly a fair question, Dr. Rawlins," I

D

replied ; " an artist, you know, does not like to talk
of what he is doing until his work is finished, and
then he usually talks too much."

" At any rate, you do not mind telling me if there
is a figure of a woman in it ? "

" There is," I said, looking at him sharply.   I
guessed what was in his mind.

" You have your own ideas of the woman,
doubtless," he continued ; "perhaps you have even
modelled her ? "

" To say the truth," I replied, " I have ; but she is
the least important figure of the group, and though I
have nearly finished the other two figures in marble,
I have only roughly worked out her position in the
statue itself."

He came closer to me.   " I am making a fresh
offer to you, Mr. Maxwell," he said, fixing his eyes
on my face.   " I will purchase your work, when it is
completed, if you will take my daughter as a model
for the woman in the group."

" I do not think your daughter will consent," I
said, with a smile ; " nor, of course, would you, until
you had seen the design of the work."

" Perhaps it would not spoil the design if the
woman's figure were clothed ? "

" Oh, I did not mean that ! " I said quickly.   " I
intend the figure to be clothed ; but still, one does
not always like to be part of an allegorical subject.
However, what would you offer for the group when
completed ? "

" You said the work would not fetch what I offered

for the statue of my daughter," he replied. "But I
require it to be completed by a certain date. I will
give you twenty thousand pounds for the work if it is
finished to my satisfaction by January 13th."

For the moment I could hardly believe my ears.
It was impossible to refuse an offer that was, as far
as I knew, absolutely without precedent in the world
of art. I would rather not have been hampered in
my design by the necessity of making a perfect
likeness of my model, but it was almost impossible
to refuse such magnificent terms ; moreover, my
work would be sold before it was finished, at a price
which would be quoted in every paper in Europe,
and though the money itself was not much of an
inducement to me, still, every man likes as much
money as he can get, and likes still better to let
people know that his work can command it.

"If that is a genuine offer," I said, "I accept it."

He held out his hand and I took it.

"It is a bargain!" he exclaimed, looking me
straight in the eyes. "It must be fulfilled by
January 13th, and fulfilled to my satisfaction."

As he held my hand and looked at me, a strange
sense of future evil came over my mind, and I was
almost sorry, for the moment, that the bargain had
been made. It was of course ridiculous, as the
transaction was made in the ordinary course of
business. There was, however, a look of power,
and almost of cruelty, in the man's eyes that I had
not noticed before, and his fingers seemed cold and
tenacious as a steel vice. I noticed, too, that the

handsome mouth was very hard, that the lips were thin, and the jaws very firm and determined. Here was a man, I thought to myself, who would hold on to anything till his grip was relaxed by death. But the feeling was only momentary—a mere flash of insight into something that lay beneath the surface. His face brightened into a smile, and he loosed my hand.

"I will do my best," I said gravely, "for my own sake; but I should like you to understand that I must have an absolutely free hand in this work. I have my own ideas, and I intend to execute them. I cannot make any bargain, unless this is understood."

"Certainly, certainly!" he replied. "When I said that it must be done to my satisfaction, I only referred to the likeness of my daughter. It was hardly necessary to make such a condition to Mr. Maxwell. It will, of course, be done to my satisfaction. The time, however, is of absolute importance."

"I can do it by that date," I said, "but I am afraid it will be very tiring work for your daughter; sitting for an artist is very wearisome work, and she is not strong."

"She enjoys very good health," he replied. "Now may I ask the subject of your work?"

"If you come and see me to-morrow, I will show you the design," I said. "I can hardly describe it to you, and if I told you the source from whence I derived my inspiration, you would laugh at me."

"Very well, Mr. Maxwell," he replied, "I will call upon you to-morrow after dinner."

" I hope your daughter's accident is not likely to prove serious," I said.

" I am afraid she will be laid up for some days," he answered, " though her ankle is not so bad as you might think from the fact that she fainted with the pain."

" I must leave you now, Dr. Rawlins," I said, looking at my watch. " I am sure you will excuse me, for I am tired."

" May I order the carriage to take you back to Ardrachan ? " he queried.

I declined the offer, as it was a fine night, and I wanted as much exercise as possible. He took the lamp from one of the tables and showed me the way. When we had reached the top of the stairs and entered the passage, we passed through the opposite door into an immense drawing-room. It was dark and empty, and as we passed through it, I could see by the light of the lamp he carried that it was full of countless treasures of art. A statue of a young woman gleamed in cne corner, and he pointed it out to me.

" By Canova," he said, with a smile. " That piece in the centre is by Flaxman. There are some genuine Murillos and Greuzes on the walls ; I will show you them one day in a proper light. I only call your attention to them, so that you may know that your statue will be in good company."

" And that picture ? " I queried, as we reached the other side of the room, and a large picture loomed through the semi-darkness. I could merely distinguish the figure of a woman holding her hands uplifted to heaven, as if in supplication, but my artistic instincts told me that it was a fine piece of work. Dr. Rawlins raised the lamp, so that the light shone upon the canvas.   Then I saw that the woman's face was distorted with the most pitiful expression of terror that I have ever seen depicted by an artist's brush. Beneath her feet lay the heavy coils of a gigantic serpent, apparently dead or sleeping, and behind her, in the distance, rose range upon range of craggy mountains.   Yet, as I looked closer, I saw that a thin veil of light hung between her figure and the background. At first it seemed shapeless, but as I gazed at the misty curtain, it fashioned itself into a dim face, with long white hair and terrible eyes, and there was a look in those eyes that made me turn my face away in horror.

"What is it?" I said quickly.

He did not answer, but I thought I saw the lamp tremble in his hands.

"It is a fine work," I continued.

"Yes," he replied; "it is by an unknown artist; but it is, as you say, a fine work.   Do you observe the frame?"

I had not noticed it, for the fascination of the picture had attracted my whole attention; but I looked at it now, and saw that it was made of ivory, yellow with age, and wonderfully carved into the shapes of serpents, twisted together in a hundred coils; and the eyes of each reptile were jewels, some blue, some green, some red, some yellow, sparkling and flashing in the lamplight.   The thing must have been priceless.

"It was made for a king," he said quietly.

His voice seemed unsteady, and I glanced sharply at him as he spoke. Then I saw that his face was drawn and haggard, and that he seemed to have suddenly changed into a weak, decrepit old man. I thought that he stooped a little more than before, and that the hard lines of character on his face had softened almost to a look of senility.

I turned away from the picture, and we passed out of the door in silence, and after traversing several other rooms, all of which were in darkness, we reached the hall, and he stood on the steps to wish me good-night.

"You cannot miss your way," he said, "as the road runs straight from these gates to the village, and straight from there to Ardrachan."

"Good-night, Dr. Rawlins," I replied; "I shall see you to-morrow at nine o'clock."

He held out his hand, and I took it. The grasp was no longer firm and sinewy, but weak as that of a child, and as the lamp shone on his face, I almost fancied I saw a tear glistening in one of his eyes. I walked sharply down the drive, and looking back when I had reached the turn through some woods, I saw him still standing in the entrance, and the rays of the lamp shining on his handsome old head. The rest of the castle was in darkness. I could only see the white circle of light where he stood, and the bowed figure looking into the night. Then the trees hid him from view, and I heard the door clang as I walked quickly down the road towards Ardrachan.

CHAPTER V

"THE GREATEST WORK IN THE WORLD"

THE next morning was wet, and a rising gale from the south-west began to drive masses of grey clouds across the hills, shrouding everything in mist.

As I worked in my studio, I could hear the roar of the wind down the clefts and gullies of the mountains, and could see the trees bending and straining, as though struck with successive blows from an unseen hand.

The air was perceptibly colder, and the sight of the damp sodden earth and the dull leaden sky made me feel thoroughly miserable. I was quite glad when my Irish terrier pushed the door open with his nose and walked in. He had been out in the garden, and was never allowed to come upstairs with wet feet; but on this occasion I forgave him and said nothing, as he crept quietly to a corner and lay down. He was miserable, like myself, and wanted company, and I had not the heart to turn him out.

The rain fell ceaselessly on the roof of the studio, and the noise irritated me. It was, moreover, difficult to see my work, for the sky was dull, and a continuous stream of water trickled down the glass and still further obscured what light there was.

I was certainly depressed; I felt as if it were the break-up of summer, and that yesterday I had seen the last of the sunshine for months to come. I am not usually affected by the weather to such an extent. Like other people, I prefer sunshine to gloom, but when I am working and my mind is fully occupied, I have no time to think about depression of spirits. But this morning I was distinctly miserable. My life suddenly seemed a failure, and it appeared to me that the work before me was all wrong, both in conception and execution, and that I should probably never do anything very great. Looking at the statue calmly and critically, I felt that after all it lacked the one touch of genius. Of course it was not finished, and the touch of genius is often but a single stroke of the chisel or pen. But still it appeared far from being even a work of promise, and I began to think that it would require either a more skilled hand or a finer intellect to bring it to perfection. Indeed, as I looked at the figures, it almost seemed that Ahriman was a very common blackguard, and that Ormuzd was little better than a prig.

I laid my chisel down for a minute, and lighting a cigarette, walked over to the dog and patted his head. As I did so, I touched his ear and he yelped. I bent down to look at it, and saw that it was bleeding slightly from a small puncture. He had evidently been fighting with something, but the wound looked too small and clean to be made by the teeth of a dog.

I turned him over and examined him for any further
signs of the contest.   I found nothing but a few small
white hairs close to his mouth, and a few specks of
blood on his under jaw.

I thought no more of the matter, and walked up
and down the studio, trying to get myself into a
more cheerful frame of mind.   But I was unsuccessful, and began to think that something besides the
external influence of the weather was working upon
my brain.   My thoughts suddenly went back to the
night before, and it struck me that I had experienced
a very similar feeling when Dr. Rawlins had taken
my hand in the laboratory and concluded the
bargain.   Then, however, it was momentary and
intense, like a sharp pain ; now it was faint and
dull, a mere weariness and sense of something wrong.

I began to wonder who this Dr. Rawlins was, and
what secrets of science he was in search of.   Then
my thoughts wandered more pleasantly to his
daughter.   Perhaps she would supply what was
lacking in the work, and give some swift flash of
inspiration to my art.   Then my cigarette burnt
close to my fingers and put an end to my meditations, and I knew it was time to start work again,
for I never allowed myself longer rest, except for
meals, than was required to smoke a single cigarette.
This habit was almost like reverting to the ancient
method of telling the time by marked candles, but I
found it a very useful guide.

I picked up my chisel and turned to my work
again, but found nothing in it to brighten my

thoughts. If anything, the group seemed still more unsatisfactory. Yesterday it had appeared full of promise and life, the groundwork of a world-wide reputation. To-day it was dull and lifeless, a mere pot-boiler, and I began to wonder if this were a forecast of what it was really destined to be, and if I had unconsciously exchanged the soul of my art for the sum of twenty thousand pounds. But in spite of my gloomy forebodings, I worked steadily on all day, and battled against my thoughts until I had almost conquered them. Then the darkness began to creep round the studio, and the gong warned me that it was time to dress for dinner.

It was a damp and chilly evening, and during dinner I gave directions for the fire to be lighted in the library. When I had finished my meal, I went in there to enjoy a pipe before Dr. Rawlins arrived. The room was large and comfortable, with books strewn all over it, on shelves and tables, and even, I am ashamed to say, on the floor itself. The curtains were of dark blue velvet, and the chairs and lounges were upholstered in the same material; the wood-work was all of black oak, and the ceiling and walls were painted a sombre brown. There was no gilt or bright colouring in any part of the room. Even the pictures were framed in black or brown wood, and the only relief to the darkness was supplied by a few small statuettes, glimmering here and there like ghosts on the top of some shelves and bookcases. Some people might have called the room gloomy, but to me it was just the place for rest and quiet, and I

was only too glad of some change from the glare of
the studio and the everlasting whiteness of the marble.
I turned the lamp low, and flinging myself into an
easy-chair, lit my pipe, and let the smoke curl peace-
fully to the ceiling.   Outside I could hear the wind
roaring like the distant sound of waves on a rocky
shore, and the rain pattering against the windows.
But within all was cheery and comfortable as a
man could wish for.   The fire crackled merrily and
gave all the light I required ; nor was I without a
companion to talk to, for the dog stretched his brown
limbs lazily in the warmth, and blinked at me as
though he wanted me to speak to him.   When I had
smoked my pipe, I began to doubt whether Dr.
Rawlins would come out on such a wet night, and I
should have given up all hope if I had not judged
him to be a man whose time was carefully mapped
out, and who would be sure to keep an appointment,
were it at all possible.   I was right in my estimate,
for as I began to fill my pipe a second time, the dog
suddenly jumped up, and beginning to bark, ran to
the window and put his paws on the ledge.   I listened
attentively, and in a few seconds heard the faint noise
of wheels, which the dog's keen ears had detected
before mine.   Then a carriage rolled up the drive
with a muffled beat of hoofs and a jingle of harness,
and stopped at the hall door.

Then I noticed something peculiar in the dog's
conduct.   He left the window, and slunk away into a
corner with his tail between his legs, just as though I
had struck him with a whip.   I called to him, but he

refused to come out into the room, and fixing his eyes on the door, began to snarl ominously. I could see the brown hair on his back ruffling with suppressed fury.

I turned up the light and poked the fire, and before I had resumed my seat, Dr. Rawlins entered. He was attired in ordinary evening dress, and looked much more European than he had done in the laboratory. Rags sprang out from his corner with every hair on his body bristling with rage. I gave him a cuff on the side of his head, and he went out yelping into the hall. I apologised, and moved towards my guest with outstretched hand.

"Well," Dr. Rawlins said briskly, shaking my hand and taking no notice of the dog, "you see I have come, though it is not a night for an old man. I fear the cold very much. I have lived abroad almost all my life."

"I am glad to see you, Dr. Rawlins," I replied. "Sit here by the fire. You will take something, of course, after your long drive?"

I passed him a box of cigars, and put my hand on the bell.

"Nothing, thank you," he replied, "but I will have a cigar if I may."

"I am glad you have come," I continued; "the weather has got on my nerves. I am quite convinced to-night that my work is doomed to failure."

He raised his eyebrows slightly and smiled.

"The weather must affect you considerably, Mr. Maxwell," he said. "Perhaps I may be able to alter your opinion. I should like to see your work as soon as possible ; my time is limited."

"We will go at once," I replied ; "but I am afraid you will find the studio cold."

"I will wear my coat, if you will excuse me," he said.

I rang the bell and told the servant to bring in his coat. When it came, he buttoned it carefully up to his chin, and followed me into the studio.

The light from the candle I carried seemed only a speck of flame in that large room, and I lit two lamps on a side table. I always kept a white cloth over the statue when I was not working. I removed this and stood aside, holding one of the lamps in my hand.

Dr. Rawlins looked at my work intently for quite half a minute ; then he walked to the table, took the other lamp from it, and returned to examine the details more closely.

"I suppose you cannot guess what the subject is ? " I said ; "it might represent so many things."

"Yes," he replied thoughtfully, as though speaking to himself, "it might represent many things, but it is clear that Evil and Good are fighting for that woman's soul. The woman is not sculptured yet, but she should have a look of terror on her face —unless, indeed, she is evil."

"Or unless she has perfect faith in the power of Good," I answered. "You give me hope, Dr. Rawlins. At any rate, I have made it clear that they are not fighting for her body."

"That is quite clear to me. What is the subject ? "

"Ormuzd and Ahriman fighting for the soul of man."

"As they have fought for ten thousand years," he replied mechanically, "and the battle is not decided yet."

I looked sharply at him. His voice was strangely husky, and his eyes seemed to be looking at something beyond the statue.

"Pardon me," he said abruptly, "I was thinking of something else. Whatever put the idea into your head? Why did you not call it 'Good and Evil,' or 'God and Devil'?"

"The name was suggested to me by a book I once read," I replied.

He turned away from the statue, and replaced the lamp on the table.

"It is a fine work," he said, coming up to me. "It might be the greatest work in the world."

I laughed. I knew it would never be that. No modern has the strength and skill of those giants of the past.

"It might be the greatest work in the world," he repeated, "if you carry out the bargain you have entered into.'

I smiled politely.

"Your daughter is beautiful," I said, "but she cannot give me the hands or the brains of Praxiteles."

"I was not thinking of my daughter," he replied. "I am not vain enough to think that she will add to the value of your work."

"I have no doubt she will!" I exclaimed

emphatically; "but she cannot give me genius. Shall we go back to the smoking-room now?"

"Yes," he replied, turning away from the statue; "I have seen enough to form an opinion. It will certainly be a great work."

I covered up the statue, put out the lamps, and taking a candle from the mantelpiece, led the way downstairs to the smoking-room. Dr. Rawlins flung off his coat, and we ensconced ourselves in two easy-chairs before the fire. For a few minutes we both watched the blaze in silence.

"You mentioned a book just now," Dr. Rawlins said abruptly. "Might I ask the title of it?"

"It was a Persian book," I answered, "and I had to get it translated for me. It was called 'The White Priests of Ahriman.' Have you ever seen it?"

"Yes," he said slowly, "I know it well." He was looking into the fire, as though in search of some face among the glowing coals. "Quite well, in fact," he continued, "and I know Persia quite well too. Where did you come across the book?"

"On a book-stall in Paris. I think it cost me a franc."

Dr. Rawlins leant back in his chair and laughed.

"There are only three copies of that book in the world," he said, "and I know half-a-dozen men who would give a hundred pounds for it. You are evidently lucky in your bargains, Mr. Maxwell," and he looked at me meaningly.

"Is there anything you have not read?" I asked, with a laugh.

"Nothing on that subject; at any rate, nothing worth reading. What did you think of the book?"

I told him how deep an impression it had made on me, and how I had actually travelled to Persia for some confirmation of the story. Then we began to talk of various places in that country, which, as far as I could judge, he seemed to know intimately, and the accuracy of his knowledge confirmed the first impressions I had of him. There was no doubt that he was of Eastern origin. An hour passed pleasantly in recounting our reminiscences and adventures; he listened rather than talked, occasionally suggesting a name that I could not remember, or telling some short anecdote to bear out what I was saying. Then, during a pause in the conversation, he looked at his watch.

"I must be off, Mr. Maxwell," he said. "I think I could talk to you all night on Persia. The country and people interest me more than any land or nation in the world But I should like to know whether you usually start in quest of truth, whenever you read a fairy tale."

"It was not a fairy tale that I read," I replied. "The man who wrote the book was a scientist and he discussed the story scientifically; not as though he were discussing the probability of a legend, but as though he were trying to find an explanation of an acknowledged fact."

"Perhaps he had the simple faith of a believer,"

E

Dr. Rawlins answered, with a smile ; "your divines discuss miracles in the same way."

"Yes," I said, "and that is what struck me so forcibly, and that is why I went to Persia."

"I suppose, then, you have also been to Palestine?"

"No ; but in this case there was an opportunity of investigating and verifying a modern miracle."

"But you found nothing," he answered, "and I am not surprised. The Kohrud Mountains are so vast and impenetrable, that if a city lay concealed in them, you might wander for a year and pass it by. If you have the book here, I should like to have a look at it. Who wrote it?"

"One Deva Dacobra," I replied.

"That is curious," he said; "the name is not Persian; it is distinctly Hindoo. Do you think you can find the book?"

"It is lying somewhere about," I said, rising from my seat and looking round the room. "I have not seen it for a long time. Ah, here it is!" I exclaimed, picking it up and bringing it forward into the light. It had been lying on the top of a pile of books in the corner. I handed it to him.

"A handsome cover," he said, looking at it closely ; "very fine work indeed. French, I suppose; they are great binders."

Then I saw him start slightly, and hold the book closer to the light. I went up and looked over his shoulder. He pointed to a small brown mark on the white vellum, no bigger than a five-shilling piece.

"Dirt," I said, with a laugh; "but I shall keep it more carefully, now I know its value."

"It is the footprint of some small animal," he replied, examining the mark closer. "Do you keep pets?"

"My dog there," I replied, "and I dare say the cook has a cat or two, and I believe the coachman has a few rats and a badger. But why do you ask?"

"It is a footprint I know very well," he said, turning over the leaves of the book; "it is that of neither a cat nor a dog, and was certainly not made by a rat or a badger. It is the footprint of a monkey."

"There are no monkeys in this part of Scotland," I said, with a laugh.

He looked at me so keenly and intently that I could hardly bear his scrutiny.

"And what if there were?" he replied, still keeping his eyes on my face. Then he took hold of my arm, and I was astonished at the power in the fingers of so old a man. "Are you sure?" he said. "Surely there is one in the village? Sailors bring them back as pets sometimes."

"There may be, of course; but I don't think it matters; I can wash the book."

He let go my arm and laughed.

"You must think me a fool," he said, "but I have a horror of monkeys, and I should be quite ill if I thought there was one in the neighbourhood. Some people feel the same thing about cats, and a cat is a much more beautiful animal than a monkey. Would you mind ordering my horses to be put in ? "

I rang the bell and gave the order. In a few minutes the servant entered to say that the carriage was at the door. I accompanied Dr. Rawlins into the hall, and noticed that he looked carefully on every side of him as he went, searching the staircase, hall, and passage with a few swift glances.

"Good-bye, Mr. Maxwell," he said, as we reached the porch and he was putting on his coat ; "you have interested me very much both by your work and conversation. When will you be ready for my daughter ? "

" As soon as she is well enough to come," I replied.

He was silent for a minute, and looked at the footman who was standing near us.

" You can go, George," I said, guessing from Dr. Rawlins' look that he had something to say to me.

The man left us alone ; we stood in the outer hall, and I could see the lamps of the carriage gleaming like two eyes through the glass. I heard the rain-drops being driven against the glass. He was silent for a few seconds. Then he said abruptly :

" You thought I jested when I said your statue might be the greatest work in the world ? "

" If you did not jest, you flattered me."

" It was no idle flattery, Mr. Maxwell. It shall be the greatest work in the world if you have ambition."

I smiled, and taking a cigarette from my case, lit it.

"My ambitions make up my life," I replied, "such as it is."

"It is well," he said. "I too have ambitions, and nothing matters, if only I realise them. I have sacrificed all, and will sacrifice all to them. What would you give for success?"

"I am not a poor man," I replied, "but I would resign all I have on this earth and live in poverty all the rest of my days, if I could give a really great work to the world—a work that would not be the sensation of the season, nor yet the fashion of a century, but one that would endure as a masterpiece for all time. Money is not everything. I should not fear death when such a work was completed."

"Life is not everything."

"I would endure pain and unhappiness."

"Even happiness is not all," he said.

"I would give up all!" I exclaimed. "My soul is in my work, and all I ask is success. But why do you look at me like that?" and I smiled.

"I knew a man once," he replied, "whose soul was also in his work. It was in the East, and he built a temple to the gods. He completed it, and nowhere in the whole world is there a building to match it for beauty or perfection of design. It was almost a living thing, and the people said that at nights it cried aloud to heaven. But the man's intellect shrivelled and shrank as he proceeded with his work, and when the topmost stone was laid by the workmen, he was found clinging to the pillars of the porch, a raving idiot. His soul and intelligence had left him and were in the work that he had completed. That man gave his all."

"I don't think I shall go mad," I said, "unless it is with disappointment."

"You shall not be disappointed," he answered, laying his hand on my arm.

I looked at him in surprise; the old gentleman in evening dress did not seem like a dispenser of the gifts of the gods. He spoke with assurance, and I laughed. He looked at me keenly, and once more I felt the same uneasiness come over me that I had experienced the night before.

"Good-night," he said, and put out his hand.

I took it and held it for a moment. Then I opened the door, and as I did so I heard steps on the gravel, and a man crawled out of the darkness into the circle of light. He was drenched through with the rain, and, I could see from the way he walked, considerably more than half drunk. He was very ragged and disreputable; I could see the bare flesh of one of his elbows, and his toes were sticking out of his boots. He was probably one of the tramps that are the terror of lonely country roads.

"They see'd 'im go 'ere," he said, in a thick voice; "they see'd 'im go 'ere. 'Ave you seen 'im, gentlemen?"

"What do you want?" I asked sharply.

The man was a powerful-looking fellow, with a

square, sullen face, a heavy jaw, and an ugly scowl.
I did not fancy him as a lodger in my grounds
for the night.

"'E was a white 'un," he said, holding himself up
by the wheel of the carriage, "they see'd 'im go 'ere,
and white 'uns is scarce."

"A white what?" said Dr. Rawlins, coming
forward to my side.

"A white monkey," replied the man; "my white
monkey."

"He is not here," I said, and then I recollected
the few white hairs and the blood I had seen on
Rags' mouth, but I thought it best to say nothing
of that. "You had better ask in the village, my
man. What are you doing with a monkey?"

"Bought 'im off a sailor in Glasgow," he said.

Dr. Rawlins was behind me, and I turned round
to him with a smile. His gaze was fixed on the
man's face, and I thought I almost saw a look of
terror in his eyes.

"Here you are," I said, "here is the owner of the
beast who walked over my book."

Dr. Rawlins did not answer, but pushed past
me into the rain and confronted the man, who
scowled at him from under his black eyebrows.

"What are you doing with a white monkey?" he
asked sternly.

"Bought 'im off a sailor, I tell yer. Can't a man
'ave a white monkey, if 'e likes. I paid 'im 'alf a
pint of gin; 'e drank it and wanted 'im back; but
I floored him and left."

" A very creditable transaction," said Dr. Rawlins, with a sneer.

" Would you know the sailor again ? " I asked. " Where did he come from ? "

" 'E sailed from Bosher, so 'e said ; but sailors are almighty liars.   I don't believe 'e's been farther than Liverpool ; 'e's gone off now on another ship back to Bosher."

Dr. Rawlins turned to me.

" Bushire, he means ; you know it, of course—in the Gulf of Persia ? "

" I know it well," I answered, for I had landed there.   " Come, you had better get off, my man.   If I see your monkey I will let you know.   Leave your name and address with the groom in the saddle-room."

The man went round to the back of the house and Dr. Rawlins stepped into his carriage.

" An unpleasant customer," I said.

" A very unpleasant customer," he replied.   " Good-night, Mr. Maxwell."

The carriage rolled off down the drive, and I watched the lamps disappearing in the distance, and breathed in the fresh cold air.   Then after the sound of wheels had died away, and the lamps had vanished round the corner, I heard the crunch of gravel, and a tall awkward figure passed the circle of light that streamed from the door, and lurched heavily into the darkness.

CHAPTER VI

HOW THE STATUE WAS MADE, BUT NOT PERFECTED

DURING the next four months nothing occurred of any particular interest to anyone but myself. The sittings began as soon as Miss Rawlins' foot was well, which was not until a week following her father's visit. And they continued almost daily, with the exception of one week when she was laid up with a severe chill, and a few days when the light was too bad to do any work at all.

On every occasion she was accompanied by a lady of severe aspect, and I should think of unimpeachable morals. I subsequently learnt that she had been hired from the village of Balath for these occasions, and was no less a person than the curate's wife. She was hard-visaged, and looked with silent disapproval at all that was going on.

The figures of the two men in the statue were considerably undraped, and I saw at once that this was a source of anxiety to her. She sat sideways in a corner of the room, and buried her face in a large brown book, which I always took to be a volume of sermons, until she left it one day in the study, and I discovered it to be an exhaustive treatise on cookery.

Dr. Rawlins himself came but rarely, for his work kept him closely confined to his laboratory. However, I had several opportunities of estimating the character of this extraordinary man, and soon came to the conclusion that there were depths in his nature that I could not fathom. From other sources I heard stories of his disposition, which were so contrary to the aspect in which he showed himself to me, that I was at first inclined to regard them as fables. His reputation in that part of the country would scarcely have disgraced the devil himself. He owned a large amount of land in the neighbourhood, which he had purchased with the castle, and there was not a man or woman connected with his estate who did not loathe the very mention of his name. I heard stories of labourers in his employ who had practically starved to death within two hundred yards of his castle, and of tenants who had been ruined, and then driven by despair to the disgrace of a prison and a subsequent career of crime.

Yet I never knew a man so devoted to his daughter. When they were in the room together, his eyes never left her face for a moment. He seemed to anticipate her every wish, and hasten to gratify it almost before it had formed itself in her mind. No labour of body or intellect was too great for him to undertake on her behalf; nothing that money could buy was good enough for her. He seemed to live entirely for her sake. And yet,

remembering the first night I met him, and how he
would not leave his laboratory to thank the man who
had saved her life, I at first doubted if he were
sincere in his display of affection ; nor was it until I
had known him for some months that I realised
how deeply and passionately he cared for his only
child, and how truly she represented all the love and
affection of the world for him.

But in those few months I discovered that the
other side of his character was accurately painted by
his neighbours, and from my own knowledge I know
that no fiend could have driven a man to hell with
more glee than he drove the Laird of Inch Ross to
disgrace and suicide. At first I had disbelieved the
tales about him, but unfortunately I discovered that
there was no doubt about their truth ; and I saw him
myself one day shatter a half-starved mongrel's leg
with a heavy stick, and laugh as it howled and writhed
on the ground. The villagers said that the soul of
the Black Knight of Balath had entered into him, and
when he passed down the street, I have seen them
draw back into their cottages and close their doors
until he had walked past the houses, as through a
deserted village.

I could scarcely analyse my own feelings towards
him. Often I shrank from his path with loathing,
and I remember when he broke the stray cur's leg,
I tore the stick from his hand, and threatened him
with it. He laughed, and I broke it in pieces on my
knee. " I am sorry you have broken it," he said ; " it
was a present from my daughter," and he never

referred to the incident again, or seemed to bear me
any grudge for the violence of my action.   Yet when
I have seen him with his daughter I have for the
moment respected and almost admired him.   Though
this one good trait of his did not alter my general
estimate of his character—for even the vilest criminals
have a soft spot somewhere in their hearts—yet it did
much to mitigate the extraordinary disgust that I
otherwise might have felt for him.

But of the high quality of his mind there could be
no difference of opinion.   I never met a man who
had made himself master of so many books and
subjects.   His memory was little short of miraculous,
and old age had not in the least impaired the acute-
ness of his perception, or the strength of that rare
gift which discerns at a glance the difference between
the false and the true.   When a man is old with the
wisdom of age, and still retains the intellect and
vigour of youth, he personifies the highest form of
intellect, and Dr. Rawlins was certainly fitted to
succeed in attaining to any knowledge that lay within
the reach of a finite mind.

And for over sixty years all his powers and energies
had been directed towards the attainment of a single
object.   It is true that his fine memory gave those
who only knew him slightly the impression that, like
Bacon, he had made all knowledge his province ; but
in reality his whole mind was focussed on one subject,
and I believe he spoke no more than the truth when
he said to me the first night we met, that his work
was a matter of life and death.   I think that he must

have taken a fancy to me, or else he discovered in me
a possible source of information, and was resolved,
like most successful men, not to neglect the smallest
and least likely opportunity. At any rate, he confided
to me the object of his experiments and investigations,
and I found that the task he had set himself to do
was no less than an attempt to break down the
barrier between the living and the dead.

I knew this to be a wall against which many human
intellects had shattered themselves in vain, and
beneath which lay the empty lives and broken hearts
of a thousand dreamers. I myself, as an ardent
biologist, had first faced it with hope, then turned
my back on it in despair, and then had turned again
to discover the supernatural agencies of the past,
which men believe to have levelled it to the ground;
but still I had found no lever to move a single one
of its everlasting stones.

I was half sorry when he told me of his ambitions.
He could not have many years before him, and it
was pitiful to think that his magnificent intellect had
for sixty years been wasted in the pursuit of a
phantom. Directed into other paths, it might have
been of the utmost service to the human race. Yet
whenever he spoke of his experiments, he spoke with
a certain note of triumph in his voice. He never
told me anything definite about his researches. He
talked of the failures of past ages, and explained
why they had failed; he even sometimes spoke of
his own want of success, but never a word of the
operations that he hoped would give him the victory.

He said, however, that he was within sight of ultimate triumph, and that he might attain to it any day and at any hour. It was painful for me to listen to the hopes of so strong a man; they were the same hopes that have filled the breasts of inquirers after truth in all ages. How many had been within sight of that city of success, and how many had seen its fair outline recede farther and farther in the distance, when they thought they stood near to its very walls! Yet I knew that the man was not a dreamer, and I felt confident that, if success were possible, he would be more likely to succeed than to fail.

But during those four months I had more opportunities of observing the daughter than the father. Dr. Rawlins came in on more than one evening to smoke a cigar with me, and on two or three occasions I dined at Balath, and sat far into the night discussing science with him. But I saw Miss Rawlins nearly every day, and she certainly provided a more pleasant study of character. It is very tiring for an inexperienced person to sit as a model for a sculptor. Not only is it painfully monotonous, but the physical exertion of remaining in one attitude for any length of time is very exhausting to those not trained to endure it. Yet she never complained, and was always bright and cheerful. I was engrossed in my work, and am afraid I was an exceedingly dull companion for a young girl; but she never appeared to notice it, nor seemed vexed that I paid her so little attention.

"I will do the talking," she said; "that is, when you are not working upon my face, and you can do the thinking."

And a very interesting and amusing little talker she was, flashing from grave to gay without an effort; at one time jesting with brilliant wit, or brimming over with childish fun, and at another displaying such depth and accuracy of thought that her father himself could scarcely have equalled it.

I often wondered why I did not fall in love with her. I have never seen a more beautiful or sensitive face, and have rarely come across a more fascinating personality; and every day seemed to disclose some fresh charm of manner or expression. She was all a man could desire, and we were brought together daily on terms of the greatest intimacy. But she never moved my heart to anything but a sincere admiration and friendship. It may be that I had no heart, and that the capacity for passionate love died ten years previously, when one for whose sake I toiled, thought, and lived, showed me the vanity of all human faith and trust. Or it may be that the frankness and freedom of our intercourse thrust the thought of any more tender feelings from my head. Or it might even be that some instinct caused me to shrink from the strange, pitiful look I sometimes noticed in those large grey eyes, and that pity, so often akin to love, was in this case allied to a fear which I could neither define nor explain; but, be it as it may, no word or look of passion ever passed between us. We were, as they say, too good friends to be lovers.

The statue progressed rapidly. I was engrossed in the work, and spared neither myself nor my model in my efforts to bring it to perfection. At the end of four months it was practically finished. Yet I looked in vain for that supreme inspiration which would make it one of the masterpieces of the world of art. I am a conscientious workman, and the modelling was as good as I had ever done in my life. The likeness of Elaine Rawlins was perfect. The whole idea was carried out exactly as I had planned it. Yet there was something wanting, and I began to fear that the conception was inadequate, and that the subject had assumed in my mind a value which it did not in reality possess. Perhaps it was that I was fastidious; Elaine said it was magnificent, and that she would be famous for all time; her father said it was the work of a great artist, but that it was not finished yet.

And I felt, too, that it was not finished, and that I was incompetent to finish it. Yet I knew that it was possible for the smallest difference to transform the whole. If one looks at a picture of a great master, and then at a good copy of the picture, it is often impossible to detect any difference between the two. The colouring may be exactly similar, and every line and detail may be the same in all respects; but yet there is a difference, and an artist, though perhaps he could not point it out, would tell you that one is a great work and the other a comparatively worthless imitation. The subtle power of a great mind is in one of them ; and no imitator, copy he ever so perfectly, can reproduce the shadows and lights of the intellect that inspired the painting. It was so with my work. I realised that at present it was an imperfect copy of what I had meant it to be. I knew that to change the whole thing to a really great masterpiece might possibly not be a labour of more than half-a-dozen hours, yet for those few hours a man might wait all his life in vain.

Then the day came when I said to myself that I could do no more to the statue, and I decided to leave off work. It was a few days before Christmas, and the snow lay deep over the whole country. I told Miss Rawlins that it was unnecessary for her to come again, and she looked quite miserable at the news, though if I had been in her place I should have been exceedingly thankful. As it was, I was very sorry myself that the sittings had come to an end, and wished that my conscience would allow me to prolong them until the day fixed for the completion of the statue. But I could not honestly continue to sit scowling at my work, unable to alter it in any way for the better. I had been doing this already for a week, and my model had patiently jested with me for my inaction ; but it was scarcely fair to the girl to fetch her seven miles through the snowdrifts that lay between here and Balath, simply that I might pass the time away in conversation. And now that the time for parting had come, I knew that I should

F

miss her very much. I had grown very fond of the child during these few months that we had been together, and though no thought of love had crossed my mind, yet I felt that a very pleasant episode in my life was coming to an end.

On that last day I managed to get a few minutes' conversation with her alone before she left the house. We were in the hall waiting for the carriage to come to the door, and I had successfully disposed of the chaperon for a little while, by suggesting that biscuits and port in the dining-room would fortify her against the cold.

Outside, the snow lay deep, and the dull leaden sky looked as if another storm were coming up from the north. It was not a pleasant day for a drive, but Miss Rawlins, who looked very charming in her sable-lined coat and her little sable toque, laughed when I expressed the hope that the journey in the cold would not injure her health.

" I love the cold weather," she said ; " and even if I hated it, I think I could face it to leave Balath for a little while. You do not know how dull it is there. I think you are the only stranger who has ever entered the house. I love coming here. It is not wrong of me to say so, is it ? " and a slight tinge of colour came into her cheeks.

I laughed.

"No, indeed," I replied. "I am very sorry our work is over ; it is quite as dull here as it is at Balath."

" Oh, but you need not be dull ; you can fill the

house with people if you like. Now I am obliged to
be lonely. My father will not allow a soul inside the
door ; he himself is at work all day in his laboratory,
and I see very little of him, though he is the dearest
father in the world."

As she said this, I wondered whether she knew
what other people thought of him, and decided that
no one could have been so cruel as to have told her.
Besides, she was carefully watched and guarded, so
no whisper of the truth would be likely to come to
her ears.

" I shall come and call sometimes," I said, with a
smile, " and hope we shall always be good friends. I
think your father will allow *me* to come."

" Oh," she cried, clapping her hands together, " I
quite forgot. You must come to our party on New
Year's Eve."

" Your party on New Year's Eve ! " I said, raising
my eyes in astonishment. " Where is it to be ? "

" In Balath, of course," she answered.

" But I thought your father never allowed anyone
into the house. Besides, he must have offended all
the people round by keeping apart from them ; I am
quite sure that I have."

" Well, it is like this," she said, with a mysterious
air. " I will tell you a secret. Father asked me
what I would like for a Christmas present, and I
said, ' A party.' He said, ' No,' and then he offered
me a pair of ponies, a diamond bracelet, a new grand
piano, and fifty other things instead. I said, ' No!
No! No!' to each one, and said it fifty times. ' I

will have a party,' I said, and then—then I cried.
Am I not a little fool?"

"You are a very wise little woman," I said. "Of
course, he gave in?"

"Yes, dear old father, he did. It was a shame
of me, wasn't it? You do not know how worn and
thin he has got the last fortnight; he is overworking
himself with his experiments. I think a party would
brighten him up."

"Excuse me," I said; "you won't think me rude,
but will the people come?"

"Of course they will come," she answered. "They
are simply dying to get into the castle. I believe
most of them believe it is inhabited by an ogre.
Curiosity will prevail over pride, and they will come
if only to find out what we are like. Probably they
will sneer and be unpleasant; but I shan't care; I
shall get plenty of fun. You will come, won't you?"

I hesitated; the fact was, I had decided to ask
Fox Faversham down to stay with me for Christmas.
He was a lonely bachelor like myself, and that very
morning I had found a letter on my breakfast table
announcing his return from Spain, where he had been
studying local colour for his next Academy picture.
My work was finished now, and I think the heart of
every man turns toward companionship at Christmas
time.

"The fact is," I said, after a slight pause, "that I
have a friend coming to stay with me; perhaps your
father would not care—"

"Bring him with you," she cried indignantly. "Of

course we shall be glad to welcome any friend of yours; how ridiculous you are!"

" Very well," I replied; "then I shall be delighted to come. But here is the carriage."

"Where is Mrs. Balquiddy?" she said, looking round the empty hall.

" Still fortifying herself, I expect," I replied; "but she must be nearly impregnable by now. Are you in a hurry?"

"Not if you have anything to say of importance," she replied, with an arch little smile.

"I want to ask you something, Miss Rawlins, but you must promise me not to be offended."

"Well?" she said.

"I want to know if you are quite happy now— really and truthfully happy?"

"Of course. Why do you ask? I am cheerful, am I not?"

"Oh, yes," I replied; "you are always cheerful and always bright, Miss Rawlins—I wish I had your temperament; but I have seen you sometimes when I have thought — well, you will pardon me, won't you? I should like to speak to you like an old friend —when I have thought that you had some great trouble, in spite of all your laughter."

"I am perfectly happy," she replied, with a merry laugh.

"There has been a look sometimes in your eyes, which I am sure ought not to be there. I have noticed it more than once, and have thought about it a great deal."

" Perhaps that is when I have been thinking," she replied—"thinking of the awful blank in my life. I am not unhappy, only sometimes a little afraid. It is as though there were a veil over a large part of my life, and I am sometimes afraid of what lies behind it."

"Nothing very dreadful, I expect; but why does not your father relieve your anxiety? I think you told me that he had never allowed you to know anything."

" I told you the truth," she replied, in a low voice. " He says that if I were to worry my brain about it, I should have another attack of the same illness; that the doctor has given him strict instructions that I am not to be spoken to about the past. I had a great fright, resulting in brain fever, and they say that any memory of the past may awaken a train of thought that would lead to some recollection of the shock and a recurrence of the attack. But I am quite happy."

" Happy is the nation whose annals are few," I said, with a smile.

" Yet sometimes," she answered, " I am afraid."

" I understand," I said sympathetically; " but I am sure there is nothing to be afraid of; it is only the fear one always has of the unknown. Your father is quite right. Rejoice in the present and let the past be. I should not care very much myself if I never recollected anything. There are advantages in forgetting; the thing cuts both ways."

" Good-bye," she said, holding out her hand,

" till New Year's Eve. Will you fetch Mrs. Balquiddy ? "

I brought the good lady from the dining-room ; she was at peace with all the world and still munched a biscuit. There was a faint stain of port about her ample mouth. I showed them both into the carriage, and stood by the window.

" You will be lucky if you get home without a storm," I said, looking at the leaden sky.

" The road is lonesome," said Mrs. Balquiddy, who had now disposed of the biscuit, "and it's no' the storm I'm fearin'. But if we get stickit in a drift, I shall be scart to death."

" You will be quite warm and comfortable, Mrs. Balquiddy, till we come to dig you out."

" Aye, and the country as full of bogles as a Dunkeld cheese is full of maggots ! It is right warm and comfortable we shall be with the bogles about ! "

" I do not think you will find anything to alarm you on the way," I answered, with a smile.

" Have you no' heard, then ? " she said, leaning out of the window with a comical look of terror on her fat face.

" I have heard of nothing to be frightened at, Mrs. Balquiddy."

" Not of the wild white beasties in the woods ? " she exclaimed, in an awe-struck voice. " My man saw one last Sabbath, as he came from the kirk to see old Elsie o' the Burn, wha's deein'. It flittered from tree to tree like a buird, and old Peter Angus

tells us of twa, but he's often in sich a state, that it
might hae been only one. And there are those in
the village who swear there are six, and that they
have all been seen in different places at once."

"What are they?" I said thoughtfully. I was
thinking of the tramp that came to the door four
months ago, and of the animal he had lost.

"Mere white beasties," she answered; "no man
has dared look sae long at one as to tell what it
might be. But the folks say the country is full
of them, and no man dare leave his hearthstone at
night."

"I must get my gun," I said, with a laugh. "Do
you know anything of these strange animals, Miss
Rawlins?"

"Only from Mrs. Balquiddy; but I'm not afraid of
them; they seem to be very small."

"Aye; awfu' sma', and awfu' ugly," chimed in
Mrs. Balquiddy.

"What does your father think of them?" I said to
Miss Rawlins.

"I told him about them one day, and he said he
didn't wish to hear the villagers' tales. Then he told
me not to be frightened, and that I should be all
right. Wasn't it ridiculous of him; as if I should be
afraid of a white rabbit!"

"Rabbits do not climb trees, Miss Rawlins," I
said.

"Well, as if I should be frightened of anything
that size, white or black."

"And he was not afraid of going out at night after

hearing of them?" I asked jestingly, but at the same time wishing to learn the truth.

"Of course not," she replied. "How ridiculous you are, Mr. Maxwell! But we must be getting home, or else we shall probably be buried in the snow for several days. Good-bye, and do not forget the party."

"Good-bye," I said, and waved my hand as the carriage rolled off down the drive.

Somehow or other I thought a good deal about this trivial conversation during the rest of the day. The look in Dr. Rawlins' eyes when he listened to the half-drunken ramblings of the tramp haunted me, and that night I dreamt that I was fighting a whole army of white monkeys, but with such success that by the time I woke up I must have slain ten thousand of them.

CHAPTER VII

OF FOX FAVERSHAM AND WHAT WE SAW
IN THE WOOD

THE next morning I wrote a letter to Fox Faversham:

"This place is just suited to you after your three years' sojourn in Spain; you want bracing northern ideas, or we shall have you painting nothing but 'love in idleness.' We are not absolutely without society, and there are no piano-organs. The station is only fifteen miles away."

On second thoughts I erased this last sentence and substituted, "You can get a through-carriage from Euston." This was not precisely the truth, as one often had to change three times after Glasgow, but I knew it would appeal strongly to a man fresh from the *dolce far niente* of the sunny South, and as my mind was set on his coming, I determined to leave him no loop-hole for excuses.

The answer was prompt and expensive. I had to pay seven shillings and sixpence for the telegram which announced his intention of coming.

Two days afterwards he arrived himself, wrapped to the eyes in a large fur coat, half-drunk with the whisky he had taken to keep the cold out, and bitterly sarcastic about the train service of Scotland.

When last I saw Fox Faversham he was a handsome young fellow of about twenty-five ; a tall and broad-shouldered athlete, who took life exactly as he found it, and laughed at his troubles and perplexities. We had gone through a good many hard times together, but there was never a time so gloomy as to cast a shadow over his spirits. He was one of those people—would there were more of them—who seem to take everything as a mere jest. Men of sour and stolid intellect call this disposition by a hard name. But the world can better afford to lose the sayings of its wise men than the light-hearted carelessness of its youth. And Fox Faversham was no fool. His mind was strong and well-balanced, and when he chose he could do some very brilliant work indeed. Nor had he the instability generally associated with the artistic temperament. He was not engaged one day in getting thoroughly drunk, and the next in giving to the world a masterpiece. He was a steady-going young man, with sound ideas and passable morals, and he contrived to hide some very sterling qualities under his cloak of gaiety.

Such was the Fox Faversham I knew three years ago. But before I had passed an hour in his company, I could see that a change had come over him since those days. In outward appearance he was the same, a trifle thinner about the face, perhaps, and with one or two lines about his mouth, but still the same light-hearted jester. Yet there was a change beneath, and I felt it instinctively rather than perceived it in his manner, though once or twice, when he thought I was not looking, I saw the smile die from his face, and I knew that at last something had crossed his path too serious to be laughed away.

After dinner he chatted of his experiences in Spain. I had been so much alone, and so occupied with my thoughts the last seven or eight months, that the society of another man was like a breath of fresh air to me. I thrust my work entirely out of my mind, and we both sat before the library fire, in our Norfolk jackets, our feet on the fender, pipes between our teeth, and whisky and soda on a little table between us, and no man could ask for a fairer paradise than this on a winter's night.

We talked of everything but Art. He plunged into the gory details of a bull-fight, and described the black eyes of the Castilian maidens, and I— for history, like charity, begins at home—gave an accurate account of the geography, archæology and society of the village in which I lived; and when this rather limited subject was exhausted, I turned to my travels in Persia, my struggles, my successes, and my ambitions for the future.

"Are you doing much work now?" Faversham inquired, after an interval in the conversation.

"Not just at present," I replied, knocking out my pipe on the sole of my shoe rather more loudly than was necessary. I did not care to talk about my work just then. I was glad to get it out of my mind for a few hours.

"Are you?" I asked, hoping to divert his attention from my reticence.

"Yes, I am painting my Spanish pictures."

"I should have thought," I replied, "—of course I am ignorant of such matters—that you would have done that better in Spain."

"Oh, no," he said; "one gets no time for that sort of thing in Spain," and certainly, if the tales of his hair-breadth escapes and adventures in that country were at all accurate, he could have had no time to do anything but hide from vengeance and justice.

"You were there three years?" I said thoughtfully; "one can do a lot in three years."

"Yes," he replied, looking closely at his pipe; "one can do a lot in three years; all sorts of things, in fact, but no painting."

"Why not?"

"You do not understand, my dear fellow," he said. "I did not go to Spain to paint, but to get the local atmosphere and colour, and the general tone of the country. I did not want to sketch churches, and peasants in native costume. It is the general idea I went to find, and I think I have found it. All my future work will be tinged with the atmosphere of Spain. I am to all intents and purposes a Spaniard."

"You are quite brown," I replied. "Is that the local colour?"

He laughed, and we talked in this strain late into the night.

As I was lighting the candles preparatory to going to bed, I suddenly looked round at him. He was behind me, and I caught him off his guard. I saw an expression of pain on his face, though it died away as his eyes met mine.

" What is it ? " he said, with a laugh. " Have you burnt your fingers ? "

" Have *you* burnt your fingers, Faversham ? " I said seriously, as I handed him the lighted candle—" in Spain ? "

" Spain is a warm country," he replied jestingly.

I pressed the matter no further, and calling the dog from his corner, went upstairs to my room for the night.

The next morning was bright and sunny, and I suggested a walk. Fox Faversham was anxious to inspect my work, but I was not at all inclined to let his critical eye see it for the first time in broad daylight, and in the end I prevailed on him to put on his thickest boots, and come out into the snow.

" It will probably kill me," he said meekly ; "but I suppose I must try and resume the rôle of a hardy Englishman as soon as possible."

So he armed himself with a heavy coat and a huge pair of American rubber boots, and expressed his readiness to start at once. As we reached the door, an idea suddenly struck me, and going back into the house I returned in a few minutes with my gun.

" Shooting ? " he queried, raising his eyebrows. " I did not know you had any shooting."

"We may see something," I replied, slipping a dozen cartridges into one of my pockets; " I have an idea that we shall."

" I wish you'd told me there was shooting ; I'd have brought my gun."

" There is no game that I know of, and I do not suppose you care for seagulls."

" Not a bit ! Is that what you are after ? "

" No," I answered ; " but about six months ago I saw a curious animal, and I had no gun with me. I have regretted it ever since, for I now have every reason to believe that it was a white monkey. Perhaps I shall see it again."

" Escaped from a menagerie, I suppose ? "

I told him the story of the tramp, and of the one or two occasions on which I had seen some signs of the animal.

" Why should you kill the poor beast ? " he said, when I had finished.

" Well, there seem to be several. The villagers apparently have seen at least three, so one of them can easily be spared. I should rather like to have it stuffed. But does not it strike you as rather a curious thing that these monkeys should be running about the west coast of Scotland ? "

" Probably there is only one, and the village whisky has produced the rest."

" That may be so," I replied, shouldering my gun, and opening the hall door; "at any rate, I should think this snow would kill some of them."

We started off down the drive. It was a glorious

morning; the sun sparkled on the snow, and the air was clear and crisp, and as we passed through the lodge gates, the whole panorama of hill and slope spread out before us like a mass of white clouds rolling away to the line of the dark blue sea. On leaving the grounds, we turned inland, and struck straight across the moor towards a patch of wood that lay about two miles away up the slopes of Ben Ardrachan. There was no path, but the snow was only four inches deep, and fairly hard.

As we walked along, I told Faversham about my work, and recounted all that had occurred since I came to Ardrachan. He was particularly interested in Miss Rawlins.

" Quite a romance," he said, when I had finished. " Of course you are in love with her ? "

I told him no question of love had arisen, and that it was all a commercial transaction. I also said I had an invitation for him for New Year's Eve.

He ventured no opinion about Dr. Rawlins, except that he was probably a criminal fleeing from justice ; but he cross-examined me very closely about the daughter, and I saw that it was impossible to remove the suspicion from his mind that I was in love with her.

At last we reached the wood. The view from this spot—one thousand feet up the mountain—was magnificent, and we stopped for a moment or two to look at it. I pointed out the towers of Balath in the distance. They looked like a black stain against the white snow. Then I turned round and leaned over the gate that opened into a rude sort of pathway through the trees. Fox Faversham came to my side, and, filling his pipe, looked doubtfully at the rather forbidding darkness. Everything was absolutely silent, save for the steady drip, drip, of water, where the sun was thawing the snow from the top branches of the trees, and the occasional sound of a lump of snow rustling to the ground. The trees were very close, and there was considerable under-growth on either side of the path, so, although the absence of leaves allowed one a certain range of vision, it was impossible to see anything on the ground, except along the white path. This was about six feet in width, and ran, as far as I could remember, right through the centre of the wood to the other side.

"A good cover for game," said Fox Faversham, "but not a good place to be in with a gun."

"No," I replied, meditatively slipping a cartridge in each barrel; "but we may as well walk along that path as anywhere. How exquisitely frosted the trees are!"

I opened the gate, and we walked slowly along the path.

"This is just the place for animals," I said. "It's the only large wood for miles, and I should not wonder if it were full of them. They like some sort of shelter in this weather."

We looked carefully for any marks in the snow, and before we had gone a couple of hundred yards

G

into the wood we found plenty of them, but nothing
that at all resembled the footprints I had seen on
my book.   Then suddenly Fox Faversham, who was
walking a few yards in front of me, stooped down to
examine a leaf by the side of the path.   He picked
it up and showed it to me.   It was dry and dead,
but it had a wet mark on it, like a print of a child's
fingers.   I recognised it at once.

"Do you mind going into the wood a little way,"
I said, "about fifty yards or so, and letting me
know if you can find any more footprints? You seem
to have better sight than I.   I will wait here with
the gun."

I expected a protest, but he went in without a
word.   I think this sort of thing appealed to his
love of mystery and adventure.   In a minute or two
he called out to me.   I took the cartridges from the
gun, and crawled in among the undergrowth, pre-
ferring to trust to my quickness in loading, rather
than have an accident.   When I came up to him, he
was quietly sitting on a tree stump.

"Well?" I said.

"Listen."

I listened attentively, and heard a faint rustling
not fifty yards away.   I looked in the direction that
the sound came from, but the brambles were too
thick to see anything.   Then I heard a funny little
sound, something between the cry of a child and the
chattering of a monkey.   I slipped cartridges into
the barrel of my gun, and cocked it.

"Fire into that bush," he said, pointing to a dense

mass of brambles round the foot of a large oak thirty yards away.

I looked sharply at the bush, and in the dim light thought I saw one thin spray of bramble move gently too and fro. I raised my gun to my shoulder, and then brought it down again.

"One cannot tell what is there," I said; "it may be a man—a poacher, perhaps."

But scarcely were the words out of my mouth, when a white thing ran swiftly up the dark trunk of the tree, and swung itself from branch to branch through the wood, getting farther away from us at every leap. I quickly fired both barrels of my gun on the chance of a stray pellet or two finding its way through the network of twigs. The shot rattled through the wood like a hail-storm, and when the smoke had cleared away, I saw the animal hanging perfectly motionless by one paw. Then it suddenly loosed its hold, and fell with a thud to the ground.

We went quickly up to it, and saw a lump of white fur huddled together among the dead leaves. It stirred a little and then lay quite still. I picked it up. It was a white monkey, and quite dead; a shot had pierced its brain, and it was bleeding from one ear. I looked at it with curiosity, and turned the body over. It was pure white, and its eyes were disgustingly pink. Its wizened little face looked strangely human, and I felt as if I had committed a murder. I laid it down on the ground, and gazed at it with a feeling of shame.

"Poor little brute!" said Fox Faversham. "I suppose you call that sport?"

I made no reply, but stooped down again and examined the animal attentively. A square inch of fur had been torn from the back of its neck, and I remembered the white hair on Rags' mouth four months ago.

"I think I'll take it back with me," I said. "You are right, Faversham, it is not sport; though there are parts of India where it is far more dangerous to kill a monkey than a tiger."

I picked it up, thrusting it into the inside pocket of my shooting coat, and began to make my way towards the path. Before we reached it, however, Fox Faversham stopped and listened with his hand to his ear. I also stopped, and now that the crunching of leaves under foot had ceased, I heard a faint cry from the heart of the wood, and then another, and then the whole of the trees seemed to be wailing, as though the wind were sweeping through them. But there was no wind, and no movement of the branches. To my imagination it sounded like a requiem. Then Fox Faversham gripped me by the arm, and pointed into the centre of the wood. In an instant it seemed to become alive with faint blurs of white, and the crying sound came nearer and nearer, and we heard what seemed like the rustling of a thousand branches.

"There are hundreds of them," cried Fox Faversham. "I think I'll get into the open," and he pushed quickly through the bushes towards the path.

I am not a very timid or superstitious man myself, but there was something unearthly in this sudden springing of the wood to life, and something terrible in the wails of these animals that swung through the trees towards us. I followed him, slipping two more cartridges into my gun as I went. There was nothing to be afraid of, and I could have confronted a million monkeys in the Himalayas. But man is the slave of his imagination, and the appearance of these animals in a place and country where one would least expect them, conjured up strange thoughts in my mind.

When we were a few yards away from the white strip of snow which showed where the path lay, I saw a dark patch against the opening like the form of a man, and when we came to the edge, a face peered in at us. I stopped suddenly, but Fox Faversham in his haste did not see the new-comer until the eyes were a foot from his own. Then he stepped back with an oath, and, moving quickly to one side, apologised. I saw now that it was Dr. Rawlins.

He did not seem to notice us, for when we stepped out past him on to the path, he did not move, but stood staring into the depth of the wood.

I think the fear of a strong man is the most terrible sight in the world. I knew Dr. Rawlins to be a man of unusual strength of will and character, and I should not have thought it possible for anything on earth to have moulded his face into such an expression of terror as I now saw upon it. His eyes were fixed on the undergrowth, wide open, staring, almost vacant. His skin was a pale yellow; his lips were partly drawn back from his teeth, till he looked like a snarling dog. I touched him lightly on the shoulder, but he did not turn.

"Let us go," said Fox Faversham, listening to the sounds in the wood; "they are coming closer; we shall have the whole menagerie on us in a minute."

"Dr. Rawlins!" I said, close to his ear, and touching him more heavily on the shoulder.

He turned quickly round on me and clung to my arm. I saw he recognised me.

"Quick, quick, Mr. Maxwell!" he cried. "Your gun! Is it loaded?"

"Yes," I replied quietly. Now that I stood in the sunlight my childish fear had vanished.

"Shoot!" he whispered hoarsely. "Shoot! For God's sake, shoot! It will frighten them; ugh! I can't stand the sight of them," and he buried his face in his hands. It was pitiful to watch him.

Fox Faversham had regained his composure now, and was looking about on the ground for stones; he had collected a pocketful, when I called to him.

"Let me introduce you to Dr. Rawlins," I said, "Mr. Fox Faversham—Dr. Rawlins."

There is nothing like an ordinary formality of civilisation to bring a man back to his senses. Dr. Rawlins' face composed itself into a momentary look of pleasure; one cannot after all forget the habits of society, and the mask of politeness fell naturally over his features.

" Mr. Faversham will think he is making the acquaintance of a lunatic," he said, with a slight bow ; " but I have an unspeakable horror of monkeys."

" Do you know that they are monkeys ? " asked Fox Faversham brusquely.

" Anyone who has lived in the East knows their cry. Listen ! "

We listened, but the wood was once more perfectly quiet. I went close to the trees and looked in. There was nothing to be seen. I began to think we had been dreaming, and turned to Dr. Rawlins. I saw that his face brightened at the silence.

" There are no monkeys there at all," he said ; " fire into the wood ! "

I took up my gun and fired both barrels among the trees ; there was absolute silence when the echo had died away.

" Thank you," Dr. Rawlins said ; " that is sufficient proof; they would have started chattering at the sound of a gun. I think I am going mad ! " He passed his hand over his forehead and seemed to be collecting his senses. " It is wonderful what hold a man's imagination will take over his reasoning powers. I heard two shots ; then a cry of something ; then, perhaps, the rustle of the trees in the wind ; your voices too, perhaps. Terror seized hold of me, and I easily imagined the rest. What an unsound piece of mechanism the mind of man is ! Of course there are no monkeys there at all ! "

I said nothing, but placed my hand in my pocket and looked at Fox Faversham. Then we all three walked out of the wood together. Dr. Rawlins was a long way from home, and I asked him to come to lunch with us, but he declined.

"My carriage is waiting at the other side of the wood for me," he said. "I must leave you here and go round to the left."

I wondered what he was doing alone in the wood such a distance from home. He seemed to divine my thoughts, for he added quickly :

"You know the wood is my property. I wanted to see what timber was ready to cut, but I must get home at once."

"Shall we walk round with you a part of the way ? " I asked.

He looked at me gratefully, but I saw that he was determined to be master of his feelings.

"Thank you very much," he replied ; "but I won't take you out of your way. You can see the carriage from here."

I looked, and saw a black mark against the snow about a mile off.

"I hope the shot has not frightened the coach-man," he continued ; "he may think I have been murdered. By-the-bye, have you killed anything ? "

"Yes," I replied ; "but nothing much."

"Birds, eh ? " he queried. "Excuse my asking, but these are my woods, you know."

"We must ask your pardon for trespassing," I said. "I think we must be going now. Good-morning, Dr. Rawlins."

He came close up to me and passed his hand over my coat.

"What have you killed?" he asked. "Show it me."

"I would rather not," I replied. "I feel a little ashamed of having killed it."

He looked at both of us keenly, and Fox Faversham, who has less control over his face than I have, looked on the ground.

"Show it to me," he repeated; "it was killed in my wood."

"I would rather not," I answered; "but if you insist—"

"I do insist."

For answer I took the dead animal from my pocket, and dropped it on the ground gently at his feet. He examined it critically. Then he looked at me, and I saw in his eyes that he was slowly realising the fact that his imagination had not played him false after all. But he kept perfect control of himself.

"Good sport indeed," he said courteously. "I killed one in India myself once, and I just managed to escape with my life. Good-morning, gentlemen," and he turned from us to walk in the opposite direction across the snow.

But on my way down the hill I turned round, and noticed that he was walking a considerable distance away from the edge of the wood.

When I got home I put the dead monkey in an outhouse, intending to send it to Glasgow in the morning to be stuffed. But when the morning came, and I gave instructions to the servant, he found nothing there but several little footprints on the dust of the floor.

CHAPTER VIII

FOX FAVERSHAM RECOGNISES A FACE

THAT evening, after dinner, Fox Faversham turned the conversation to my work, and asked me why I was so unwilling to show it to him.

"I believe it is all a fraud," he said, while we were drinking our coffee. "You leave your honest business of perpetuating dowagers in marble, and give out that you have gone to execute your life work, but as a matter of fact, I believe you have come here to be lazy and enjoy yourself."

"It seems a good place for amusement, doesn't it?" I answered sarcastically.

"I am not quite sure about Miss Rawlins," he replied, with a meaning look.

I rose from the table, and, handing him a cigar, told him to come upstairs with me at once and see the statue.

He rose to his feet with a smile.

"The workers of darkness fear the light," he said; "and I suppose you think that this is a suitable hour of the day to show it to me. Will you take the lamp with you, or do you think that a match will show it off to the best advantage?"

"I am not ashamed of it," I replied; "but I absolutely insist upon your seeing it now. I do not wish to be asked any more questions about it, and I should like to get it off my mind."

I took the lamp from the table, and led the way to the studio, Fox Faversham stumbling up the stairs after me, and muttering something about the advantages of electric light. I opened the door, and pointed to the ghostly figure that glimmered out of the darkness. The sheet was over it, and it appeared as shapeless as a cloud.

"It looks like a white elephant," he said, as we walked towards it.

"I will take off the cloth in a minute," I replied. "Do you mind holding the light?"

He took the lamp from my hands. I carefully gathered up the bottom of the sheet from the floor, and with a dexterous sweep of my arm flung it off the statue.

"There it is," I said, looking at him anxiously, for he was known to be a very fine judge of sculpture.

But it was only for a second or two that I saw his face. His eyes travelled quickly from the figure of Ahriman to that of the girl, and making a step forward, he looked closely into her marble face. Then he gave a cry of surprise and horror, and the lamp fell from his fingers with a crash. We were in darkness.

"Hang you, Faversham!" I said. "What is it?" and I fumbled in my pocket for a match.

But he made no reply, and when at last I had

found the box and struck a light, I saw that he was pale as death.

"Are you ill, old chap?" I said gently, for he looked ghastly in the flickering flame of the match.

"Yes," he replied hoarsely, "I am ill; for God's sake, tell me what that is?"

I struck another match, and going to the table lit two candles. The floor was strewn with oil and broken glass. It was fortunate that the safety apparatus of the lamp had worked successfully.

"What is the matter, Faversham?" I asked quietly. "What have you seen?"

He pointed to the statue.

"I do not understand," I said; "that is only the work I spoke of. I think I told you the subject. You had better have a cigar and soothe your nerves. I can't have you seeing things."

He took a cigar from my case, and lit it with trembling fingers.

"Who is it?" he repeated. "You needn't look at me like that. I am quite myself; but who is the woman in the group?"

"Miss Rawlins, of course," I answered. "You have a very bad memory, Faversham. I told you all about it."

"Oh, yes, of course," he replied, speaking as if in a dream; "it is Miss Rawlins. It is very cold in here; let us go downstairs," and his teeth chattered.

I replaced the cloth on the statue, and we settled ourselves by the library fire. I poured him out a stiff glass of brandy and water, and he drank it greedily. I noticed that his hand still trembled. Then he leant back in his chair and puffed silently at his cigar. I did not speak to him, for I thought it best for him to open the conversation; and for quite five minutes neither of us spoke. In my own mind I guessed the probable cause of his agitation, and decided that he had met Miss Rawlins before and that he had perhaps been in love with her.

At last the silence began to get foolish. Faversham had closed his eyes, and was pretending to be asleep.

" Well," I said sharply, " what do you think of my work ? "

He half opened his eyes, and looked at me sleepily.

" Eh ? What did you say ? I'm sorry, Maxwell, but I was dozing."

" What do you think of my work ? " I repeated.

" It is magnificent," he said ; " it is a masterpiece. The likeness —the resemblance is extraordinary."

An expression of pain crossed his face, and I thought I saw his lip quiver.

" You have met Miss Rawlins before ? " I queried, looking away from him into the fire.

He was silent.

" I am an old friend, Faversham," I continued, " and I have no wish to touch on anything that is painful to you. But we shall, of course, see Miss Rawlins at Balath when we go to their dance ; and if you would rather not go, please tell me."

" I shall certainly go," he replied, pulling himself together with effort. " I have never met Miss Rawlins before."

" Oh, I thought you recognised the face perhaps."

" Is it a good likeness ? " he asked.

" It is considered so. I am not satisfied with it myself; but, at any rate, Dr. Rawlins considers it is worth twenty thousand pounds."

" A fabulous price for any work of art," he replied. " But you are sure the likeness is good ? "

" You will see Miss Rawlins in a few days ; then you can judge for yourself."

" Then I shall see the living image of someone I once knew in Spain."

My mind went back to the night before, and the question he had turned away with a jest. I saw that the subject was very painful to him. His fingers were nervously gripped together, and there was a curious look in his eyes. I tried to turn the conversation by asking him what he would like to do in the morning, but he took no notice of my question.

" Yes," he continued slowly, as if speaking to himself, " someone I once knew very well in Spain, and someone I once cared for a good bit."

" Perhaps it is the same," I said. " People change their names ; but then, of course, you would have recognised her father when you saw him in the woods."

" It is impossible for it to be the same," he replied, in a low voice, " for the girl I cared for is dead."

He bowed his head in his hands for a second, and then sat up sharply, as if ashamed of his emotion.

" I am awfully sorry, old chap," I said.

I did not in the least know what to say to him.

Men so rarely confide their deepest emotions to each other, that they have no supply of words to express their sympathy. Fox Faversham was, as a rule, a man who never talked about anything serious, and certainly not cf his emotions, except as a' subject of jest. This fact made the scene doubly painful to me, and I knew that the shock of seeing what was apparently a marvellous likeness to the dead girl he had loved must have unnerved him terribly, or he would never have confided so much to me. As it was, the emotion was only momentary. Directly I mumbled a word of sympathy, he pulled himself together, and commenced to re-light his cigar.

"I must apologise, Maxwell," he said. "It was rather sudden, you know, and one can't always control oneself."

"No, indeed," I replied. "If you asked me to pick out a striking example of iron will and indomitable purpose, I should select Dr. Rawlins. Yet you saw his face this morning, and how he positively clung to my arm in terror."

"I have been thinking of that old chap's face," he said, "and of all you have told me about him. In my opinion there is something wrong. Does anyone know anything of his past life?"

"No one in this part of the world, though of course there are all sorts of rumours in the village, where his brutal conduct has made the entire population his enemy. I believe the most favourable tale of him reports that he is a pirate from the Indian Ocean."

"What do you think yourself?"

"He is a gentleman," I replied, "and a man of great wealth, devoted to his daughter, and absolutely heartless to others; a man of great intellect, but entirely wrapped up in a single scientific pursuit."

"Is that all?"

"No; I think there is something else—something that is perhaps the key-note of his life, but I cannot discover what it is. It is not science, nor yet love of his daughter, though to all outward appearances these two things monopolise his thoughts. It may be some circumstance in the past connected with both, but the idea does not seem to be a very probable one."

"It is a very extraordinary idea."

"He is a very extraordinary man," I replied, "and the undefined idea is strong in my mind. I cannot tell you why. I suppose it is an impression. I am very sensitive to impressions."

"I should say that the key-note of his life is Fear," Fox Faversham replied.

"You have only seen him once."

"But I saw the hunted look in his eyes. He is probably, as the villagers say, a criminal living under an assumed name."

"Do criminals shriek with terror at a few harmless monkeys?"

"Yet I have seen a man with a gun frightened at them," he replied, with a meaning smile.

"Yes, frightened; but not absolutely wild with terror. Why, Faversham, the man was off his head with fright. I should say that there is something in his past life connected with these animals, and the sight of them brings back some terrible memory."

"It might be merely an instinctive antipathy," Faversham said.

I smiled. Though Dr. Rawlins had stated this to be the case, I knew that his will was sufficiently strong to conquer any outward expression of such an aversion.

"It might be," I replied; "but it is very unlikely. What is it, Rags?"

The dog had risen from his basket and was over by the window, sniffing at the bottom of the wainscoting. Then he scratched and whined, and looked back at us for approval.

"I suppose there are plenty of rats in this house?" said Faversham.

"I have never seen one. What on earth is the matter with the dog?"

He had got his paws up on the window-sill, and seemed to be trying to poke his nose through the glass. I rose from my chair and pulled up the blind. There was nothing to be seen but the white snow and the dark masses of shrubbery outside. I threw open the window and a draught of cold air swept through the room. Rags jumped on to the window-sill and barked. Then he sprang out and made across the snow into the bushes, where we heard him rustling about, as if he were hunting for something. Faversham came to my side, and looking out, pointed to some marks in the snow about ten yards away from the house. In spite of my remonstrances he

H

insisted on getting out of the window, and tramped through the snow in his thin shoes to examine them.

"One of those confounded monkeys," he said, and whistled to the dog.

Rags came trotting out of the shrubbery, and looked up at him, wagging his tail.

"Come in, Faversham," I said; "you will catch an awful cold."

He did not answer, but looked down the drive, and seemed to be listening for something. The dog barked furiously, but he laid one hand on his collar. Then I listened, too, and heard the soft tread of something walking through the snow.

"A caller," said Faversham, turning his head towards me.

Then suddenly there was the noise of a scuffle, a man's cry of anger, and an awful screech, as of something in pain; then a moment's silence, and a crash of something being thrown into the shrubbery. I saw the dog pulling violently at his collar, and Faversham began to walk quickly down the drive. Then I heard the sound of voices, and in a few minutes he came back into the light again, accompanied by another man.

"Here is Dr. Rawlins," Faversham cried. "Go round and open the door, Maxwell; he is hurt."

I opened the door and they both came inside. The dog slunk along behind them, and, running past us, went back to the library. Dr. Rawlins was pressing one of his hands to his lips and sucking it hard.

"What is the matter?" I asked.

"Nothing," he replied, raising a smiling face to me; "a mere scratch—the bite of a monkey. I killed him and flung him into your shrubbery. I hope you will pardon me."

"Come into the library," I said, rather curtly. I could not think what the man was doing in my grounds at this time of night.

He came in, and as he sat down by the fire I was astonished to see the change that had taken place in his appearance since the morning. He was certainly a trifle untidy and disordered, for there was snow on his coat and on the knees of his trousers, and his hand was bleeding, but he looked at least twenty years younger, and his eyes flashed with an expression of triumph that I had never seen in them before. I offered him a cigar, and when he had lighted it, he leant forward in his chair, and looked me steadily in the face.

"The work of my life is over, Mr. Maxwell," he said quietly. "I have attained success."

"I congratulate you heartily," I replied, holding out my hand.

He took it, and his clasp was warm and firm as that of a man of thirty.

"May I congratulate you, too?" said Faversham.

"I thank you both," the old man replied quietly. "The discovery came this afternoon about five o'clock; I have been near it for a long time. Once I worked for twenty-four hours on end, and all the time was so near to it that I seemed to touch it with my hand ; but it has always evaded me until to-day, and now, after forty minutes' work in my laboratory, the one link required came clearly into my mind.   I tested it again, and yet again, and found no flaw in it· In the world of science there will no longer be any distinction between living and dead matter.   The formula that life can only spring from life will be cast away into the scientific dust-heap.   The battle of the scientists is over, and the victory I have gained for the upholders of Abiogenesis is such that Huxley never dreamed of."

He rose to his feet and knitted his fingers together. If I had not known him well, I should have thought he was uttering a prayer of thanks.   His eyes flashed, and his body seemed more erect and full of vigour than I had ever seen it before.   Yet he was a very old man.

"For sixty years!" he exclaimed.   "For sixty years!   Neither of you can know what success means after sixty years of failure.   I could not keep the news to myself and my daughter, so I came round here.   Mr. Maxwell will sympathise with me."

"My success has not come yet," I answered gravely; and Fox Faversham looked at me, wondering what I was talking about.

"But it shall," Dr. Rawlins answered, as if to himself, "it shall!"

"How did you get here?" Fox Faversham asked abruptly.

"My carriage is in the village," he replied, "at the

Thistle Inn ; I thought I would spare the horses this last hill."

I did not believe him ; I had never known him spare anything, nor did I believe he had come over from Balath simply to tell me of his discovery, however important it might be. I thought it quite likely that he had left his carriage in the village because he had been somewhere else and did not wish the coachman to know his movements. Fox Faversham glanced meaningly at me, and I fancied he was thinking much the same thing.

"You are sure of your success," I said—" quite sure that you are not mistaken ? "

For answer he pulled something out of his pocket and handed it to me. It was a small piece of rock about the size of a walnut. I turned it over, and there did not seem to be anything remarkable about it.

"What is this ? " I asked.

"An ordinary piece of granite," he replied, "such as you may chip off the cliffs any day of the week. Will you do me the honour to place that piece of stone in a glass jar, seal the lid very carefully, so that it may be air-tight, and keep it for a few days ? "

"Certainly ; but what will happen to it ? "

"You will see. It is a sound piece of stone, is it not ? "

I examined it carefully, and tried to break a bit off the edge, but unsuccessfully.

"It is perfectly sound," I replied. "I will carry out your instructions."

"And now to turn to another matter," he continued, "and one probably of more interest to yourself. You will excuse me talking business for a minute, Mr. Faversham?"

Faversham nodded, and Dr. Rawlins drew an envelope from his pocket and handed it to me.

"A small Christmas present, Mr. Maxwell," he said.

I opened the envelope and drew out a cheque for twenty thousand pounds.

"Thank you, Dr. Rawlins," I said quietly, as if the receipt of such a sum of money was of every-day occurrence; "I will write you out a receipt. I suppose from this you consider the statue finished?"

"Yes," he replied; "I do not think you can improve it."

I flushed, for he had perhaps thrown a slight accent on the word "you."

"I have not received any assistance," I replied, going to the writing-table.

Faversham rose at the same time; he was annoyed at being excluded from the conversation, and announced his intention of going upstairs to change his wet socks and slippers. When he had gone I handed the receipt to Dr. Rawlins, who folded it up and put it away in his pocket.

"No," he said, "you have received no assistance. But I shall not take the statue away for a fortnight."

I smiled sarcastically.

"If you are satisfied, it is all right," I said. "I

have my life before me ; my battles are yet to come, and I may win success."

" All my life is behind me," he replied grimly, " and my battles are over."

I looked at the strong, handsome old face, bright with its triumph. But even success had not softened a line of the cruel mouth. I wondered what his battles had been like, and if the list of the slain was a long one. I wondered, too, if he had really found his peace at last.

" ' Call no man happy till he is dead,' " I quoted.

He looked keenly at me, and a shadow came over his face.

There was a moment's silence ; the clock ticked loudly, and Rags gave a funny little whine ; he was chasing rats in his sleep. Then I heard Faversham come hurriedly downstairs, and he burst into the room.

" A fire on the hill ! " he cried. " Come and look at it ! "

We hurriedly put on our hats and coats, and going out of the hall door, walked about a hundred yards down the drive until we came in sight of the mountains behind the house. From there we could see the white mass of Ben Ardrachan towering in the moonlight. From the dark patch of wood upon its slopes leaped half-a-dozen thin tongues of flame, and the black smoke poured along the mountain side.

" It burns well for wet wood," said Faversham.

" There is five thousand pounds' worth of timber

in it!" exclaimed Dr. Rawlins.   Then we heard the
sound of wheels on the drive, and his carriage came
up to us.   "You will excuse me," he said, "but I
must go down to the village."

The coachman turned the horses, and he stepped
into the carriage.

"Can we help you at all?" I said.

He pointed to the wood.   The wind on the upper
slope of the mountain had caught the flames, and
they were sweeping along from six different points
with a fury that nothing could extinguish.

"I am afraid it is too late," he said, with a smile.
"We shall see you on New Year's Eve, I hope.
Good-night!" and the carriage rolled off.

Faversham looked at the wood thoughtfully.

"The servant told me that it had been burning
for two hours," he said.   "Dr. Rawlins has not been
here for more than half an hour; how odd he should
not have noticed it!"

CHAPTER IX

A LINK WITH THE PAST

THE grim darkness of Balath Castle was transformed into a fairy scene of splendour on the night of the ball. The dreary corridors and halls were carpeted, and sparkled with hundreds of candles. The cold grey stone, which took the place of wall-paper in many of the apartments, was concealed with rich tapestries ; rare flowers were in profusion ; the grand staircase glowed like a conservatory ; and every table and niche seemed to be bursting forth in a summer glory of blossom. Where previously I had only seen dust and darkness, there was light and colour, and where I had hitherto only heard the dull beating of the waves at the foot of the cliffs, there was the sound of music and laughter. Even the broken ruins had not been left to frown in protest against the gaiety. They were hung with thousands of small lamps, and far out at sea the sailors must have wondered what new landmark had appeared for their guidance on the coast.

The great banqueting hall, which I had never entered before, was set apart for dancing. It was fifty yards in length, and over thirty in width. A gallery ran all round it, and at one end this was wide enough to accommodate a band of about thirty musicians. The floor had been specially laid down for the occasion, and appeared to me to be perfect.

The drawing-rooms were thrown open for the use of those who wished to sit out the dances. They needed no further decoration than their priceless works of art, but whereas they were usually in a state of semi-darkness, which rendered any just appreciation of their treasures impossible, to-night they blazed with a thousand candles, which gave too much light, I should fancy, for some of the dancers who wanted to sit there.

If I had any doubts about Dr. Rawlins' invitations being accepted, they were at once removed by the sight of the string of carriages outside the entrance to the castle. I learnt afterwards that the invitations had been couched in such a form that the people were led to believe that he had just recovered from a long illness, and that the festivities were a kind of thanksgiving. In any case, as Miss Rawlins suggested, curiosity would probably have overcome any sense of pique. I had every reason to believe that of all the residents in that part of the world, I was the only one who had ever entered the private apartments of the castle. Everyone in the neighbourhood looked upon the place as somewhat uncanny, and many who were there for the first time must have been grievously disappointed to find nothing very gruesome or mysterious within its walls. It was certainly to-night merely the house of a rich man shown off to the best advantage.

Miss Rawlins looked more fair and radiant than ever. It was evidently one of the red-letter days of her life. She met us at the foot of the great oak staircase, looking like a fairy queen. She was dressed in white, and her only ornaments were a string of magnificent diamonds round her throat, and a band of them sparkling in her dark hair. I was interested to see what kind of meeting there would be between her and Fox Faversham, and I watched them both closely as I introduced them. She showed absolutely no sign of recognition, but I saw the blood leave his face when he looked at her. However, he simply bowed and made a common-place remark ; then he booked a dance on his pro-gramme, and I, being an old friend, managed to secure two for myself. She introduced us to some charming girls, and feeling that she had done her duty as hostess, left us.

I and Faversham were not alone together until quite an hour later in the evening ; he looked very tired and pale as he crossed the room to where I was standing. He obviously had something to say to me.

"Come out into one of the corridors," he said ; "it is too hot in here."

We went outside and sat down on a lounge under a large palm.

"Well?" I said interrogatively.

He passed his hand across his forehead and then turned to me and gripped hold of my arm.

"Look closely at me, Maxwell," he said. "I am

sane enough, am I not? All this evening I have had an idea that I am going mad."

I looked at him. His face was pale, and there was a wild light in his eyes. I was not prepared to say that he was quite himself, but I told him that, barring traces of temporary excitement, he spoke and acted like a sane person.

"I am under some delusion," he said. "This Miss Rawlins—who is she? What do you know about her? I have been watching her all the evening. Do you know for a fact that she is this man's daughter?"

" She is believed to be so," I replied, "and I have no reason to believe she is anything else."

" Well, she is not," he whispered hoarsely, " unless indeed I am a raving lunatic. Her name is Alice Borrodaile ; she died three years ago in Spain, and I saw her laid in her grave."

I looked at him pityingly. It seemed indeed that his mind was unhinged. Doubtless he had brooded so long over the death of the girl he had loved, that his disordered fancy had caught at a striking resemblance, and fashioned it into the form of the dead girl herself.

" Nonsense ! " I said sharply ; " this is not the age of miracles."

But directly I had spoken, it occurred to me that the words were opposed to all that I had been searching for in the fables of the past.

He looked at me contemptuously.

" I am not a fool," he said quickly. " I tell you that the girl is Alice Borrodaile."

"She is probably very like her," I replied; "perhaps it is an extraordinary resemblance."

"She is more like her than you know," he said. "Alice Borrodaile had the small white mark of an old scar on her forehead. I have heard her tell me how it was done when she was a child. When you next pass Miss Rawlins, look at her closely and you will see that mark. An extraordinary resemblance indeed!"

I was silent. If this mark were actually there, and not the creation of his disordered brain, the resemblance presented a problem that could not be solved by derision.

"Why does she not recognise you," I asked, "if it is the same girl?"

"I do not know," he said pitifully—"I do not know, Maxwell. I cannot understand it all. It is hell to me. I think my brain is going."

He rose slowly to his feet and looked wildly about him. I was concerned about his health; his mind certainly appeared to be giving way.

"Look here, old chap," I said quietly, "if I were you, I would not worry about it at all. Will you come home now and have a quiet smoke by the fire? I can easily make an excuse."

"Not till my dance," he murmured; "not till my dance with her. I would stay if it meant madness."

I tried to persuade him to leave. I foresaw no possible good to him from such an opportunity of conversation as the dance would give. But he was firm on this point, and as I heard the band beginning

to play the music for the next waltz, I left him to find
my partner. Miss Rawlins happened to be talking
to her as I came up, and I scanned the former's face
with a keen glance. Faversham had spoken the
truth. The mark was so small that I had not noticed
it before, for one can see a person every day and
fail to note such things, and no one but an ardent
lover photographs such trifles in his mind.

My partner was a charming little girl with fluffy
golden hair and laughing blue eyes. If she referred
to me afterwards in the confidences of her bed-
chamber as a "dull old stick," I should not blame
her. She certainly deserved a more attentive partner
for this dance ; but we had scarcely started that
solemn procession round the room, which is irrever-
ently styled "a waltz," when the question I had put
to Fox Faversham, asking him if Miss Rawlins had
recognised him, came back into my thoughts, and
then like a flash came the recollection of Miss
Rawlins' story of her life. She remembered nothing
since her illness three years ago. It was quite
possible for Fox Faversham to have been her lover,
and for his face to have passed completely from a
mind that had apparently been wiped as clean as a
slate. Yet her father did not recognise him, and her
name was Rawlins, not Borrodaile.

I began to have grave suspicions that there was
something very wrong in the whole business—unless,
indeed, Faversham was really insane, and was
weaving a tale out of his disordered imagination.
It was possible that he had met the girl before, and

had loved her ; that he had heard she was dead, and
that perhaps he was intentionally deceived on this
point by her parents.   It was quite possible that she
had not died, but had recovered—that he had seen
her laid in her grave was perhaps an exaggeration on
his part, or, at any rate, a delusion of his fevered
brain.   He must have been maddened with grief at
the time, and in a state to have imagined anything.
Then perhaps the girl's parents died, and she was
placed in the hands of a guardian, who adopted her,
gave her his name, and spoke of her as his own
child.   It was all possible, if not probable ; at any
rate, it was a conceivable solution, but it depended
entirely on the assumption that Fox Faversham was
mistaken as to her death.   The whole thing was
like a chess problem, and it was impossible to solve
it accurately in the middle of a dance.

My meditations were interrupted by the plaintive
expostulation of my partner, as I steered her with
some force into a middle-aged couple.   I apologised,
and turned my thoughts to the matter immediately
in hand, which was to make myself agreeable to a
charming little lady.   We subsequently turned our
dance into a more or less dignified romp round the
corridor, and ended it at the supper table, to our
mutual satisfaction.

I danced steadily all the evening till about half-
past twelve, and then came two blank spaces on my
programme.   I had left them open intentionally, in
case I wanted a quiet smoke away from the chatter
of feminine frivolity.   My next dance after this

interval was with Miss Rawlins, and it was the second dance she had given me. I left the ball-room without attracting the attention of my hostess, who at intervals prosecuted the customary search for idle young men, and found my way to the drawing-room. There were several couples in it, and passing through the room, I reached the suite of apartments that lay to the right of it. They were quite deserted; in fact, I do not suppose that any guests knew of their existence; they opened one into the other, and the one at the far end was generally used as a smoking-room. The next room was the library, and the two were only divided by a pair of heavy curtains. These were partly drawn back, and probably for this reason, or perhaps because guests were not supposed to wander into this part of the house, there were no lights in the further room. I threw myself into a chair, and lighting a cigarette, closed my eyes, and began to think about Fox Faversham. I must have felt very tired, for I had scarcely smoked for five minutes when I fell asleep.

I remember I dreamed about Faversham, and just as he was talking to me about Miss Rawlins, I opened my eyes and looked round the room. To my surprise he seemed to continue the conversation, and I noticed that his voice had got suddenly louder. Then I rubbed my eyes, and I knew that I was no longer dreaming; that I was awake, and that Faversham was actually speaking to someone in the next room. I heard a woman answer him, and recognised Miss Rawlins' voice.

They were both hidden from me by the curtain, and I was uncertain how to act. I did not know what they might have been saying, and if I disclosed myself, they might not believe that I had been asleep at all. On the other hand, if their talk had been merely conventional, I could disclose myself without causing any embarrassment. I decided in my own mind that they had probably been only talking on ordinary matters, and I was just going to give a loud yawn to attract their attention when Miss Rawlins crossed the room and came into sight. She was evidently agitated, and there was a look of alarm on her face. In a moment Faversham was by her side ; his face was like that of a madman, and the girl shrank from him as he looked at her. I sat motionless in my chair. I had no wish to hear what might follow. It was even dishonourable for me to remain, but at that moment I could not have moved from my seat for all the scruples of a Puritan. It was too late ; it was evident the crisis I feared had come.

"I do not remember ever having met you before, Mr. Faversham," she said, with an effort at calmness.

"Probably not," he replied, in a low voice ; "yet we have met before."

"I think not," she said quietly—"at least, not in the last three years."

"No, not in the last three years," said Faversham ; and then all his restraint left him, and he gripped her by the wrists.

"Who are you ? " he cried. "Who are you ? For God's sake, tell me who you are !"

I

She gave a little cry, but kept her presence of mind. She was a brave girl, and though she thought she was in the power of a lunatic, she did not scream or struggle.

" Leave go of my wrists, please, Mr. Faversham," she said, in a quiet voice. He loosed them, and she stepped back a pace or two. " How dare you insult me ? " she cried, and turned towards the door.

He walked swiftly past her and leant against it.

" Not till you hear me," he said. " I will compose myself, Miss Rawlins, but you must hear me. I am not mad ; indeed, I am not mad. You do not know what I am suffering. Let me tell you."

" Very well," she replied ; " but if you dare to touch me again, I must ask you to leave the house."

" More than three years ago," he said quietly, " I met you in Spain. You do not remember it ? "

" I do not remember it," she said gravely.

She saw now that this meeting was in the buried past of her life, and that this was something more serious than the ravings of a lunatic.

" I can only believe that all your memories of that time are dead. If you remembered your existence at all you could not have forgotten me."

" I remember nothing," she said, in a strained voice. " But before you go on, Mr. Faversham, let me tell you that three years ago I had a very severe illness, and remember absolutely nothing that happened before it."

" Thank God you have told me that ! " he cried. " I knew there was some explanation."

" Well, Mr. Faversham ? " she said.

" I cannot go on," he cried ; " I cannot, now you
have told me that. I have no right to re-open the
past for you. Yet, if I might, and without offence,
it would mean so much to me. But I dare not do it."

" Please go on," she said.

I half rose in my chair to interfere, but had not the
courage to show myself. Besides, there was something here that had to be thrashed out, if either of
them were to have any peace of mind for ever after.
I saw that, with a woman's intuition, she already
guessed the secret on his lips, and realised that her
dead past held a serious episode. I admired her
strength of mind ; she was determined to hear the
story, though she guessed what it would be, and
shrank from the hearing of it. Perhaps she thought
it would be well to get it over, or perhaps she looked
at it from an impersonal point of view, as though she
were about to hear the tale of some other woman's
love.

" Very well," said Faversham ; " but you will not
be offended ? I will be calm. I will speak as though
it concerned neither of us. You will try and believe
that I speak the truth."

" I am sure you will speak the truth, Mr.
Faversham."

" Thank you," he said simply ; " I will try and make
it as unobjectionable as possible."

He was as cold now as a piece of ice. Yet I could
see from his eyes that his passion burnt within him
like the fires of hell.

"When I knew you in Spain," he said quietly, " I loved you." He stopped apologetically. I saw her white bosom heave, and she looked on the ground. " I loved you," he continued, " and you gave me more than all the rest of the world can ever give me again. You gave me your love."

"Yes?" she murmured, keeping her eyes on the ground.

" I thought you were dead. I have never thought of anything else since. Thank God you are alive, though I may never see you again!"

My previous suspicions were confirmed—he had not spoken the truth when he told me he had seen her actually laid in her grave; he only *thought* that she was dead.

" Please go on," she said, and so tenderly that I wondered whether the recollection of the past was coming back to her.

" I recognised you directly I saw you," he continued. "Can you wonder I am not myself? I recognised you when I saw Maxwell's statue. It was like the dead coming to life. Oh, can't you remember?—can't you remember?"

"I remember nothing," she murmured, but so faintly that I could hardly hear her voice.

He buried his face in his hands. Then he suddenly stretched them out as though he would tear down the awful veil between the present and the past.

" It is too horrible," he whispered hoarsely. " Yet you were mine, and I have held you in my arms. I have kissed your lips. You gave me all your love.

Can't you remember?" He moved a step towards her, as if he would clasp her in his embrace again.

She shrank back. "Mr. Faversham!" she said indignantly.

The tale was becoming too realistic.

"I am sorry. I forgot. I said I would be calm. I am very, very sorry, Miss Rawlins."

"I will go back to the ball-room," she said wearily. He moved away from the door and opened it. "I must think," she said, pressing one hand to her forehead, "think quietly, and speak to my father. You will believe me, Mr. Faversham, when I say how sorry I am to have caused you pain. I will speak to my father, and if—at any time it—should be possible—I mean—I mean— Oh, let me go, Mr. Faversham!"

The door was open, and there was nothing to prevent her leaving the room. But she stopped and looked at him, and I saw a dark flush come over her face. I thought that perhaps, after all, the veil was not so thick but that love would tear some small rent in it. He bowed, and touched her hand with his lips.

"If I have not behaved as a gentleman should, Miss Rawlins, you will, out of your tender heart, forgive me. I have some excuse. I thought to-night I had lost my reason; but you have restored it to me. I understand everything now."

She looked him frankly in the face, and I saw pity in those large grey eyes.

"I understand," she answered; "the link with the

past is broken. No power of mine can bring the pieces together. They lie in the hands of God."

They were both silent, and through the open door came the faint sound of music, mingled with the murmur of the sea on the rocks beneath the castle.

" I do not understand," she said at last; " I do not understand my father—why he did not speak of such a thing as this."

He glanced keenly at her. I saw that it was on the tip of his tongue to say, " That is not your father. Your name was not Elaine Rawlins when I loved you ; like you, I do not understand." But Faversham behaved like the true gentleman that he was, and did not add to the difficulties of the situation.

" Perhaps he had his reasons," he replied quietly. " Let me take you to your next partner. But first I should like to ask a favour of you ? "

" I will grant it if I can, Mr. Faversham."

" It is only this. I love you now as dearly as I did in that forgotten past; but I will not speak of it again until I have the right to do so. Only, if you are in any trouble or difficulty, I should like to be able to help you and to be your friend. It would be a great consolation to me to know that you would let me do this."

She held out her hand, and he took it. I saw the mad passion leap into his eyes at the touch of her fingers, but he merely clasped them for a few seconds, and said nothing. Then they passed out of the room together, and I was alone.

I felt thoroughly ashamed of myself for having

heard so much that was not intended for my ears, but I expected that Faversham would probably tell me everything the next day, and that my conscience would be relieved of its burden. In a minute or two I rose from my seat and went back to the ball-room. The dance I should have had with Miss Rawlins was over, and I saved her the trouble of apologising by a quick confession that I had been asleep, and that I should never forgive myself. Five minutes after, Faversham came to me and suggested our departure. I could see that he was thoroughly worn out, so I ordered the carriage. He was very silent as we drove home swiftly through the snow, and it was only when we were near Ardrachan that he spoke, except in answer to my remarks.

Then he told me in a few brief words that he had confessed everything to Miss Rawlins, and that the past was a blank to her.

"Did you know of this illness of hers?" he said sharply.

"Yes," I replied; "but I did not feel justified in telling you what she confided to me. How did she account for the change of name? I suppose you told her you had heard that she was dead?"

"Of course," he replied.

"But you told me that you had seen her laid in her grave. Why did you exaggerate, Faversham? The two are very different things. In the former case I could have found an easy explanation."

He was silent, and there was no sound for a minute or two but the beat of the horses' feet in the snow.

"I spoke the truth, Maxwell," he said hoarsely. "I am perfectly calm now. It is not a delusion. I spoke the truth as I would speak it before God. I saw her dead, and I saw her in her grave."

"It is incredible, Faversham," I replied. "You were not calm at the time of her supposed death; you were mad with grief."

"It is true!" he cried vehemently. "It is absolutely true! There is some devilry in this that I do not understand, but I will get to the bottom of it. I will learn the truth, Maxwell, if I have to drag it out from Dr. Rawlins with my fingers on his throat."

CHAPTER X

FAVERSHAM ate very little at breakfast the next morning, and there was a dull, heavy expression about his eyes, as if he had not slept during the night. We talked about ordinary matters, but I could see that his mind was occupied with other thoughts. He said no more than politeness required, and once or twice apologised for not catching the substance of my remarks. The weather was suffic:-ently depressing; the air had suddenly become warmer, and a fine, drizzling rain had begun to melt the snow. The sky was grey, and heavy black clouds were slowly coming up from the west. It was impossible to do anything with comfort out of doors, so, after breakfast, we went into the library and resigned ourselves to a day of inaction. I stared disconsolately out of the window, and Faversham sat gloomily in a chair by the fire, with an evening paper, sent on to him from Glasgow by post, lying unopened on his knee.

"I mean to get at the truth," he said suddenly. "I have not slept all night. I have turned over a thousand things in my brain, and have arrived at no conclusion. What do you really think is the truth, Maxwell?"

I turned away from the gloomy landscape and strolled over to the fire.

"Let us look at this matter calmly, Faversham," I said. "Can you consider it absolutely dispassion- ately? I know it will be hard."

"I think so," he replied. "At any rate I can listen to what you have to say."

"Well, let us look at the absolute facts," I said, sitting down in a chair opposite him. "Here, on the one hand, is Miss Rawlins, the daughter, or the alleged daughter of Dr. Rawlins. She does not know you, and her father does not know you. They came to Balath three years ago, and, as far as I can discover, nothing else is known about them. On the other hand, you say that three years ago this girl was known by the name of Alice Borrodaile, that you met her in Spain, that she died, and that you saw her after she was dead."

"Those are the facts," he replied quietly.

"Well," I continued, "the facts would easily agree if it were not for one point. It is quite possible she was in Spain three years ago; it is quite possible that Dr. Rawlins is not her father, and he does not remember you, because he has never seen you. It is quite possible—in fact, it is certain—that she herself would not remember you, as she has forgotten every- thing that happened before three years ago. It is quite possible that she has changed her name; all these things occur every day in life. But the one point that is inexplicable is, that you saw her dead, and she is now alive. The whole mystery boils itself down to that."

"Well," he replied, nervously fingering some embroidery on the chair, "what is the explanation?"

"There are two or three explanations," I said. "The first is that you are mistaken in supposing her to be the same girl. The second is, that you are mistaken in supposing that she died."

"I am mistaken on neither point," he replied, rising from his chair; "it is impossible for a man to be mistaken about two facts of that sort unless he is mad."

"Unless he is temporarily mad, Faversham," I said gently, looking at his agitated face.

"You think I am mad," he answered, as he paced up and down the room, "and I suppose that is the third explanation? But I assure you I am not."

"I am certain you are not," I replied, "but even the sanest of us have our delusions in moments of grief or passion, or, in fact, on any of those occasions when the human mind is stirred to its lowest depths."

"Well, now I will give you an explanation," he said, and then he stopped suddenly.

"Well?" I said.

"It is this. The dead has been raised to life."

"The age of miracles is over," I replied.

"Is it?" he said, with a tinge of sarcasm in his voice. "I thought, Maxwell, you had tried to prove that it was not. I have read articles of yours on the subject. What, then, has been the object of your researches into the mysteries of life and death ? "

" The result has been a failure."

" Yet this man, Dr. Rawlins, has succeeded," he continued.

" He says so," I replied ; " but, at any rate, he had not succeeded three years ago. And you are no scientist, Faversham, I am afraid ; he does not claim to have found the means of bringing the dead to life ; the dead body from the scientific point of view is living matter. What he does claim to have done is to have introduced the germs of life into absolutely dead matter, such as stone or iron—by-the-bye, what about that piece of granite he gave me ? I think I will have a look at it."

I rose from my chair, and going over to a small ebony cabinet in the corner, took out a glass jar and brought it over to the window so that I could examine its contents in the light. There was apparently no change in its appearance. Then somehow or other the jar slipped through my fingers and fell with a crash to the floor. I stooped down to pick up the broken pieces of glass, and, to my surprise, I saw that the stone had been shattered into fragments. There was no piece larger than a grain of wheat, and most of it had crumbled into fine dust. I called Faversham, and he picked up some of the dust in his fingers and looked it.

" I should not care to build a house of that stone," he said. " Faugh ! What a smell ! "

There was a faint odour of decayed matter rising from the floor. I took up a few grains of the stone and sniffed it. The stench was horrible ; it might almost have been putrid flesh.

"This is a matter worth investigation," I said, and going to the cupboard I took out my microscope and set it on a table by the window.

Then I placed the powder on the glass slide, and adjusted the lens to the right focus. As I did so, I gave a cry of surprise. The small particles of stone were stirred and shifted by thousands of minute living specks no bigger than a grain of dust. The stone was alive. It had decayed like a piece of vegetable or animal matter.

Faversham came up and looked through the eye-piece, examining the stone attentively for a minute.

"And yet you say the age of miracles is over ? " he said, when he had finished his examination.

"A trick," I replied, "or else Dr. Rawlins is a greater man than I thought."

"He is more than that," Faversham cried ; "he is a devil. I tell you that Balath holds some secret; there is something extraordinary about this man. I guessed it when I first saw him, and I am sure of it now. You have noticed it yourself. What is the meaning of this poor girl's loss of memory? What is the meaning of the extraordinary appearance of all these monkeys in a part of the world where it is most unlikely that one has ever been seen before ? They could not all have come over with sailors. Why is this man, Dr. Rawlins, sick with terror at the sight

of them? Why is he obviously an Oriental under
an assumed name? You have asked yourself these
questions and cannot answer them. There is something wrong, Maxwell; something very wrong.
There is a secret locked up in that old castle,
but I will tear it out, if it costs me my life, and
if I have to blast the walls with dynamite to get at
it. And the secret is bound up with the death of the
girl I loved, and love still."

He flung himself into a chair and buried his face
in his hands.

"Let us go out for a walk," I said; "it is better to
get wet than miserable. There is no answer to these
questions; there is something wrong about the
whole business, and I will do my best to help you
to find out the truth. But sometimes the truth is
better left unknown."

"January the 13th," he said, as if speaking to
himself—"January the 13th. Why is the statue to
be finished by that date?"

"I am sure I do not know," I replied. "In any
case, we need not worry about it now. Come out,
and get some fresh air."

After a good deal of persuasion, I induced him to
leave the fireside and go for a walk; but he insisted
on going up into the hills to look at the wood which
had been burnt. I tried to induce him to go in
another direction, as I wished to keep his mind off
the matter as much as possible. But it was of no
avail. He said he would either do that or stay
indoors. So we climbed the hill in the drenching

rain, until we reached the wood, which was one of the most desolate sights I have ever seen.

The trees had been almost completely destroyed. Here and there a small clump of them had escaped the general destruction, but most of the wood was simply a mass of charred stumps and ashes. Some of these were still smouldering, in spite of the damp weather, and as we picked our way over the blackened ground, we felt the earth in places still warm beneath our feet. But the steady rain, almost as fine as mist, was gradually beating the whole place into a wet mass of black and sodden ashes, and a faint cloud of vapour hung over everything, like a fog rising from the sea. Before we had gone very far into this scene of desolation, Faversham stooped down, and picking up a piece of wood, examined it closely.

"I thought so!" he said. "I wondered why the wood burnt so well; a good deal of it must have been damp."

He handed the charred fragment to me; it was one of the staves of a barrel.

"Petroleum or tar," he said. "I expect we shall find more."

He was right; we searched carefully, and found three similar pieces in different parts of the wood.

"Dr. Rawlins?" he said, with an inquiring glance at me.

"He wished to make a clean job of it," I replied. "We ought to find some bodies."

We looked carefully, but only found one little

charred lump of skin and bone. However, the destruction had been so general, and had been spread over so many acres, that it would have taken us a week to thoroughly examine and turn over the piles of fallen trunks and tangled debris.

"They could hardly have escaped," said Faversham. "I noticed that the fire started in several places. These points formed a circle, and the animals were probably too terrified to stir till they were surrounded by a ring of flames."

"Let us go back, Faversham," I said; "this atmosphere is awful."

Indeed the place was like a Turkish bath. We were both pouring with sweat and soaked with steam and rain. Our hands, clothes, and faces were as black as soot; there was nothing to be gained by further examination. Faversham was much better away from the place, and, personally, I did not much care what we found. So we left the wood, and taking a sharp walk farther up the hill, we returned home another way, and got back to lunch at two o'clock.

The footman said that in our absence Dr. Rawlins and his daughter had called, and had asked to see the statue. The man had thought that there would be no harm in allowing them to do so, as he knew that Dr. Rawlins had purchased it. They had, he said, spent quite an hour in the studio, but could not wait until our return.

"I wanted to see Dr. Rawlins," Faversham said.

"I wish we had stayed at home; I have a few questions to ask him."

"It is perhaps better you were out, then," I replied, "for he might not have given you very pleasant answers."

"I could, at any rate, have seen her," he said roughly.

"If you take my advice, Faversham, you will not see her again. It will only give you pain."

"It may be possible to revive the past," he answered; "who knows that it is impossible? Perhaps some voice may break through the silence, and perhaps some ray of light may pierce that veil of darkness. Who knows? At any rate, one can start afresh. I may win her love again."

After dinner that evening we sat comfortably by the fire in the library; the house was perfectly silent, except for an occasional sound of laughter when a door opened into the servants' quarters. For some reason or other I was unaccountably depressed. Outside, the rain was pattering gently on the windows; but within, the fire and lamps were burning brightly. Both Faversham and the dog were in the room with me. There was absolutely nothing in my surroundings to account for the strange feeling of nervousness which had come over me. But I had a vague sense of something being wrong. It is not unusual, I believe, in one's experience. A man sometimes wakes up in the middle of the night, and a sudden idea seizes him that a burglar or some other unauthorised person is

K

in the room. He hears no noise, but he cannot get
rid of the idea, and it is not until he has lit a candle
and discovered that it was only fancy, that he can get
to sleep again. A similar idea had seized me to-night.
I was sure there was something in the house which
ought not to be there, and I felt so restless that only
the fear of Faversham's ridicule kept me from going
through all the rooms to see what was the matter.

However, I struggled against the feeling, and
turned my thoughts to the work I had just completed. Faversham was gloomy and silent, and my
meditations were not interrupted. I began to recall
every line and curve of the statue, and wondered
why I was so dissatisfied with it. I knew that the
conception had been good, but I felt that the execution of it fell far short of what I had dreamed of.
In truth, I do not suppose that any work, whether
of author, artist, sculptor, or musician, has ever
realised the dreams of its creator. But in this case
the difference between the design and its accomplish-
ment seemed to be almost immeasurable.

" Let us go and look at your statue," Faversham
said abruptly.

He had not spoken for ten minutes, and it was
curious that he should have broken in upon my
thoughts with a remark that almost seemed to be
suggested by them. I wondered if his mind had
been travelling along the same line of thought.

" Why ? " I asked sharply, as if the idea were
ridiculous.

" I want to see it," he said simply.

"Well, you can go if you like; what on earth do you want to see it for?"

He was silent, and I guessed he merely wanted to look at the face of the girl he loved. I had a suspicion that he visited the studio every day. I questioned him no further, but, rising from my seat, lighted a candle, and we made our way upstairs to the studio. But, as I opened the door, a sudden draught extinguished the light, and I felt a current of air sweeping through the room. I was unable to relight the wick until I had closed the door.

Then I saw that one of the windows was wide open, and that there was a pool of water on the floor beneath it. I put the candle down, and went over to close it.

"What fool has done this?" I exclaimed sharply. "Servants have strange ideas of ventilation," and closing the window with a crash, I fastened it, and looked through the glass into the garden.

"Come here!" said Faversham suddenly.

The cloth was, for some reason or other, off the statue, and was lying in a white heap on the floor.

He was looking earnestly at the sculptured figure of Elaine Rawlins. I came over to his side, and he pointed to some small brown marks on the white stone. They were footprints of some small animal, and it required only a momentary glance to see that they were similar to the one I found on my book in the library. I noticed, with a feeling of horror, that one of them was right across the beautiful mouth.

"What does this mean, Faversham?" I asked.

"It means that Dr. Rawlins was here this morning," he cried, "and no doubt this thing has followed him."

We looked at each other for a few moments in silence. Then Faversham walked over to the window and stared out into the darkness; but I stepped back a pace or two from the statue and stood gazing fixedly at it, in the hope that some sudden flash of inspiration might come upon me, and that I might discover some way to remedy its faults. For quite five minutes I watched it with a glance that might have almost read the soul of any living thing. I exerted the whole power of my mind to draw the secret of my failure from its stone, and I concentrated all my will and thought on that block of marble.

Then, as I gazed, a curious thing happened. The statue gradually grew misty and faint in outline, and I felt as if I were looking into the eyes of a mesmerist. Then it seemed to quiver and grow clear again, and as it grew more distinct I could have sworn that I saw a flicker of life pass over the face of the girl. It was probably only a delusion, for my brain was dizzy with looking so long and intently at a single object. But it seemed very real to me then, and stepping quickly back, I put up my hands to my face for a moment, and closed my eyes. When I opened them again I saw Faversham watching me.

"What is the matter?" he said.

"Merely a delusion, Faversham!" I cried; "but examine the statue. Does it seem to you to have changed?"

He looked at it carefully, and replied that it appeared to him to be just the same. I looked at it again. He was quite right. There was no change in it at all. But somehow or other I fancied that it gave me more pleasure to look at it now than it had ever done before, and I began to think that, after all, it was not such a failure as I had imagined. It certainly appeared to have grown insensibly nearer to my ideal.

Then I remembered Dr. Rawlins' promise, and that he had visited it this morning. And, with this recollection in my mind, I looked at it again, keeping my eyes steadily fixed on it. As I did so, the same mist came over my sight, and I was positive that something moved in the room. It was not Fox Faversham, for he was standing behind me. One curious fact I noticed was that the room seemed to be hung up before my gaze like a painted picture seen through a mist. It was, I suppose, only the natural result of looking so long at one place. I saw nothing clearly but the statue, which my eyes were fixed upon. But I had a dim impression of the rest of the room, and I was positive that something had moved. Then a thick mist came over my eyes again, and I felt quite giddy.

"Open the window, Faversham, for a second," I said, "and let's have some fresh air. I do not feel very well."

He opened the window, and a blast of wintry air swept over my face. I took a deep breath of it, and everything became clear again. I think I must have almost mesmerised myself by staring so fixedly at the white marble.

" I think we have seen enough," Faversham said. " Shall I cover the statue up ? "

I nodded assent, and he went over to where the large white sheet lay piled up in a heap on the floor. He took hold of one corner, and, as he did so, I saw the centre of it heave and tremble for a second, as though he had shaken it into new folds. But he had merely raised the corner gently from the ground, and could not have disturbed the middle part at all. He noticed the movement, too, and swept the whole of the sheet up quickly, creating a draught that made the flame of the candle shoot up horizontally in a thin flickering line. Then, in the momentary semi-darkness I saw him stoop quickly, and something white scuttled across the room like a flash of light, went swiftly up the curtain, and disappeared through the window into the darkness. Simultaneously there was a crash of broken glass. I saw that Faversham had thrown a heavy block of marble, and had missed his mark. We looked at each other.

" It has been here all the time," Faversham said, after a pause. " Curse the brute ! What does it want ? I wish I had been a thought quicker, and a little more accurate in my aim ; I'd have broken its back."

" Let us go downstairs," I said ; " there's something I don't like about these animals, though, of course, they are perfectly harmless. Bah ! I can smell it now."

I walked to the window and closed it, and we went
downstairs, locking the door after us.

We smoked in silence for a few minutes, but I did
not enjoy my pipe. The faint, horrible odour of that
white animal was still in my nostrils, and seemed to
destroy the favour of the tobacco.

" Have you a revolver ? " Faversham asked
suddenly.

" Yes," I replied.

" Can you lend it to me to-morrow ? "

" What do you want it for ? " I asked, looking at
him keenly.

I was not quite sure that he was in a fit state to be
trusted with a weapon of that kind. Just now he
looked too much like the kind of man who cared
little for his own life, and less for the lives of others

" I am going to Balath to-morrow," he replied. " I
probably shall not want the revolver, but still it may
be useful. There is a look in Rawlins' eyes that I
do not like. I do not think he would stick at anything if I really inconvenienced him, and I intend to
inconvenience him a good deal."

" What do you intend to do when you get there ?
Do you want me to come ? "

" I would rather go by myself," he answered. " I
am going to get to the bottom of the whole business,
if I can. I don't think I shall go in by the front
door, but I may do so."

" I think you are unwise, Faversham. Knowledge
is not to be gained in this way, but only by time,
which lays all secrets bare."

" And often takes two thousand years to uncover them. Thank you, Maxwell. I may seem impatient, but I prefer to trust to myself. A great deal can be done in a quiet, unobtrusive way. I sometimes think I should have made a good burglar."

" The revolver is here," I said, and crossing the room to my writing-table, I unlocked a drawer, and handed the weapon to him.

It was a Webley, Army pattern, of modern make, and he looked at it approvingly. I gave him a box of cartridges ; he filled the chambers, and placed half a dozen in his pocket.

" On second thoughts," he said, " I will go to-night. There is no time like the present."

I tried to dissuade him. It was a wretched night, and the roads were three or four inches deep in slush. But he appeared to have made up his mind, and seeing that no arguments were of any avail, I tried to persuade him to ride over ; but he insisted upon walking, stating as his reason that he would have to put up the horse at the inn, and that it would attract attention in the village.

" In any case, I wish you would let me go with you, Faversham," I said.

" No, Maxwell," he replied, " you had better not. This is my affair, and I shall see it through all right alone. But you might fill my flask with brandy, and get me some sandwiches. I may not be back to breakfast."

I rang the bell, and gave the necessary orders.

He went upstairs, and reappeared in a few minutes

in an old shooting coat, breeches, and gaiters. Then
he put on a heavy overcoat, placed the sandwiches
and flask in one pocket and the revolver in the
other, and put on his cap. He was determined to
start at once, and I went to the hall door to see him
off.

" This is a mad trick, Faversham," I said ; " I wish
I could stop you. Have you plenty of tobacco and
matches ? "

" Plenty, thanks. I'll probably be in to breakfast,
but do not wait for me."

" Remember this is a law-abiding country, Faversham."

He looked at me. His face was very stern and
pale, and his mouth set with hard determination.

" I will remember," he said ; " but all the same I
intend to find out the truth. Good-night, Maxwell."

I saw him go down the drive into the wet darkness, and closed the door. I felt that I had done
wrong in letting him go alone. Poor Faversham,
half mad with grief and the uncertain terrors of this
strange web of mystery that seemed to be clinging
round the place, was no fit person to go in search of
the truth with a loaded revolver in his pocket.

I did not sleep much that night. I lay awake
trying to piece many different things together in my
mind. But when at last I did manage to close my
eyes, the thoughts still whirled round and round in a
confusing tangle. Then the air of my dream was
overshadowed with a great darkness, and the white
face of Elaine shone through the gloom like a misty

star.   Then the bare white throat seemed to thicken,
and the dark hair melted into the forehead, and the
burning eyes shrank away, until the whole face looked
like a shapeless mass of snow, but quivering and
changing like a cloud.   Then it formed itself anew,
and the grinning face of a white monkey mocked me
in the darkness.   Then that, too, faded into mist, and
from the mist there came the semblance of a white
skull, with glowing eyes in its deep sockets, and the
dark hairs of a living man streaming from its bony
head.   And through all these changes I saw, like a
thin veil of gauze flung across the scene, the face of
Dr. Rawlins.

CHAPTER XI

FAVERSHAM did not appear at breakfast the next morning, but about eleven o'clock Dr. Rawlins and his daughter drove over from Balath. The latter looked extremely ill, and there were dark circles round her eyes, as if she had not slept for the last two nights. Doubtless her interview with Faversham had been a great shock to her. I felt very sorry for the poor child, and wished that my friend had never come to stay with me. She brightened up, however, when she shook hands with me, and chatted pleasantly about the success of the dance.

Dr. Rawlins himself had an anxious look on his face. Indeed, I had noticed during the past two months that he was ageing very rapidly. The faint wrinkles on his handsome face had deepened into dark lines. I noticed, too, that he had acquired a habit of looking sharply and suddenly about the room, as if he expected to see something. Yet there was no sign of dimness in his flashing eyes, nor any indication of weakness in his determined mouth.

While I was talking to his daughter, he strolled

over to the drawing-room window, and seemed to be searching the garden with keen eyes.

"How is your friend?" he said, suddenly turning from the window.

There was a peculiar smile on his face, and I wondered whether he knew where Faversham was.

"He is quite well," I replied, with a laugh. "He is walking off the effects of your dance."

Miss Rawlins turned her head away, and pretended to examine some Japanese ivories on a side-table.

"The dance has been too much for Elaine," he said. "I warned her against the excitement, but she would have her way. She is not at all well."

"I am all right, father," she broke in cheerfully. "Mr. Maxwell will think I am an invalid," and then she turned the conversation to general subjects.

I began to wonder why the Doctor had called, but I was not long left in doubt.

"You will want to know what brings us here so early, Mr. Maxwell," he said. "I wished to take some photographs of the statue. A friend of mine in London is very much interested in modern art, and this at present is the only way in which I can show your work to him. We called here yesterday, but the light was too bad to take any pictures."

"The statue is yours, Dr. Rawlins; of course you can photograph it."

"We need not trouble you, Mr. Maxwell," he said, producing a folding Kodak from the pocket of his overcoat; "it may take an hour, and I am sure your time is valuable."

I hesitated for a moment. It was obvious he did not want me. Then I made up my mind. My dressing-room window looks out upon the glass roof of the studio.

"I am rather busy, Dr. Rawlins," I replied, "so I hope you will excuse me, and you too, Miss Rawlins— unless, indeed, you are going to stay with me downstairs?"

"No," said Dr. Rawlins sharply, "I trust a great deal to her judgment; she knows more about photography than I do."

"And Mrs. Balquiddy is not here," Miss Rawlins said, with an arch little smile. "It would be most improper."

"Let me, however," I continued, "have the pleasure of showing you to the door of the studio."

I wanted to observe Dr. Rawlins' face when he saw the footprints on the marble.

We all three made our way to the studio, Miss Rawlins laughing and chatting merrily as we went upstairs, though I knew her heart was very sad. What a charming child she was! If Faversham ever won her back to him, he would get more happiness than most men deserve.

"I am afraid you will find the room very cold," I remarked, as I opened the door; "one of the windows is broken."

I rang the bell, and when the servant came, told her to paste a piece of paper over the aperture, and get the village glazier to mend the pane some time during the day.

"If you have a fire lit," I said, striking a match, "it will be fairly warm, and I suppose you will not be very long."

"We can keep on our hats and coats," Miss Rawlins said. "It is a shame to give you so much trouble."

I lighted the fire, and it crackled merrily. Then I looked at Miss Rawlins and saw that she had suddenly turned very white, and that her eyes were staring fixedly at the wall.

"Are you ill?" I said quickly.

"No, no, I am all right," she replied faintly, holding on to the back of a chair; "I felt a bit queer —that is all."

"Go and get some brandy, please," Dr. Rawlins said, going quickly to her side, and taking her hand. "What is it, my child—what is it?"

"I am all right, father; it is nothing."

He looked at her anxiously, his old face full of tender distress.

I ran downstairs and brought up a wine-glassful of brandy; but when I returned, she was sitting on the sofa, and there was a bright flush on her cheeks. She sprang up as I entered, and laughed.

"I am perfectly well," she cried, waving me away, "and I am a teetotaller. Don't tempt me."

I could not persuade her to touch the brandy, so I placed the glass on the mantelpiece, and walking over to the statue, took off the cloth. Dr. Rawlins came over to my side, and I watched his face. He gave a slight start as he saw the brown marks on the marble, and shot a quick glance at the window. He at once connected the two events. Then he stooped down and examined the footprints more closely.

"What is it?" I said, pretending that I saw them for the first time.

"An uninvited visitor," he replied curtly, "and one whose visits you will do well to discourage. I should have that pane mended at once."

I looked carefully at the marks; they seemed more numerous now than they did the night before. A few of them were tinged with red, and there were one or two drops that looked like blood on the white stone. I went to the window and examined the broken pane. There were some white hairs sticking to the sharp edge of the glass.

"If I were an animal," I said, "I should be sorry to get through that broken pane."

Indeed, I had thought it so impossible that I had taken no steps the night before to stop up the opening; the hole was in the centre of the pane, and nothing could have got through, except by clinging to the broken edges of the glass.

Dr. Rawlins made no reply, but had dipped his handkerchief in the brandy, and was wiping out the stains.

Miss Rawlins treated the whole thing as a joke, and seemed immensely amused. In a minute or two the housemaid came with some paste and paper. I went downstairs for a little while, knowing that nothing of any importance would take place while Jane was in the studio, and then went up to my dressing-room. The window was open, and by leaning cautiously out, I had a good view of the glass roof of the studio.

My curiosity was not rewarded by any discovery of importance. In the first place, the glass roof was none too clean, for the melting snow had left a thin deposit of dirt upon it. Secondly, a view obtained from directly overhead is not a very satisfactory one. However, I saw Dr. Rawlins standing in various parts of the room with a small black box in his hand. He was obviously doing what he had said, and was taking photographs. There was nothing mysterious in his actions. Miss Rawlins sat on a chair watching him. I saw this much and no more, and felt rather a fool for taking the trouble to watch such uninteresting operations.

I had seen enough ; whatever mystery there was about these two was not going to be revealed in a glass-covered studio open to the view of at least a dozen windows ; in fact, it was probable that Dr. Rawlins knew I was watching him. I left the dressing-room, and went downstairs to the library, and in about a quarter of an hour I heard the Doctor's voice asking for me in the hall, and they were both shown into the library.

" I think we have done it justice," said Miss Rawlins ; " we have photographed it in every way but upside down."

" Perhaps you might have done that from one of the bedroom windows," said her father, looking at me with a faint smile.

I noticed, however, that he had a hunted expression in his eye, and that his face had almost a look of despair on it. I imagined a man might look something like that when he was watching his dearest hopes being shattered, and the fabric of his life crumbling to the ground. Then he held out his hand.

"Good-bye, Mr. Maxwell! I hope the photographs will be a success. I shall send for the statue on January the 12th," and he turned to go.

At that moment, however, there was a clattering of hoofs on the drive, and a violent ring at the bell, and a minute later Faversham strode into the room.

His face was white, and his eyes bloodshot. He was spattered thickly with mud from head to foot. His left hand was bound with a piece of linen, and the bandage was wet and crimson with blood. In his right hand he held a heavy hunting-crop. He entered without a word, and closing the door, leant his back against it.

Dr. Rawlins looked at him inquiringly, as one might look at a lunatic, and Miss Rawlins shrank to her father's side with a little cry of surprise.

"My dear Faversham," I said, "do you see Miss Rawlins is here?"

His cap was still on his head, but when I spoke he took it off, and, crumpling it up in his hand, bowed ever so slightly.

"Have you had an accident, Mr. Faversham?" asked the Doctor; "you quite startled us."

L

" I shall startle you more before I leave the room,"
he replied.

His voice was hoarse and broken. Dr. Rawlins
shrugged his shoulders, and turning away from him,
made some commonplace remark to his daughter. I
was uncertain how to act. It was evident that
Faversham had discovered something of the very
highest importance, but I did not want a scene.
There was Miss Rawlins to be thought of.

" I think we must go, Mr. Maxwell," said Dr.
Rawlins, looking at his watch, " or we shall be late
for lunch."

He paid no more attention to Faversham, who
stood glaring at him with a white face, than if the
young fellow had been a footman.

Faversham smiled and crossed his legs, tapping
one of his gaiters with his hunting-crop.

" I do not wish to seem rude," he said, " but I have
something to say to you before you go. Would you
mind waiting a few minutes in the drawing-room,
Miss Rawlins ? " And moving to one side, he
half opened the door.

" Do you wish to go, Elaine ? " her father asked.

" I would rather stay," she replied, in a low voice,
edging a little closer to his side and taking his hand.

I think she imagined that he was in danger, and
wished to be near to help him. Faversham's face
certainly boded no good.

" You see, sir," the old man said courteously, " that
my daughter's wishes are to stay. It remains with
you to respect them or not."

"Go, Miss Rawlins!" he cried. "Go, Miss Rawlins! Go — for your own sake — I beseech you!"

"I will stay," she said firmly, "unless my father wishes me to leave him."

The old man looked at her for a moment tenderly, and then kissed her, linking his arm in hers.

"Well, Mr. Faversham," he said, "tell us quickly what you have to say."

"It will be no news to you," replied Faversham, ' but I will tell you, Maxwell, and you, too, Miss Rawlins — though I would have spared you the pain. First, I will tell you that this man "—pointing to Dr. Rawlins with his hunting-crop—" is not the father of Miss Rawlins. Then I will tell you that his name is not Rawlins. And then I will tell you that every hour Miss Rawlins stays with him at Balath is at the risk of her life."

As each sentence fell from Faversham's lips, the lines round the Doctor's mouth grew deeper and more determined. He let go of his daughter's arm, and advanced a step towards Faversham ; his lips were slightly parted, showing a thin line of teeth between them. He looked for a moment as if he were going to spring at him, and I saw Faversham's hand tighten on his hunting-crop. But the attitude was only momentary, and it could scarcely have lasted for two seconds. He turned to me, and laughed heartily.

"I should obtain medical advice for your friend, Mr. Maxwell," he said. "Elaine, we will go home.

Perhaps you will allow us to pass, Mr. Faversham, now that you have given us such interesting information ? "

" What I have told you, Dr. Rawlins, is only what you already know ; but I will tell you something that perhaps you do not know—that I met Miss Rawlins three years ago at Malaga in Spain, and that her name then was not Elaine Rawlins but Alice Borrodaile. I would say more if she were not here, but when I say that much you will see that the game is up. All secrets are laid bare in the long run, Dr. Rawlins ; there is always some little chink to let a ray of light into the darkness. I happen on this occasion to be that little chink. This is a lonely part of the world—it was most unlikely that anyone from Malaga would come here ; but still the world is very small, after all. I have come here, and am the only link between her present and her past. I intend to save her from you, and she knows that I will gladly give my life to do it."

" Father, father ! " cried the girl ; " I am afraid ; he is mad ! Take me away, please."

" You hear your answer, Mr. Faversham," said Dr. Rawlins, with a cold smile.

" She shall not return to Balath with you," Faversham exclaimed violently, " if I can prevent it. Maxwell, you will help me. I swear to you that I have found out everything, and that if we let her return, we may be answerable for her death. I will tell you all afterwards. I cannot now while she is here. But Dr. Rawlins must return to Balath alone."

I was in a very uncomfortable situation. On the one side was Faversham, who, though half mad with excitement, had probably some very good reason for what he had said. On the other, Dr. Rawlins, cool and polite, my guest, and insisting merely on ordinary courtesy, and with him this girl, implicitly trusting in him and clinging to him, while she trembled with fear under the look of Faversham's eyes, and seemed only anxious to be out of the house.

"I will leave it to Miss Rawlins, Faversham," I said.

"She cannot judge!" he cried. "She does not believe me. How can she judge, when she does not know? It all seems so impossible. Of course she does not believe me."

"Where, Mr. Faversham, did you obtain this interesting information?" asked Dr. Rawlins sarcastically.—"From the villagers?"

"I have been in Balath Castle from about two o'clock until 10.30 this morning," Faversham answered. "I have here in my pocket the story of your life." And he touched the left side of his coat with his bandaged hand.

Then for the first time did Dr. Rawlins' face show any real anxiety; but it was only for a moment.

"Truly, Elaine," he said, "we have been entertaining a noble gentleman unawares. Are you sure, sir, it is the story of my life? What book have you selected to honour me? What novelist has painted a hero so much resembling your most uninteresting servant?"

"It is the story of one who was a curse to all who

knew him—the story of Deva Dacobra, outlaw, murderer, and patricide!"

"You honour me," he replied, with a mocking bow; "but I will take no advantage of you. Elaine shall decide between us, and the advantage shall be all on your side."

He went up to the girl, who was as white as death, and kissed her. She smiled back at him, and gave him a look of such great trust and tenderness that I had little hopes for Faversham.

"Elaine, my child," the old man said, "you have heard this man's story. Try and imagine for a moment that he is not mad. Suppose that my name is not Rawlins; suppose that you are not my daughter; suppose even that you are in danger at Balath—though I think you know the danger cannot come from me. Take this for a moment as if it were all true; as if I had told it to you myself. Would you, under these circumstances, rather go back to Balath, or find such protection as these young men would give you? They are, of course, men of honour. You would have nothing to fear from them."

She glanced for a moment at our faces.

"They are honourable gentlemen, father," she replied—"one, at least, would give his life for me; but I love you, and would not leave you, if all they say were true."

There was silence for a minute; then Faversham tucked his hunting-crop under his left arm and slipped his right hand into his pocket.

"Well, Mr. Faversham," said the Doctor, "we will wish you good-day. I regret that I cannot leave by the window."

But Faversham did not budge an inch from the door.

"Faversham!" I said sharply, "you heard what Miss Rawlins said?"

"I heard," he replied mechanically, his eyes fixed on the girl's face. "Her mind as well as her soul is his. He speaks through her lips." And as he uttered these words he drew his right hand out of his pocket, and I saw the dull blue light on my revolver.

This was going too far. I strolled over quietly to his side.

"Please move from the door, Faversham," I said, "if you have any of the feelings of a gentleman."

His face was working horribly; he was quite beside himself; he was evidently meditating whether he would kill Dr. Rawlins where he stood, in the presence of the girl. I slipped my fingers round his wrist, and laid my other hand on his elbow. The movement seemed to arouse him to definite action. He tried to wrench his arm free from me, glaring like a madman, but I was the stronger man of the two, and one of his hands was disabled. I twisted his arm back suddenly with all my force, and the weapon dropped on the floor. As he staggered back from the door, I picked up the revolver and placed it in my pocket; he said nothing, but sank into a chair and buried his face in his hands. I then held the door open, and Dr. Rawlins and his daughter moved towards it. Neither of them spoke. The girl had hidden her face during the brief struggle, and I saw that she suffered deeply.

Then Faversham leaped suddenly from his chair, sprang across the room, and flinging himself on his knees before her, seized her hand.

"Forgive me! Forgive me!" he cried, "but do not go—for God's sake, do not go!"

He gripped the girl's wrist so hard that she gave a little cry of pain, and looked at him in terror.

"Faversham!" I said sternly, "you forget yourself! This lady is in my house."

He rose without a word and walked to the window. I saw Dr. Rawlins and his daughter to the door, and watched them till the carriage had disappeared round the corner of the drive. When I re-entered the library, Faversham was still standing at the window. I went up to him and laid my hand on his shoulder. He turned round, and I saw that all the passion had left his face.

"Thank you, Maxwell," he said simply. "You have saved me from myself. I should have killed him in her presence—but it may have to be done yet, if we would save her."

"Sit down and tell me all about it. Have you had any breakfast?"

"Sandwiches," he replied. "I am not hungry, but a little tired."

He was shaking from head to foot, and I insisted upon his sitting down by the fire. I then went to the cupboard and poured him out a stiff glass of brandy, which he drank greedily.

"Well?" I said, when he had drained the glass to the last drop.

"I will tell you everything," he replied; "there is not much to tell. The clue to the whole mystery lies in this little story, which I happened to come across. It would convey nothing to a stranger; but I think, when you read it, you will see that it conveys everything to you and me."

He stopped and drew from his pocket a thin round tin, such as architects use for plans, and laid it on the table.

"Shall I read it now?" said I.

"No. I will tell you how I got it. By-the-bye, I have something else," and he took from his pocket a key which he laid down beside the roll. "For further use," he explained, "if we require it. It opens the door from the garden into the servants' quarters."

"You have not wasted your time."

"I have not," he replied. "I will tell you everything. I had a stiff walk to Balath. It was pitch dark, and pouring with rain the whole time. I lost my way twice, and did not reach the castle until one o'clock. I had a sandwich and a drop of whisky, and set to work to find an entrance. I walked round the whole place, and inspected every foot of the walls, and every window. The windows were all barred, and most of them six feet from the ground. There were two or three side doors, but of course they were all locked. I began to realise the folly of my errand, and wondered if I could make any excuse for ringing at the front door, and so gain admittance under false pretences. But I decided that the time of night rendered any such course impossible. They were all in bed, and the whole castle was in absolute darkness.

" I eventually decided to climb up a part of the ruined wall farthest away from the inhabited portion of the castle. I did so with considerable difficulty, for it was at least fifteen feet high, and I found cut glass at the top ; I have torn my left hand considerably. I got inside, and wandered about the deserted ruins. I could see nothing, but I remembered hearing you speak of an entrance from this side. I think you used it once when Miss—I will call her Miss Rawlins —showed you over the ruins. I found it after searching some time, but it was locked. I cursed myself for a fool—as if any door was likely to be left open in a house so carefully guarded from the public as this ! However, I had brought one or two tools with me ; I did not show them to you before I started ; they once helped me out of a serious difficulty in Spain. I could not have used them on any of the other doors, because I should have made too much noise, but here, on the side of the house where there were only kitchens and outhouses, I was not likely to be heard, especially as the wind was roaring through the broken walls and towers.

" Once inside, I took off my boots, and groped my way through the kitchens and passages until I reached the hall. From there I remembered my way, and found the drawing-room. There was no sound in the house, and I had six hours of darkness before me. In that time I must have ransacked every room except the bedrooms. I did not waste a minute. I was able to light a candle, as all the rooms were shuttered, and no light could show through the windows. Then I opened every drawer and every cupboard, read every paper and document, and examined everything for some clue. I had no sense of shame. I was dominated by a single idea, and that was to elucidate the mystery that hung over the life and death of the woman I loved. If anyone had interrupted me, I think I should have shot them without hesitation. I searched for six hours and found nothing. Then I put all the rooms as straight as possible, so that my visit might not attract attention for some time — I closed every drawer and tidied every cabinet. No one would notice that the whole place had been turned upside down, until they found the locks were broken, which might not be for days.

"Just as I was going, however, I saw this tin case thrown carelessly on the bookshelf in the library. I had noticed it before, but, owing to the fact of its being left about, I did not think that it was likely to be of any importance. However, I picked it up now, and hesitated ; it was just a chance. At that moment there was a faint sound of movement in some distant part of the house, and I knew that I should have to go in a few minutes ; however, I noticed that there was a padlock on the case, and I resolved to see its

contents. I burst it open and found this—a mere
story. I just glanced at it, and was going to throw
it away when the words ' white monkey,' caught my
eye, and I slipped the case into my pocket.

" Then I went back by the way I came, but
unfortunately I was too late ! The servant had
come down to the kitchen, and was lighting the
fire ; the window looked out on the place I had
to cross to reach the wall. I took out the key from
the inside door I had broken open, and hid myself
in the cupboard. There I stayed until ten o'clock,
when I heard one of the servants say that the Doctor
and Miss Rawlins had just started out on a drive to
Ardrachan. In a few minutes I seized my opportunity, and slipping out, reached the hall. You
know how desolate the place is ; they cannot keep
more than three servants, I should think. I saw no
one, and, trusting to luck, opened the front door and
walked boldly down to the village. I read the
manuscript on the way, and when I had finished
it I made more haste. I went to the inn, hired a
horse, and dashed straight off, hoping to catch
Dacobra before he left here."

" What do you call him ? " I asked.

" Deva Dacobra is his name."

I seemed to have heard the name before, and
puzzled my brain for a minute or two. Then I
recollected the Persian book I had bought in Paris
—" The White Priests of Ahriman," by Deva
Dacobra. A faint glimmer of light came into my
brain.

" Is that his name ? " I said thoughtfully.

" I believe that to be his name," Faversham replied.
" Read this," and opening the tin case, he drew out a
roll of manuscript, and handed it to me.

The story was written on parchment, in a clear
round hand. It was—like the other book—called
" The White Priests of Ahriman." I turned over a
page or two, and glanced at them.

" Shall I read it to myself ? " I asked.

Faversham did not answer, and, looking at him, I
saw that his eyes were closed. He was absolutely
worn out, and I did not disturb him. I lit my pipe
and began to read.

The following was the story written on the
parchment before me, word for word:

CHAPTER XII

"THE WHITE PRIESTS OF AHRIMAN"

A WILDERNESS of stone! Gigantic cliffs rising six hundred feet into the air; great loose boulders lying scattered about, and heaped up, like potatoes flung suddenly from a sack; countless heaps of small pebbles and broken shale, continually shifting and running down in little streams, as if touched by some unseen foot. Nothing but stone, ascending and ascending until the white snow covered its bareness, and the great peak of the Kuh Hazar towered far above the clouds into the sunlight, and watched over the most desolate mountain range of all Persia.

At the foot of the mountains the vegetation grew thick and luxuriant, and the lower slopes, running gently into the valley like the roots of a great tree, were green and cheerful. But here all life seemed to have died, and a barren land of loneliness was piled up, tier upon tier, almost as far as the eye could reach. It was as if some terrible volcanic upheaval had swept away all life, whether of plant or animal, and torn the whole surface of the country into deep gorges and crumbling cliffs. There was almost complete silence, only broken now and then by the cry of a raven or the rustling of a small stream of shale as it slid down the mountain-side.

It was the last place on earth where anyone would expect to find a human being, unless, indeed, it were a criminal fleeing from his fellow-men. Not only was there no chance of supporting life for any time, but the difficulties in the path of the traveller were almost insurmountable. On the level ground his progress was hindered by the great boulders worn smooth and slippery by the storms of centuries, and on the slopes, even if he were not confronted by an inaccessible cliff, his feet sank several inches into the loose shale, and at every step forward the bank quivered and slid away beneath his feet.

Yet there was a man creeping and crawling along over all the obstacles like some great insect. He progressed upwards at the rate of about a quarter of a mile in an hour ; at one time creeping between boulders, or cautiously scaling them with hands that must have been as tenacious as the feet of a fly ; at another swinging himself from cleft to cleft along the sheer face of the rock. Any moment a slip might have meant instant death, or the more terrible agony of slow starvation with broken limbs, through burning days and bitter nights. But never for a second did he seem to lose his foothold, or even hesitate on his course. Very slowly, but with absolute sureness, he moved on to his destination—if indeed a man could have a destination in so strange a place.

Once or twice he stopped for breath, and rubbed

his hands swiftly over his brown naked arms to relax the strain on the muscles. Then, when he had done the same to the muscles of his legs, and looked at the fastenings of a curious little straw basket that hung round his neck, he resumed his journey.

The sun was setting now, and the valley below was quite dark. The shadow of the night was running up the mountain swiftly, like the dark waters of a rising tide. For a moment or two the rocks were tinged with fire, and then the light died from them, and one by one they faded into the greyness. Then the higher summits of the mountains glowed with crimson and gold, and for long after the night had come, the great peak of the Kuh Hazar stood out like a rose-coloured spire against the sky.

The sunset had lit up the swarthy features of the traveller for a short time, and then had left him in the twilight. But he still moved on, though his course was now a thousand times more difficult. Even his indomitable energy realised this, and perching himself on a ledge of rock, he took a piece of food from his pouch, and chewed it contemplatively. Then unhooking the little straw basket from round his neck, he put it up to his ear. Something rustled and stirred within, and apparently satisfied at the sound, he replaced the basket, and waited with patience for the moon to rise above the great spur of the Kohrud Mountains. It was already shining on the flat country beneath him, and was flooding the valley with its light. It was not long before it surmounted the cliffs, and he could continue on his way.

He proceeded still more slowly than before. The moon, even when it is at its full, as it was that night, is not a trustworthy light to travel by, and the deep shadows which it casts are even more dangerous and uncertain than total darkness. So he redoubled his caution, but never faltered on his upward journey. Some of the wild native races of the East have an extraordinary power of sight, sharpened by long and continual practice to a pitch of excellence that is incredible to more civilised races. And certainly no European, however sure of foot or steady of nerve, could have undertaken that ascent in the moonlight. But this man crept on, absolutely undismayed by any difficulties, and with apparently no more concern on his face than if he had been walking on a country road in the daytime.

At last, after the ascent of an almost perpendicular cliff, the traveller came to a great tableland, stretching nearly half a mile to the base of still further heights that rose black and misty into the moonlight. Here he stopped and scanned the stone plateau, as if in search of something. Boulders were scattered everywhere over the rocky surface, and here and there gleamed the white bones of small animals that the vultures had carried to these heights to devour. But nothing moved in that silent wilderness.

He gave an exclamation of disappointment, and sitting down on a rock, waited patiently with closed eyes. For nearly an hour he sat thus, as motionless

M

as the rock around him. Then something dark rose
with a swish, and fluttered into the air a hundred
yards away, and there was a flapping of wings overhead. He looked up, and something passed between
him and the moon. It was a vulture. Then another
soared up, and yet another, until the whole air
seemed to move with the beating of their wings, and
they circled away in hundreds into the darkness.
The man looked keenly across the tableland, for he
knew that something must have disturbed them.
For a few seconds his keen eyesight could detect
nothing, but suddenly he caught sight of a small
white object about three hundred yards off. It
might have been merely a skeleton, but it seemed
more solid and more definite, and even as he looked,
it moved, and began to come a few yards nearer to
him with a ridiculous hopping motion. Every now
and then it stopped, but only for a few seconds, and
then it came on again, and when it was within a
hundred yards, he could see that it was some small
white animal. He reached out his hand to pick up a
large stone. He was not quite sure yet what it was,
and he thought perhaps it would be well to kill it.

But when it approached a little closer, he saw that
it was only a small white monkey, and he laid down
the stone. The animal advanced to within ten paces
of him and sat down, mowing and grimacing. He
rose and moved towards it, but as he advanced it
retreated across the plateau, and made towards the
great mass of rock that towered against the sky
half a mile away. He followed it in silence, for now

he knew that it was the guide for which he had been waiting.

Before long they had passed out of the moonlight into the shadow of the great cliff, and the animal became only a blurred white speck in the darkness. But the man kept his eye fixed upon it, as it danced before him like some will-o'-the-wisp, and in a few minutes a solid wall of rock, nearly one thousand feet in height, rose within a couple of yards of him. The animal stopped for a few seconds and touched the rock with its paw; then it scampered along to the left, and the man followed, until they reached an opening. It was a narrow chasm, no more than twenty feet in width—a mere split in the huge mass of stone, as though the mountain had been dropped on the earth and cracked in two.

The animal disappeared into the darkness of the gorge, but the man kept close behind it. The two walls rose on each side of him to so great a height that the moonlit sky above looked no more than a thread of dark blue across the blackness. He could not see an inch before his face, and only the soft patter of little feet and the occasional crunch of small pebbles told him that his guide was still moving before him. He laid one hand on the smooth wall of the rock and felt his way cautiously. It was no easy journey in the absolute darkness. He continually struck his feet against large stones, and stumbled to his knees; and now and then he encountered sharp, projecting points of rock, that cut into his flesh. But, torn and bleeding, he went slowly on, and though his limbs dragged wearily, he seemed to be animated by some indomitable purpose.

Suddenly he fell over a large boulder, and one of his hands touched something soft and furry. His guide had evidently stopped, and was close to him. Rising to his feet, he spread out both his arms, and to his surprise touched the rock on each side. He had not noticed how the gorge had narrowed, for while moving he had only kept his hand on one side. It was not more than five feet in width at this point. The animal made a curious little chattering noise, and he waited to see if it would move on. When about a minute had elapsed, he stooped down, and again his hand encountered the soft fur; it was evident that it was going no farther down the ravine.

He began to feel all round him for some opening, but there was apparently nothing but solid rock. Then again he touched the animal, but this time it was on a level with his head and clinging to the rock. He understood that he had to ascend. He felt carefully, and found that it was perched upon an iron bar driven firmly into the stone, and projecting from it about eighteen inches. There was another one two feet below it, and, drawing himself up, he secured a foothold. Then he commenced the ascent. The bars were set one after the other, about a foot apart. It was child's play after what he had gone through, and no more difficult than walking up a ladder. He ascended quite five hundred feet, then,

as he reached one of his hands up to catch hold of
the next bar, he encountered nothing.

He moved his hand a little to the left towards the
face of the rock, and still there was nothing ; but
feeling cautiously about, he touched a small soft
paw, and found that the animal was sitting upon
the floor of some opening in the cliff. He quickly
clambered into the tunnel—for such it was—and
rose cautiously to his feet. He found that he
could stand upright and touch the rock on both
sides. The darkness was absolute and the silence
only broken by the sound of his own footsteps as
he made his way slowly into the heart of the
mountain.

When he had proceeded about a quarter of a
mile, he heard the whisper of little voices in the
distance. He stopped to listen. The sound came
rapidly closer and closer, and with it the noise of
tiny footfall spattering and scratching on the rocks.
Then, as he moved on, innumerable little soft things
began to bump against his legs and hamper his
progress. Some of them clambered up his body,
swinging themselves on to his shoulders, clinging
to his arms, and fingering the straw basket. Once
even perched itself on his head and pawed his
hair and eyes.

He stopped, and, for the first time on his journey,
a sickening sense of fear came over him. He knew
what they were — merely a swarm of harmless
monkeys. He was a Hindoo, and had seen many
thousands of them in his own country. But he knew

that no monkeys were to be found in Persia, and this fact, combined with the darkness and the sense of his helpless position in the heart of these many million tons of rock, began to work upon his nerves. Besides, he felt a shrinking disgust at being literally overrun by these animals. The air was heavy with the smell of them. As he moved, he seemed to plough through a sea of fur. He carefully shuffled his feet along the floor and pushed them aside, squealing and chattering, only to have them pressing in again more closely and thickly than before. And no sooner did one spring from his shoulder than another ran swiftly up his back and took its place. At last he could stand it no longer, and standing still, he struck out with his hands, and cried aloud with fear. The noise and chattering only redoubled, and they sprang so thickly upon him that he sank to his knees. Then he heard the sound of something like a human laugh, and before he could cry out a second time, there was a swift rush of animals past him, the pattering of feet died away in the distance, and he was alone again in the darkness.

He rose to his feet, panting and gasping for breath, and stretched out his hand to lean against the wall—but his fingers touched nothing. He moved several yards in every direction, groping for something solid, and lifted his hand above his head. But all the rock seemed to have vanished, except that which lay beneath his feet. The roof above him might have been the roof of heaven, only he knew that no sky

was ever so dark as that inky blackness. Then an
idea seized him, for he was not without resource.
He gave a sharp cry and listened. The sound
echoed and re-echoed, and seemed to reverberate
from rock to rock in the distance, until it died away
in a low murmur. His keen ear told him something
of what he wished to know, and he realised that he
was in some enormous cavern, stretching far away on
all sides, and rising above his head to a height of
probably several hundred feet. But that was not the
only answer to his cry ; for scarcely had the echoes
died when he heard a small laugh close behind him.

" Who art thou ? " cried a clear voice, speaking the
Zend language—the ancient tongue of Persia. " And
why dost thou cry aloud in the place of silence ? "

" I am Deva Dacobra, the Hindoo," the man
answered, in the same tongue.

" Whom dost thou seek ? " the voice asked.

" I seek the Priests of Ahriman."

" The temple of Ahriman is here, and we are his
servants, and we do his will," the voice continued.
" Why hast thou come ? "

" For the gift of life, as Zaki, the son of Hasan,
told me."

" It is well—if thou wilt pay the price ? "

" I will pay the price," the man answered, " and
will do it gladly."

As he spoke, a hand touched his arm by the elbow
and slid down to the wrist. The hand was cold and
hard like a hand of bone, but the man did not flinch,
though the grip tightened on his flesh like a vice.

" Thy hand is in mine," said the voice, " and thou wilt speak the truth. Hast thou prayed to him whom thou knowest of ? "

" I have prayed thrice three hundred prayers."

" And thy life—hast thou lived it faithfully and fruitfully for him ? "

" I have earnestly tried to do so."

" Hast thou slain ? "

" The blood of seven deaths is on the hand you hold."

" Is it the blood of the innocent ? "

" They were innocent and harmless to me and mine," the man answered.

" Hast thou defrauded the widow and the orphan ? Hast thou betrayed thy friend ? Hast thou been a scourge and a strife to all thy land ? "

" My name is cursed by all who know me."

" By all, Dacobra ? " the voice repeated, and the bony fingers tightened on his pulse.

The man was silent, and his hand tried to shake itself free.

" Answer, Dacobra," the voice said sternly.

" By all but one," the man said, in a low voice.

" Is there any living soul who can recall one kind word, one gentle action of thine ? "

" There is one," the man said, between his teeth.

" It is well, Dacobra," the voice replied. " Still, it were better for thee if there were not one."

The man's muscles tightened, and he drew himself up to his full height.

" I am a man," he cried, " though for this one

thing I have made myself less human than the jackals that prowl about these mountains. Since I was fourteen years of age, and I exchanged my soul for wisdom, my life has been a curse to all who knew me; my path has been a path of fire and sword, of robbery and violence, of deceit and dishonour, of broken faith and shameful lust. My father died by my hand, cursing me with his last breath. My mother fled the house, a shrieking maniac, when she saw his blood upon my hands; and the great river that bore her body to the sea was more merciful to her than I. My sister starved upon the mountain rather than be near me. I have been hunted as a beast of prey, but I have rent the hunter in pieces. And all this I have done for the love of wisdom and the reward thou canst give me. Yet I am still a man, and there was one I could not harm; for she has shared my soul with the love of knowledge—and I love her."

"Her name?" the voice asked sternly.

"Zuhrah, the daughter of Sadik, the silversmith. But there was only one—there was only one!"

"It is well," said the voice; "and those who give their lives to the pursuit of knowledge shall have their reward. Come with me!"

Dacobra felt a pressure upon his arm, and followed where he was led into the darkness.

The voice spoke no more to him, and when he had gone a few hundred yards he felt the fingers loosen on his arm, and he was told not to move from the place where he stood. Then the footsteps died away in the distance, and he was alone.

Before many minutes had elapsed, however, he heard the sound of several feet coming towards him, and as they came nearer, he heard voices, and heard, too, the sound of something being dragged along the floor towards him. Then, one by one, the people— whoever they were—began to pass him, and as each passed he felt the touch of a small, cold hand upon his arm. He counted ninety-nine, and then the hundredth grasped his hand and stopped.

"We are here, Dacobra ; the circle is complete," said the voice, and he recognised it as the voice he had heard before. "Thou standest in the presence of the Givers of Life. In darkness we were born, in darkness have we lived, in darkness we shall live for ever."

"In darkness we were born, in darkness have we lived, in darkness we shall live for ever," repeated the other voices, and the man realised from the sound that they formed a circle round him.

"Thou hast come for the gift of a life. Dost thou know the price ? "

"The price of my soul and of my own life when I am dead."

"Dost thou understand that thy life, even as this life we give thee, will pass from form to form for ever; that we bestow it where we will; that it is ours, and that there will be no sleep for thee after death, and no rest for all eternity ? "

"I understand."

"Dost thou understand that this life is given
into thy power for but sixty-three years, and that
at the end of these years we shall claim it from thee
again?"

"I understand."

"Dost thou swear to pay the price willingly when
the time shall come?"

"I swear it," the man answered.

"Kneel at my feet, and place my hand to thy lips,
and swear it by him whose servants we are."

Dacobra placed the cold, skinny hand to his
mouth, and it seemed to him to taste of blood. Then
he swore the oath. As he did so he felt a dozen
hands laid upon his head, and a shudder passed
through his frame.

"Rise, Deva Dacobra," said the voice. "The power
is in thee. Thou canst bestow the life where thou
wilt. To no living thing canst thou give it, but only
to the dead thing that has once lived; and the dead
shall live again with the life that thou givest it."

Deva Dacobra rose to his feet, and unhooked the
little basket from his shoulder.

"As Zaki, the son of Hasan, told me," he said,
"and as I read in my searches for the truth, I have
brought this with me."

The basket was taken from his hand.

"A snake!" said the priest, and a low laugh echoed
from lip to lip round the circle. "It is alive, and it
must die!"

"Be careful, great priest; there is poison in its
fangs!"

The priest laughed again, and Dacobra could hear the stirring of leaves and the low hissing of the reptile. Then the hissing died away, and he heard a soft thud upon the floor. He involuntarily stepped back, for his legs were bare, and an angry snake is not a pleasant neighbour in the darkness.

" It will not harm thee, Dacobra. Take it in thy hand."

Dacobra went on his knees, and groped cautiously on the rocky floor till he found something like a ball of scaly rope, quivering and writhing and knotting itself together in the agony of death. He shuddered, and drew his hand away.

" Take it in thy hand, Dacobra," the priest repeated. The young man touched it again, and as he did so, the muscles relaxed, the knots uncoiled, and it lay limp and lifeless in his hand. " Now the other hand, Dacobra," and the priest took hold of his fingers, and leading him a few steps forward, told him to kneel. Then the man felt another hand placed in his, and soft, warm fingers, like the delicate fingers of a child or woman, touched his own.

" Thou hast but to will the passing of the life and it shall pass," said the priest.

" It is a woman," said Dacobra, in a low tone of horror, dropping the hand and passing his fingers swiftly over the face. " It is a woman, and she will die."

" Thou hast boasted of the hardness of thy heart," the priest said, with a laugh ; " moreover, the life is not hers. The girl died three years ago in the night,

but before dawn came we gave her life again, and her
father never knew that his daughter had been dead.
The life is ours, and we give it now to thee."

"Yet I might take her with me," Dacobra said,
lifting the limp hand once more. "It is a fairer
casket than the snake."

"Thou art a philosopher, Dacobra, but still a man.
Thou wilt find it more easy to take her life from her
in the dark."

"And the woman?"

"Her body will return to the grave, where it should
have lain these last three years."

"It is well," Dacobra replied; "the reptile will be
more convenient for my purposes," and as he spoke
he willed that the life should pass.

A slight shudder passed through the frame of the
woman, and the hand that lay so lightly in his own
gripped his fingers for a few seconds like a vice of
steel, till he almost called out with the pain. Then
the grip relaxed, and the arm dropped heavily to the
floor. As it did so, he heard a faint hissing, and the
cold coils of the snake stirred in his hand; he felt
quickly for the basket, dropped the reptile in, and
closed the lid.

"It is over," said the priest. "Pray thou for so
painless a death."

Dacobra was silent. He remained on his knees,
and out of curiosity touched the face and body of the
woman. They were still warm, but the heart had
ceased to beat.

The priest divined his thoughts.

" Thou wouldst like to look on thy handiwork, Dacobra? Perhaps thou dost not believe that she is dead?"

" I would look," the young man answered.

A strong desire had come over him to see the face whose light he had quenched for ever. It was more a wish to see the evidence of his power than any morbid curiosity.

" Thou mayest look," the priest answered. " We fear not the light, for we cannot see."

Dacobra fumbled in his pouch, and drawing out a flint and steel, struck them together till a spark had caught the tinder. Then he fanned it with his breath till he was able to ignite some resinous shreds of pine that were thrust into his hand. He cast them flaming on the floor, and lighted a short torch of thickly tarred rope. Then he turned to the body, but someone had covered it over with a thick white cloth.

It was a strange sight that he now saw before him. So vast was the cavern in which he stood that the flame of the torch seemed only to be lost in the awful depth of blackness, and the light fell neither on roof nor wall. Around him stood a circle of men clad entirely in white. They were all very small of stature, and not one of them could have been more than four feet in height. Their faces were old and wrinkled, and absolutely hairless, and their skin of a dead white colour. Their eyes were also white, and seemed to be covered with some sort of scale, like the eyes of those fishes which have been found in subterranean pools. It seemed to him that they resembled the skulls of dead men. One of them stood apart from the others within the circle, and Dacobra supposed that he was the one who had been addressing him. On the floor, a few feet from him, lay the motionless body under the white cloth. And in the distance, as far as he could see in all directions, small white shadows seemed to be flitting in and out from the darkness to the light. He held the torch above his head and looked at the body.

"Wouldst thou see, Dacobra?" said the priest, "or art thou afraid to look?" Then he moved towards the young man and stood by his side.

"I am not a child and afraid of the dead," Dacobra answered.

For reply the priest unhooked the basket from the young man's shoulder, and held it to his ear. Then he moved away, gave it to one of his companions in the circle, and returned beside the body.

"Thou canst look, Dacobra," he said.

Dacobra stooped down, and taking hold of one of the corners of the cloth, swept it from the face, and looked. It was the face of Zuhrah, the daughter of Sadik, the silversmith—the face of the only living soul he had ever loved.

He gave one sharp cry of pain and horror, and the torch dropped from his nerveless fingers. It had scarcely touched the ground when a foot was placed on the flame and he was again in darkness.

For a few minutes his reason struggled against the flood of passion that was overwhelming him. He muttered to himself: "I can save her. I can save

her. The power that took away can give again."
His hand fumbled wildly for the little basket. Then
he remembered that it was gone. The priests had
foreseen this, and had taken it from him. He leant
forward and kissed the cold face, and rising to his
feet, shrieked curses and lamentations through the
echoing vault. He strode like a madman from place
to place, his muscular fingers groping for something
to kill. His hand encountered nothing. The circle
of priests had disappeared. He was alone with the
dead body, to which he returned again and again,
now taking it up in his arms, now kissing the face,
now caressing the cold fingers. Then in his mad
delirium he lost his bearings and could not find the
body, and wandered to and fro, seeking it, till the
darkness and agony seemed to close in upon his brain,
his reason left him, and he lurched heavily forward to
the ground.

When he came to his senses, he felt the cold air
blowing past him, and stretching out his hand, found
that he was at the entrance in the side of the cliff.
He raised himself up to a sitting posture and peered
over the edge, wondering if it were not best to throw
himself into the chasm. Then he heard a voice
behind him.

"As well thou as another," it said. "Her life was
ours, and we have given it to thee."

"Give her body back to me! Give her body back
to me and I will go hence as empty as I came."

"No, the bargain is made, Dacobra. Give thanks
to us that thy sacrifice is complete. This tender spot

in thy heart was not worthy of one who would serve our Master. Now thou art all evil and all wise; and well wast thou named Deva, 'the Spirit of Evil.'"

"And yet,' murmured Dacobra, "in the creed of my forefathers Deva is a 'Spirit of Good.'[1] I am not all evil. I will love this soul till death, and would give all the souls of the world to purchase its freedom from thee."

"For sixty-three years it is thine; then thou art ours."

"Is there no price—not for myself, but for this girl's soul?"

"It has been in a thousand forms. How canst thou love it? It is the body thou lovest. This was the soul of Parysatis the Beautiful, who gave herself for all eternity to Ahriman two thousand years ago."

"Is there no price for its freedom? Is there no price?"

The priest fixed his sightless eyes on the young man and came closer to him.

"Aye, if thou canst do the impossible, there is a price."

"Nothing is impossible. Nothing in all the world if I can give her freedom."

"Thou art young, Dacobra," the priest answered, "and already learned beyond the wisdom of grey-beards upon earth. Long years are before thee, and if any mortal could find out that which has baffled the immortals for centuries it might be thou. Show

[1] Deva is "a Spirit of Good" in the Vedic religion, but ' a Spirit of Evil" in the Zoroastrian Creed.

N

us how the stone and iron may live and change like men and trees. Break down with thy finite intellect the barrier that an infinite mind has set between the living germ and the dead matter that has never thrilled with life. Do this, Dacobra, if thou canst, and we will give this soul its freedom."

The old priest laughed as he spoke. He might as well have asked him to take the earth in his hand and cast it back into the sun.

The young man made no reply, but felt at his side and found the basket there. Then, rising to his feet, he heard the rustle within, and placed his lips to it with reverence.

" Well, Dacobra ? " said the priest.

" Nothing is impossible," he replied, in a low voice, "and I will perform the task that thou hast set me to do."

The priest laughed.

" Farewell, Dacobra," he said ; "thou art young and I am old, but when *thou* art old we shall meet again."

The Hindoo began to descend the steps, and close behind him the little white monkey that had guided him to the place, swung itself from bar to bar, and followed him into the moonlit plain.

When he had crossed the tableland, he turned, and saw that it was still behind him. Then a wild passion seized him, and taking a heavy rock in his hands, he left nothing of it but a motionless lump of fur and blood for the vultures to pick at.

CHAPTER XIII

HOW WE RESOLVED TO FIGHT, BUT FOUND A FORTRESS

I LAID the manuscript on the table, and leant back in my chair, thinking out the whole question to a definite conclusion. Faversham was right. This tale was a possible solution. Once given the fact that it was in the power of this man to transmit life, and there was no difficulty in finding the link between Alice Borrodaile and Elaine Rawlins. Alice Borrodaile had died. This man had stolen her body and transferred to it the life which was in his gift. Once admit this fact, and the whole thing was clear. But could anything so contrary to Nature be admitted as a fact? The cold reasoning of the scientist replied in the negative. And yet, after all, science is progressive, and the impossibilities of one age are the accepted facts of the next. Our knowledge of the origin of life is still in its infancy. There are few scientists who would dare to say that such a transmission of life is absolutely impossible, for life, like electricity, is an invisible force, and is only known to us by its manifestations. Those who talk of protoplasm and say they have discovered the

secret of life, might as well say that electricity is a
piece of copper wire.

I recalled the reasoning I had read so carefully in
the Persian book I had picked up in Paris, the clear,
cold reasoning of a scientist, yet, as it now appeared,
written by the very man who held in his hands the
manifestation of its truth.   I went over to the bookshelf, and taking down the translation of the book,
referred to several passages again.   I remembered
how at the time I first read it, I was struck with
the fact that the author seemed to be discussing
the actual occurrence, and not a mere theory.   The
explanation was obvious to me now.   Here, in my
hands, was the narration of the fact wrapped up in
the guise of a story, with all those details which
would attract and hold the reader's fancy.   It was,
doubtless, for publication after Dacobra's death.

Yet, assuming the truth of the tale, Dr. Rawlins
had still to be identified with Dacobra.   The identity
was obvious to my own mind, and Faversham had
at once jumped to the same conclusion.   Dr.
Rawlins had not denied it, and even the perfect
control he usually kept over his features had broken
down when Faversham accused him bluntly face to
face.   Besides, the accumulative evidence was tremendous.   Here was a fact, and the only fact which
explained the identity of Alice Borrodaile and
Elaine Rawlins.   Here was a man, evidently of
Eastern origin, yet bearing an English name, a man
whose whole life had been devoted to a single task,
the same as that set by the White Priests of Ahriman

—the breaking down of the barrier between the animate and the inanimate in Nature. Here, too, in the west of Scotland, were the same white monkeys mentioned in the story, and here the fear of a strong man, which could be readily explained by his connection with these animals in the past. The fear, too, was obviously not physical, but doubtless owing to the fact that the lease of life was nearly up, and that these animals were the forerunners of him who would claim the life again. The White Priest was undoubtedly coming, if the story were aught but a fairy-tale. " I am old and thou art young," he had said, " but when *thou* art old we shall meet again." The story explained everything. No reasonable person could doubt that Dacobra and Dr. Rawlins were one and the same man.

Then I remembered that the man had triumphed, that he had performed the task set him, and that the White Priest would come in vain. A great joy filled my heart, for Elaine had become very dear to me. But Faversham had not remembered this fact. He had said that every hour she stayed in Balath was at the risk of her life. He had forgotten, or perhaps he did not grasp the significance of Dr. Rawlins' discovery. Poor Faversham! I looked at him as he lay asleep in the arm-chair; his face white and tired, his lips twitching nervously even in his dreams. What good could come out of this for him? If the girl's life were taken, there would only be the renewed and redoubled agony of her death; if she were spared, only the vain longing

for the body of the woman he loved, now inhabited
by the life and soul of another. I knew that all
fresh efforts to recall the buried past would be in
vain, and that never again would he storm that
citadel of love. The soul of Zuhrah, the daughter
of Sadik, the silversmith, was set as far from him as
the stars.

He slept on quietly and showed no signs of
waking, so I did not rouse him for lunch, but
took the meal by myself, and spent most of the
afternoon in the studio, carving my name on the
foot of the statue.

It was nearly seven o'clock when Faversham woke.
He had a bath, shaved, and changed his clothes for
dinner, and when he came down, he looked more
like his old self, and it was difficult to imagine that
he was the same Faversham who, in the morning,
would have taken the life of a man in cold blood.

After dinner we thrashed out the whole question
calmly and logically, as we might have discussed a
scientific problem. We read the story over again
and studied every word. We strung together all
the facts in Dr. Rawlins' life that had come within
our own knowledge, and reconciled them with the
facts in the story. At the end of the discussion
there was no doubt in our minds that the story
was true, and that Dr. Rawlins and Dacobra were
one and the same person.

"Well, Faversham," I said, when we had discussed
the matter down to a final point, "what is our part
in this business?"

" To save this girl," he replied.

" From whom ? "

" First, from Dacobra."

" Dacobra loves her with all his soul, and would not harm her."

Faversham laughed bitterly.

" You do not understand, Maxwell," he said. " If Dacobra has failed, and if this tale be aught but a fable, her life will be taken from her on January 13th by one against whom Dacobra himself, with all his devilries, is powerless. Dacobra is a man of iron will and determination, and he will save her soul from this endless slavery at any cost. He will stick at nothing. Now, if you were in his place, what would you do ? "

I thought for a moment, and then saw the trend of his thoughts.

" I should take the girl's life," I answered, " and then kill myself."

" Naturally," he replied. " This life apparently can only be passed from one to another by physical contact. If she were killed her life would vanish, and it would be impossible to pass it into another ; and that is why Dacobra will kill her, and that is why we must save her from him."

" The Priests would have foreseen so simple an escape as that."

" They relied on the man's love of life. He would naturally put off the escape until the last possible moment. While they both lived, the soul was with him. He worships that soul, as a devout man worships his God. He would not curtail his time with it by a single hour. Then the Priests would probably rely on his untiring and fruitless efforts to perform the task they set him up to the very last minute. They were right; and if Dacobra has failed to find that single path to safety, he will not part with the life till the last hour, perhaps not till the last minute given to him."

"And if we save her from him," I said thoughtfully, "what then? What are we against Dacobra's master?"

"Perhaps we are nothing," he replied, "yet we can deal with him afterwards, and if the worst comes to the worst, we can do what Dacobra would have done."

"Are you quite sure, Faversham," I said, "that you believe in the story? Remember this is plain, prosaic old England, a country of steam power and electricity, of red brick villas and orderly streets. The glamour of the East is not on you; there are no gigantic mountains and tablelands, no gloomy gorges and deep precipices; no mysteries; nothing that a man can fail to understand if he has intelligence. All is open and plain to the daylight. It is a country of law and order, and the policeman is the symbol of dull and uninteresting safety. It is different in my case. I can believe the tale, for I have been in places where nothing seems incredible, and where the things a man cannot fathom are as countless as the sands; in a land where the dark mysteries and subtle forces of Nature have lain undisturbed through all the centuries. But you have no such aid to the imagination. If I were in your place, I should scoff at the whole thing as a fairy-tale."

" Belief is forced on me," Faversham replied quietly. " When a man has seen the dead raised to life, he can believe anything. But let us discuss the facts. We must take this girl from Balath. What is our plan of action ? "

We spent the rest of the evening discussing our chances of effecting an entrance into the castle and achieving our object. There were a hundred things against us. We had first of all to get in ; then we had to persuade the girl to come with us (it would be impossible if she maintained the same attitude as in the morning); then, if she refused, we should have to take her away by force ; and, lastly, we had to get out of the castle. The law, too, was against us, and in fact I did not see anything in our favour except that we were strong and earnest men, and were moved by a common determination to effect our object. However, we plotted and planned till far into the night, and finally decided to enter the castle by stealth, if possible, and then to exert such force as was in our power to get out again.

I myself very much doubted if we should get in at all. Dr. Rawlins would certainly be on his guard after Faversham's conduct in the morning, and I think the latter began to regret that he had not been silent until an opportunity for striking a decisive blow had arrived. He told me that he had relied upon my assistance, and certainly, if I had known what I knew afterwards, I should have been inclined to stand by his side in the matter.   I doubt, however, whether I should have had the courage to use force, and detain Miss Rawlins against her will ; and even if we had done so, it is certain that Dr. Rawlins would have at once sent for the police.   Our story, if we had been foolish enough to tell it, would have been laughed at, and our hands would probably have been tied just at the moment when we wanted to deal with the matter.

It was for this reason that we finally resolved to put off any attempt to enter Balath until a day or two before January the 13th, for a failure would perhaps mean destruction to all our plans.   We decided to spend the next few days in reconnoitring the place, and not to make any effort to take Miss Rawlins away until the night of January the 12th.

The next morning I wrote to an old friend of mine in Glasgow, asking him to hire a small yacht and crew for three months if possible.   I enclosed an Ordnance map, with the position of Balath marked clearly on it, and gave detailed instructions.   They were to lie off the castle from noon of January the 12th, and put off in a boat when they saw a red light burning on the shore.   The yacht, I said, was to be secured at any price, and a handsome bonus promised to the men.   I also earnestly requested my friend to bring his wife with him, saying that I was meditating a trip to the Mediterranean, and that I hoped they would make up their minds to be my guests for at least a month.   I knew that both loved the sea in all weathers, and the promise of any adventure would bring Alan Steyning from the ends of the earth.

During the next few days we had a great deal to arrange. We made one or two expeditions along the beach to Balath, and examined the shore carefully for a suitable landing-place at all states of the tide. We also made a thorough inspection of the cliff at this point, and I chose a place where it would be just possible for a good climber to ascend or descend, if he were put to it, and marked it at the foot with a large white stone.

This work was not without its dangers. One day we were caught by the tide, and spent several hours on a small ledge of rock, with eight feet of water below us ; and on another occasion a piece of granite, weighing at least half a ton, crashed down from the top of the cliff within two feet of Faversham's head. I was not sure that the fall was altogether accidental, but saw nothing to confirm my opinion beyond the fact that there was a flat smooth mark on one of the edges of the stone, which looked as if it had been made by some steel instrument.

It was not until January 7th that we decided to make our first inspection of the walls of the castle from the top of the cliff. It was impossible to do this in the daytime, and we resolved to ride over there after dinner. I ordered two horses to be saddled, and when they were ready, we dashed off along the road to Balath. The moon was shining brightly, and our path was clear before us. In less than an hour we were at the village inn, and the church clock struck ten as we drew rein before the door. We decided to leave our horses there, and walk the rest of the way. The inn-keeper looked curiously at us, and hazarded some observation about the lateness of the hour. I did not enlighten him as to our business, but said we should return shortly, and ordered supper to be laid for two.

We then left him, and skirting the village, walked along the top of the cliff towards the castle, till we saw a dark mass rising against the sky, about half a mile ahead. There were no lights in any of the windows, and it might almost have been a piece of rock standing black and silent in the moonlight. We sat down for a moment on a piece of granite, and looked at the gloomy pile of stone. Below us the sea rolled darkly against the foot of the cliffs. By looking over the top we could see the foam curling along the coast like a thin white snake.

"What is that?" Faversham said, pointing towards the castle.

I looked, and at first saw nothing but a dark mass of stone against the sky. Then I noticed a hazy line of something stretching a little to the left of the walls along the ground. It might have been mist, but we could not actually see what it was in the distance.

We moved on carefully and in silence. Thick clouds were now hurrying up from the west, and we could hardly see each other's faces. It is wonderful how quickly the light can change to darkness when the moon goes behind a cloud. Then suddenly a row of tall black lines rose dimly before us, and

stretching out my hand I grasped an iron bar at
least an inch in thickness. We both stopped and
looked at each other. This was something new—the
work of the last few days. We were expected, and
the place had been barricaded like a fortress. The
moon came out again, and we sank to the ground
lest we should be observed. Then I looked up, and
Faversham swore a deep oath. Between us and the
castle walls, now less than a hundred yards distant,
rose a palisade of iron railings ten feet high, and with
bars set about six inches from each other. Beyond
this, at a distance of ten yards, rose a similar palisade.
The railings were crowned with a revolving *cheveux-
de-frise*, and there was no foothold between the top
and the bottom.

"Great heavens, Faversham!" I cried, "the place
is fortified.

I looked up at the windows; the moonlight,
instead of being reflected on the glass, shone on
the dull black of iron shutters. There were three
little holes in each of these, small circular spots of
light. They looked like little yellow eyes winking
at us in mockery of our discomfiture.

Faversham looked at them in gloomy silence.

"Let us examine the place thoroughly," I said.

We crept along the palisade, feeling every bar of
the railing as we went, until we came to the edge of
the cliff again, on the far side of the castle. There
was no break in that line of iron; the railing made a
semi-circle, cutting off all access to the building from
the land. On the other side, or, as it were, the

diameter of the circle, was the wall, rising sheer from
the top of the cliff to a height of forty feet.   There
was no entrance of any kind, and I wondered how
the inhabitants were going to get in and out, except
by the postern door.

We examined with particular care the two ex-
tremities of the railings.   It was just possible, if
they had been only carried to the top of the cliff, that
we could have swung round them, but the work had
been well done, and Dacobra left no loophole of this
sort.

"It certainly looks as if he expected us," I said,
"and I have now no doubt about the story.   A man
does not fortify his house like a prison without
a purpose.   He intends that there shall be no
interruption to his devilries."

Faversham laughed.

"You flatter yourself, Maxwell," he said.   "He
holds us very cheaply in his estimation.   It is not for
us that he has prepared this pleasing reception, but
for one who, I fancy, will make no more of that
palisade than you or I would make of a five-barred
gate."

"We must get in from the beach," I said ; "the
postern door is our only chance."

Faversham looked over the edge of the cliff and
shook his head.

"It is possible," I said, "though I expect you
would break your neck if you tried it in the dark ;
but I have done a good deal of mountain climbing,
and this is child's play to me.   I have been on a

place as steep as that and with no more secure a
foothold than that would give, and have known
that if I slipped it meant a fall of a thousand feet."

"And when you have got down?" Faversham
asked.

"There is the postern," I said.

"Locked, of course."

"Yes, probably," I replied; "but one must not
neglect a chance. Anyhow, it may be possible to
climb the cliff again, and find some way up the
wall to a window, or else on to the roof."

"The chances are against your doing anything of
the sort," he replied; "but we can easily get
something to scale the palisade with."

"Every inch of that railing is watched," I said,
pointing to the windows; "and now I come to
think of it, perhaps it is quite as well that we
were prevented from entering the castle on the
land side. Dacobra would not hesitate to shoot
us, especially as his own life is nothing to him.
He will not think of the wall on the cliff. Only a
very desperate man would attempt to scale that in
the dark."

Faversham gripped me by the hand.

"This is my work, Maxwell," he said, in a low
voice. "The girl is nothing to you, and you shall
not risk your life. If I cannot get down the cliff, I
will get in some other way."

"You could get down with a rope, perhaps," I
replied; "but you could not scale the cliff again,
much less the wall of the castle. I doubt if I can do

it, but I am used to this sort of thing, and with luck may be successful. You can stay at the top and watch the rope, if we want it. If we don't, and the boat comes, you can swing down and join us."

" It is my work, Maxwell," he repeated.

" It is any man's work to save life," I said, and then I laid my hands on his shoulder. " Faversham, old chap, remember who this girl is! Alice Borrodaile is dead. This woman is nothing to you. She is Zuhrah, the daughter of Sadik, the silversmith. Forget, Faversham, forget! And, when we have saved her, never think of her again."

He did not answer, and I saw that his face was ghastly in the moonlight.

" It is my work as well as yours, Faversham," I continued, " and I will risk my life gladly ; but I would rather she died than you should suffer all your life because of her. That soul can have no sympathy with you. That girl is not the girl you loved. Alice Borrodaile is dead, and think of her as dead, and only remember when last you looked on her in Spain."

He did not answer, and, turning away from the edge of the cliff, we made our way back to the village, had supper, and rode to Ardrachan in the moonlight.

CHAPTER XIV

THE FAITHFUL HEART OF A WOMAN

BY January 12th all arrangements were complete·
Alan Steyning had chartered a hundred ton steam
yacht, and on the evening of January 10th I received
a letter from him, saying that he and his wife would
sail from Glasgow early next morning, and hoped to
arrive at their destination a few hours before the time
I had fixed. But the *Fire Fly* was evidently over-
due, for both I and Faversham went out on the top
of the cliff after lunch and scanned the horizon in
vain for any signs of her. I did not feel easy in my
mind; during the last two days the wind had risen,
and there was a heavy sea rolling in from the west,
so that it was quite possible she might be a few
hours late. There was, in fact, considerable cause
for anxiety. It might be impossible to land a boat,
and if this mode of escape failed us, there was only
a remote chance of getting out of the country.
Dacobra would leave no stone unturned to stop
our flight; but, once at sea, it would go hard with
us if we could not escape—at any rate, for a time.

I had often wondered why Dacobra had not made
his escape by sea to some hiding-place, until the evil

day was past. But probably his life was bound up
in such a network of invisible threads that it was
impossible for him to break loose from them.   I
guessed now that his movements were watched day
and night.

Before dinner I wrote a few instructions for the
ordering of my household, and placed them in a
sealed envelope, which I handed to my valet, with
orders to open it if we did not return by the morning.
In another envelope I placed a letter to my lawyer
concerning my private affairs.   I am a little ashamed
to confess this, now that I am still alive; but at the
time I was impressed with the fact that our errand
was a serious one, and even so unromantic an occurrence as a slip of the foot might mean death for
me.   After dinner I ordered the horses to be got
ready, slipped into my pocket one thousand pounds
in notes, which I had drawn from the bank the day
before, and carefully filled the chambers of my
revolver.   Faversham wound up a hundred foot coil
of rope, and wrapped up the powder for the red light
in a piece of oilskin.   We rode quietly down to the
inn, and walked straight from there to the edge of
the cliff by the first palisade.   There was no danger
of our being seen.   It was a nasty night, blowing
half a gale already and threatening to become worse.
There was no moon, and not a light to be seen on
land or sea.

We looked over the waters for any sign of the
Fire Fly.   I had arranged that she should burn
three white lights on her foremast.   But the whole

sea was wrapped in darkness, and only a black gulf of howling wind and roaring waves stretched away from beneath our feet.

"This is serious, Faversham," I said, holding on to one of the iron bars, and supporting myself against the wind.

"Perhaps we cannot see her," he replied. "I expect the air is thick with spray, and the lights of these small boats are not easily seen in weather like this. I should like to burn a red light now, but I suppose you did not provide for any signal of that sort."

"No," I said. "We must do the best we can. I think I will descend the cliff at once."

We fastened the rope securely to one of the railings. I turned up my sleeves at the wrists and put one leg over the top of the cliff.

"Good-bye, Faversham, for an hour or two," I said cheerily. "I have a whistle in my pocket. If I blow it three times, go for help. Keep your eyes open for the yacht. If I succeed, I will come to the foot of the cliff and give a signal; then you must burn one of the red lights and come down below."

Faversham held out his hand and said nothing; but I could feel his thanks in the strong grip of his fingers.

At that moment one of the windows of the castle opened, and a strong white light shone out into the darkness. Faversham sank to the ground, and lay flat in a small hollow. I slipped over the top and hung for a moment with my face against the side of the cliff. Then the light slowly passed over the circular palisade, searching every inch for a radius of two hundred yards.

" Be careful, Faversham," I whispered. " Watch and listen as if your life depended upon it." Then I descended carefully to the beach.

As I moved cautiously towards the postern door, I caught my feet in a piece of cordage and stopped to disentangle them. I thought the cord might be useful to me, and I tried to pick it up from the stones; but there was a dead weight at either end. Feeling in my pocket for a knife, I ran my hand along the cord to cut off as long a piece as I could. It was attached to a large stone, and I quickly severed the strands. Then I passed my hand along it to the other end and encountered something soft and wet and furry. It was a dead monkey, and the cord was knotted tightly round its throat. I did not dare to strike a light, but by passing my fingers over its little body, I could easily guess what it was. I cut the cord again, and rolling it up, thrust it into my pocket.

When I reached the postern, the tide was nearly up to the foot of the cliff. I looked up at the castle and inspected it carefully. The only signs of life that I could detect were four small circles of light, each about the size of a penny piece. I judged that they would be in the shutters of the big drawing-room window which looked out on to the sea, and which was about six feet from the top of the cliff. Suddenly, as I looked, one disappeared and appeared again; then another did the same thing; and then another. There was evidently someone there, moving between the light and the window.

Then fortune favoured me. I saw a large break in the clouds, and a star shining clearly in the west, and in a few seconds the whole scene was flooded with light. I saw at a glance the position of the window, and that it was heavily shuttered with iron. Then my eye ran quickly over the surface of the cliff and castle wall, taking in every crack and projection that might offer a foothold. I did not waste a second. I glanced at the moon and saw that with luck it would shine out for about ten minutes. Then I commenced to climb. The cliff was firm and the footholds were good ; moreover, a long thin weed of great strength grew deep in the cracks and crannies of the rock. The climb was not a difficult task for a mountaineer with nerve and experience, but it would have been folly for Faversham to have attempted it.

I reached the top in safety, and to my delight saw that at this place the castle wall was not flush with the face of the cliff. There was a ledge at least two feet wide, and about ten feet in length. I rested on it for a minute to get my breath, and continued my examination. Then I saw that on either side of the shutters the iron hinges were so large and so clumsily fastened into the wall that they each formed a sort of hook. My mind went swiftly to the rope in my pocket, and taking it out, I examined it closely. It was new cord, three-eighths of an inch in thickness, and I calculated that it would bear my weight, if I were careful. I tied a loop at each end, and stood up on the ledge. I could just reach my hand up to within a foot of the hinges, and tried to throw an end over each of them. Here, at any rate, was something to support some, or all of my weight, until I had thoroughly inspected the windows. The only danger was that the hinges would not be securely fastened in the wall. After a great deal of care, and many attempts, and considerable strain to the muscles of my feet and hands, I got the rope fixed to one of the hinges ; then I carefully made my way to the other side of the window, and attached the other end. The rope swung in a curve just below the window ledge.

I tested it first by leaning upon it heavily with one hand. Then I threw all my weight on it, my toes just touching the ledge in case of accidents. It stood the strain well, but I heard the iron hinges grate in their stone sockets. Then, holding on to the rope with both hands, I found small footholds in the old loose stones of the wall, and raising myself up, managed to scramble into a sitting posture on to the rope. It was as comfortable as a swing, save that my knees were pressed hard against the wall, and I could not help thinking of the black depths below me. I was just in time, for I had scarcely settled myself when a dark mass of clouds obscured the moon. I put my eye to one of the holes, and to my surprise I noticed that the window was open, and I should be able to not only see, but hear what was going on inside. I thought it a little odd that it should not have been shut on such a stormy winter's night, but it was a most fortunate circumstance, as now only the iron shutters lay between me and my entrance into the house.

Miss Rawlins was in the room, and as far as I could see, alone. I could not be quite sure of this, as my range of vision was limited, but she was reading a book, and this seemed to indicate that she was by herself. I had not seen her for several days, and was shocked to see how much she had altered. Her face was deathly white, and she seemed much thinner than when I saw her last. She turned over the pages of her book in a listless, tired way, as if she were not thinking of its contents, and, pressing one of her hands to her forehead, winced as if she were in pain.

I did not watch her for more than a minute. If she were alone, this was my opportunity to get into the house and do my best to save her. No more favourable chance could have come my way. It was better than if I had found the room empty, for in that case I should have had to look for her in the house. I arranged my plan of action in a few seconds. I would tap on the shutter, and if she hesitated to let me in—which was very unlikely—would hint at my perilous position and appeal to her mercy. Once inside, I would lock the door, state my errand, tell her something of the awful truth, and persuade her to come away at once if she would save her life. If she consented, we could probably find some means of escaping through the postern. If she refused, I would do all a man could to take her out by force, though in my heart I felt that the task would be an almost impossible one. If I failed, I would whistle to Faversham, and then stay by her to protect her to the last. I gave one look behind me to see if the lights of the *Fire Fly* were visible, and was disappointed to see nothing but the darkness; then I turned back to tap gently on the shutter. But before I did so, I looked through one of the holes and saw that I was too late. The door opposite opened slowly, and Dacobra stood in the entrance. I swore under my breath, and slipping my right hand into my pocket, grasped the butt of my revolver. Then I laughed and took my hand out again. It had not come to that yet.

He entered the room and closed the door. Miss Rawlins looked round at him and smiled. He came over to her with a half-frightened look in his eyes, and laid his hand on the soft coils of her hair.

"Well, darling," he said tenderly, "are you better?"

"Yes," she cried, "of course I am; there is so much to amuse me. How are the fortifications? and when do you expect the enemy? It is quite like mediæval times. What a silly old father you are! I believe you are doing it all to amuse me and keep me in good spirits. If anyone is going to attack you, why don't you send for Muckle Mickie, as they call the village policeman?" and she laughed merrily.

He did not answer, but looked at her with infinite sorrow in his eyes. Then he pulled up a chair and sat down opposite her.

"Elaine," he said gravely, "I have much to tell you, and yet I cannot tell you all. I could tell you nothing if I did not know you loved me."

"You are the best and dearest of fathers," she said, taking hold of one of his lean brown hands.

"I have tried to be so," he continued. "I have tried to make you happy, and to give you all that you desired. I do not think you can remember a harsh word or an unkind action of mine?"

She was silent, but gave him a look of gratitude.

"Yet," he went on, "wherever my name is known, men have cursed it. I have lived a long and bitter life, Elaine, but to-night, when I tell you the truth, will be the bitterest moment of it all."

I saw the agony on the man's face and pitied him. Elaine saw it too, and her face reflected the dark shadow of its pain. I could see, too, that she was frightened. It is anticipation that strikes terror into the hearts of women like Elaine, but when the worst is known, they face it bravely, and go to death with a smile on their lips. I had no fear for her conduct in this crisis, so great an admiration had I conceived for her courage and strength of mind.

"These palisades you see, Elaine—these iron shutters—they are grim reality, strange though it may seem to you in this prosaic nineteenth century. When the work was started, I told you it was an amusement for my spare time. As it progressed and you did not believe me, I jestingly told you that it was being erected to keep out our enemies. Yet I did not really jest."

"Mr. Faversham?" she cried, in a low voice. "Mr. Faversham? He would not hurt us, and Mr. Maxwell will restrain him till his brief madness is past. Oh, father, they are Englishmen—brave, honourable men ; they would not hurt a girl and an old man."

"Mr. Faversham is as sane as you or I," he said hoarsely. Then he stopped. He was afraid.

"As sane as you or I, father?" she repeated mechanically.

I think a suspicion of the truth was beginning to dawn on her, but she looked at him inquiringly.

"As sane as you or I," he said. "Elaine, the words he spoke in his wild anger were the words of truth."

"Truth," she said, with wide-open, staring eyes. "The truth? No! no! It is impossible."

"He did not lie," the old man continued.

"He did not lie?" she queried, still in the same even voice.

"In the first place, I am not your father, Elaine."

She looked at him for a moment or two, and then dropped her eyes.

"I am all the more grateful to you," she said slowly, "for adopting me as your child. I have known no other father."

"I am no relation of yours. I am so old that your father might be my son. Secondly, my name is not Dr. Rawlins."

"It does not matter," she said, in a low voice, yet I could see that the iron had entered into her soul, and that each deceit of the one she loved was a fresh stab to her heart.

" And lastly," he continued, in a voice so low that
I could hardly catch the words, "and lastly—oh,
Elaine—my child—Elaine ! "

She rose quickly to her feet with a look of horror
on her face. Dacobra put out his arms appealingly,
but she shrank from him, and I could see that this
movement of aversion was more bitter to him than
the bitterness of death.

" Elaine ! " he cried piteously.

A shiver passed through her slender frame and she
hid her face in her hands. Then she moved swiftly
forward, and flinging herself on her knees, seized his
hand and placed it to her lips.

" Forgive me, father ! " she cried.

He placed his hand on her head, and for a space
of five minutes neither of them moved or spoke.
Then the old man raised her face and kissed her on
her forehead.

" I should not have spoken, Elaine," he said, " but
I wished the choice to lie in your hands."

She rose to her feet, and I saw that in those few
minutes all the girlhood had died out of her face, and
that the soul of a strong woman shone from her eyes
—the soul of Zuhrah, the daughter of Sadik, the
silversmith ; the soul of Parysatis looking through
all the centuries.

" Tell me all," she cried, and sitting down on the
couch, she took hold of his hand. " I trust you.
Tell me everything. I know that you will speak the
truth."

" Fox Faversham spoke the truth," he answered,

"and he would take you from me. But I will fight
him for you as long as I have breath. Yet it is not
for him that I have made a fortress of Balath. It is
for one from whom, if he lay hands on you, I am powerless to protect you, nor if the armies of England
were at your back could they save you from him—
one who is human and yet not human ; a creature of
flesh and blood and yet eternal ; all-powerful over
those who have been given into his power, yet
helpless to harm a child whose soul has not been
given to him. Such a one is coming, and to-morrow
he will be here. Your life and soul are in his power.
He gave—and he will take away."

" My life and my soul ? " she asked slowly, clasping
her hands together. " My life and my soul ? "

"I speak the truth, Elaine," the old man cried.
" By all I hold most dear—by your own dear self—
I swear I speak the truth."

" Tell me everything," she said, in a low voice,
looking fixedly across the room with vacant eyes.
" Tell me who I am—the story of my life—that
break in my memory ? "

" The story matters not," he replied. " I would
spare you the truth, Elaine ; yet this much I will
tell you."

He rose to his feet and crossed the room to where
the strange picture in the ivory frame hung on the
wall. Then he laid his hand tenderly upon the
canvas.

"Do you know who this is, Elaine ? " he said,
without turning his, head.

"My mother; have you not told me so?"

She looked at him pitifully. All the fairness of her faith and trust was crumbling like Dead Sea fruit.

"A lie!" he cried. "Another lie! This is the form of one that I have loved, and that I still love with all my heart and soul. That body is dust, and my love has passed from the coarse clay of passion and desire into the eternal love of a soul. And that soul is still on earth, and shall be with me till he who gave it shall take it away. It has lain in bondage threw all the centuries, moving from form to form, knowing neither rest nor happiness, nor the silence of that sleep which is given to men with death. Sixty-three years ago this woman died, and for sixty-three years have I battled day and night to give her soul freedom. But I have failed, Elaine— failed, and when I thought success was certain! And the price must be paid to-morrow. Do you know who this is, Elaine?"

The girl did not answer, but cowered in a heap on the sofa, and covered her face with her hands.

"Do you know who this is, Elaine?" he repeated, coming to her side.

Still she did not move, and he touched her gently on the arm. Then she suddenly gave a cry, and rising to her feet, pressed her hands to her forehead and sank unconscious to the floor.

The old man fell on his knees beside her, and murmured unintelligible words. He fetched some water and sprinkled it on her face, calling her name in a piteous voice. Then he raised her limp body in his arms, and laid it on the sofa, and for ten minutes tried to restore her to consciousness by every means in his power. Then the girl suddenly opened her eyes and sat bolt upright, staring vacantly at the picture.

"Are you better, dear child?" Dacobra said, taking hold of her hand.

For a few seconds she did not answer him. Then indeed a strange thing happened.

"Is that you, Dacobra?" she said in Persian, and her voice had a far-away sound, as if she spoke from the depths of some ravine.

During my stay in Persia I had picked up sufficient of the language to be able to understand her.

Dacobra started and looked sharply round the room, as if someone else had addressed him.

"Is that you, Dacobra?" she continued, never moving her eyes from the painting on the wall. "I have waited long for you, Dacobra, and if my father knew he would kill me. I sometimes think that if thou dost truly love me, thou wouldst leave me for ever."

"I love thee, Zuhrah," he replied, in the same language, looking not at the girl as he spoke, but at the picture on the wall. "I love thee, dearest, with all my soul, and I will never leave thee."

"Where are the roses, Dacobra?" she continued— "the red roses thou didst promise me? Ah! I see their crimson petals peeping from thy hands. Why dost thou hold thy hands behind thy back, Dacobra? Ah! It is blood, Dacobra! It is blood that lies red on thy hands."

" There is blood on my hands, sweet star of the mountain, and I would shed the blood of all the world for thee. This is the blood of one who spoke ill of thee."

" Where is the silver charm, Dacobra, to keep the evil spirits from me ? Do I see it glittering in thy girdle ? Nay, it is the steel of thy knife that glitters."

" That steel is a charm," he answered, " that will keep the evil from thee, dear heart."

" Let us go, my lord," she cried, still with fixed eyes and expressionless face. " It is dark. I hear the nightingales in the mountains. The scent of the roses is in the air. Let us go and dream of love— Ah! what is that? what is that ? Why didst thou not bring the charm, Dacobra ? The evil spirits are near us. I hear them crying to me. The air is cold with the beating of their wings. It is winter. Dear heart, protect me, protect me ! "

As she spoke she rose to her feet and pointed to the wall. The tones of her voice froze my blood cold with horror, and I looked to where she pointed, half expecting to see something. But there was nothing there, and she sank back on to the sofa, and, muttering something in so low a tone that I could not hear the words, she closed her eyes.

Dacobra still looked at the picture, nor did he turn round till the girl gave a deep sigh, and stirred slightly by his side. Then he seemed to awake from his stupor, and watched her face anxiously. In a minute or two she opened her eyes again.

" Where have I been ? " she said in English. " Ah !

I remember. It was dark and in some Eastern land. I have been there before—once or twice before, when I have fainted. What does it mean ? Ah ! I remember now."

She raised herself up to a sitting position, and stared at the picture.

" I understand," she said quietly ; " I understand. To-morrow, you said ? Why have you not told me everything ? "

" Elaine, dear child," he replied, " if it would give you a moment's peace or a moment's happiness to tell you, I would do so. But if you can trust my word, do not ask me."

" I can trust you," she said. " You would not deceive me. But is there no escape ? "

She seemed quite calm now. I had judged her rightly. In a supreme moment of terror, such as this, her strong will asserted itself and strangled her fears with fingers of steel.

" There is no escape but one, Elaine," he replied, drawing out two small white pellets from one of his pockets, and placing them in the palm of his hand. " It is death in any case, Elaine. But this will mean rest for all Eternity. There are two here, Elaine —one for you and one for myself. Promise me that when the hour comes, and you know that this is no idle story of a fevered brain—promise me this, Elaine ; that you will face your death with a calm and thankful mind."

She held out her hand, and he placed one of the pellets in her palm.

"I promise," she said softly ; " I promise, dear father, —I will call you father still—that if this be all true and not a fancy of your brain, and that if there should be no escape but by this road, I will not be afraid to travel along it."

Her face was lit with a smile. It almost seemed a smile of triumph. He stooped and reverently kissed her hand as though she had been a queen.

" Elaine," he said humbly, "you are the bravest and noblest of all women in the world, and when the time comes, it is not *you* that will be afraid."

He rose, and walking over to the picture, looked at it earnestly.

The girl rose to her feet—white and imperious— with flashing eyes.

"Whoever I am," she cried, "and whatever it is that comes, I do not fear. We will fight—fight— fight—and if we are not strong enough—well, you have given me that which will prove too powerful for our enemies."

With these words she walked over to the door, and looking back for a second at Dacobra, passed out of my sight. For a minute he did not move. Then he looked at his watch and came straight towards the window. I slipped my right hand quickly on to the butt of my revolver, and gripped the window-sill tightly with my left. I heard the drawing of a bolt, and ducked my head below the ledge. Then the iron shutters were thrown back with a clang. I raised my head slowly, and I and Dacobra were face to face.

P

CHAPTER XV

HOW I FLUNG THE GAUNTLET IN DACOBRA'S FACE

DACOBRA started, but said nothing. Then he smiled, and taking a small penknife from his pocket, opened it thoughtfully, and began to trim one of his nails. When he had finished, he carefully laid the hand which held the knife on the sill close to the cord, and looked out into the night. He could not see my revolver, as my right arm was still by my side, below the level of the window.

"Good-evening, Mr. Maxwell," he said pleasantly. "No, I would not raise my right arm if I were you. You might startle me, and if my hand slipped on to the rope—well, it would be a nasty fall."

I did not answer, and, to say the truth, felt a little foolish.

"I think you have mistaken the entrance," he continued. "Could you not get an answer to the bell?"

"Stop this fooling!" I said sternly, looking him straight in the eyes. "I have come to have a talk with you. The reason for my mode of entrance will probably suggest itself to you."

"Pray come in," he said, extending his hand, "and

allow me to assist you. I must apologise for the awkwardness of the entrance—no, your right hand, if you please."

I slipped my revolver back into my pocket, and put up my hand. He gripped it firmly, and helped me through the window. When I was in the room, he laughed. He was evidently not afraid to be alone with me, though he was practically at my mercy. Perhaps he relied upon his knowledge of human nature. It is difficult for an ordinary sane being to kill an unarmed man in cold blood. Then his eyes seemed to gaze past me, far out to sea, as though he expected to see something. He walked close up to the window and leaned out, scanning the darkness intently.

"The storm is rising," he said. "Do you see a light out at sea?"

I came to his side and looked, though I did not know what light he expected to see, unless the chartering of the *Fire Fly* had come to his knowledge. But there was nothing there. It was all darkness. The wind swept round the castle with terrific force, howling and moaning like the voice of a lost soul. Beneath us the waves thundered on the rocks, and even at this height the salt spray was driven in our faces.

"I see nothing," I said, turning away from the window with a heavy heart.

The old man peered a minute or two longer into the night, and then, crossing the room, he took a small portable electric light from the table, and let the rays play over the castle walls and the face of the cliffs. Then he withdrew his head sharply, and closing the iron shutters with three strong bolts, shut down the window inside.

"Well, Mr. Maxwell," he said, "will you not sit down?"

There was a cruel sneer on his lips, and I could hardly believe him to be the same man that I had been watching through the hole in the shutter. All the tenderness had died out of his eyes; his face was a cold mask of stone, and his voice was hard and bitter.

I did not answer him, but studied him carefully, wondering what motive he had for allowing me to enter the house, and what line of conduct he was likely to pursue. I did not think it necessary to offer any explanation, and I did not suppose he would demand one. We understood each other.

"Will you not sit down?" he repeated.

"No, thank you," I replied. "I think I can say all I have to say in about three minutes."

"You will excuse me, then. I am an old man and am tired," and he sat down in a chair a few feet from where I was standing.

"Well, Dr. Rawlins, or Mr. Dacobra, or whatever your real name is, you probably understand that I know everything?"

"Knowledge is power," he replied quietly, "except in the hands of fools, who cannot use it to the best advantage."

"I intend to use such advantage as youth and strength can give me."

" Really ? "

" I intend to take that poor girl away from here to-night, and place her in safe hands. By a lucky circumstance I have become acquainted with her story. Whether it be true or not, it is certain from what I have heard that she is in danger, and she must leave Balath to-night."

" It was indeed a lucky circumstance," he replied, with a sneer; "yet I have heard the thing called by a less pleasant name. It was also a lucky circumstance, I presume, that your friend, Mr. Faversham— another honourable gentleman—has sunk to the level of a common thief."

"Words!" I replied; "words! A life is at stake, and we are men enough to forget that we are gentlemen. But I am not here to talk. Where is the girl? Will you ring the bell and have her sent for, or shall I go and seek her out myself? "

" You cannot have listened very attentively at the window," he said, "or you would have heard her decision in this matter."

" You abuse her love and devotion towards you," I answered sharply. " Too great a coward to kill her yourself, you thrust the choice of life or death into her own hands at a time when her mind is disordered with fear."

" There was only one choice that she could possibly have made. Look here, Mr. Maxwell! Do you believe this story, or do you not? "

" I do not know. It seems incredible."

" Well, I will put the facts to you either way. If

you do not believe it, do you suppose that I should wish to put an end to her life and mine for the sake of a fairy tale ? "

" It is possible that you are mad."

" It is possible, but I know that you do not think so. You have weighed the matter carefully, and the truth of this story is, in your mind, the only solution."

" Well, if it be true ? "

" Then I tell you, Mr. Maxwell, that when the Priest comes, no power on earth can save the life and soul of this girl from him."

" It is possible that you are mistaken," I replied. " Suppose that when he comes he does not find her here."

The old man smiled wearily.

" Do you think I have not weighed that chance ? " he asked. " There is no place on all this earth where they would not find her. They have watched and followed me for sixty-three years. I will give you an instance. I once purchased a yacht, and thought that I would sail the whole wide world ceaselessly, with hundreds of miles of sea as a barrier between me and my pursuers. Yet, before the year was out, in spite of every precaution, I saw that we were still followed. We entered a port in Australia, anchoring some two miles out, put ashore in a boat, and then sailed off again. As they hung the boat on to the davits, a white monkey jumped out of her. I had the satisfaction of seeing it sink through the green water with a lump of coal at its neck. But I

saw the uselessness of it all, and it would be a
thousand times more useless now. It would mean a
flight of terror for weeks, and perhaps for months,
with this shadow chasing us remorselessly, and with
a certainty of ultimate capture. No, Mr. Maxwell,
there is no escape but death."

"Why then these palisades, these iron shutters—
or perhaps they are for my benefit?"

"You flatter yourself, Mr. Maxwell," he replied.
"They are useless. They will perhaps give us a few
hours longer, but if they were of paper they could
not be more useless to affect the end."

"I have a yacht in the bay," I said quietly. "I
am going to take Miss Rawlins on board. The wife
of a friend of mine will look after her. I will chance
the ultimate failure. But I will do my best, and you
can come too, if you like."

"You are very kind," he replied coldly; "but we
shall have to decline your offer. Our plans are made,
and we are the best judges of our own actions."

"Well, you can stay," I said; "but the girl
comes."

For reply he rose from his seat, and walking to
the window, opened it, and flung aside the shutters.

"Do you see your yacht?" he said, with a sneer.

The moon was shining faintly through a stormy
mass of clouds, and I could see the white foam of
the waves dancing across the dark waters. The
wind hissed like the lash of a whip. There were
no lights upon the sea.

"If she is there," he continued, "I am sorry for

her. Heaven help the men who try to land a boat
on this coast to-night!"

I recognised the truth of what he said, and in my
own heart realised that it was hopeless to look for
any assistance from Alan Steyning. An almost
impossible task lay before me, but I was resolved
to see it through till failure was absolutely forced
upon me. It was certain that I should need
assistance, and I began to feel in my pocket for
the whistle. But to my horror I could not find it
anywhere; it had probably dropped out of my
pocket while I was climbing the cliff. It was
evident that I should have to act alone.

Dacobra closed the shutters and the window.
"Well," he said, "are you satisfied?"

I did not answer, but began to calculate my
chances of overpowering and gagging him before
he could arouse the household with his cries. Even
if I did so, it was doubtful if I could find the girl,
and still more doubtful if I could get her away from
the castle.

"Well?" he repeated, with a smile on his lips.

A sudden fury seized me like a burst of madness.
I sprang forward and clutched him by the throat
with one hand. I am a fairly strong man, and
could have choked the life out of him if I had
wished to do so. His hands closed round my wrist
like a steel vice. I only wanted to hold him till I
could throw him limp and speechless on the floor, and
then bind and gag him. I gripped him so tightly
that he could only give a faint, gasping cry, and

pressing my other hand firmly over his mouth, bore him backwards towards the sofa. He loosed my wrists, waved his arms wildly in the air, and then caught hold of my waist.

Then before I knew what had happened, I was looking along the barrel of my own revolver. The man's arms were of unusual length, reaching, in fact, almost to his knees. He had not lost his presence of mind when I clutched hold of him; but he had quietly slipped his left hand into my pocket and taken the weapon. I let go of him, and striking up his arm, stepped back sharply. I read my death in his eyes. He would have fired if I had kept my hands on him. He staggered back on to the sofa and gasped for breath; then he changed the revolver from his left to his right hand.

"Throw up your hands," he said faintly, "or I will shoot you."

I was at his mercy, and obeyed him.

"Now walk backwards," he continued. "You will find a chair behind you." Then he covered me point blank. "Do not move," he said; "I am an excellent shot."

He rose and walked a few steps backwards, never taking his eye from mine. He evidently thought it possible that I might have another weapon concealed on me. Then he rang the bell, and in a minute or two the tall Hindoo entered.

"You will take a piece of rope, Deya," he said, "and bind the gentleman hand and foot."

The servant salaamed, and turned to leave the room.

"You will find a piece of rope here, Deya,"
Dacobra continued, with a smile. " It is hanging on
the shutters outside the window. The gentleman was
thoughtful enough to bring a piece with him."

The man went to the window, opened it, and
began to draw back the bolts of the shutters.

" Look through the eye-holes, Deya," he continued.

The man did so.

" Do you see anything ? "

" Nothing but darkness, Sahib."

" Do you hear anything ? "

" Nothing but the sea and wind, Sahib."

" Open the shutters, then, but carefully."

The man did so, and cutting off the rope, closed
the window again. Then he bound me tightly round
my wrists and ankles and left the room.

" An ideal servant," Dacobra said. " Now we can
talk things over quietly."

"You devil ! " I cried hoarsely.

He laughed. I was bound and helpless, and he
could afford to be pleasant. He placed the revolver
in his pocket, and taking a cigar from his case, cut
the end off, and lit it carefully.

" Is there anything you would like to know ? " he
said, leaning back on the sofa. " I do not mind
telling you everything, for I'm sure you will not
tell anyone else."

" Don't rely upon my honour," I said bitterly.

" I do not," he said. " I rely upon your silence."

There was no mistaking what he meant. I began
to wonder whether Fox Faversham would come to

look for me, and whether he would manage to effect
an entrance.

"I might remind you," I said calmly, "that I am a
well-known man, and that if I am missed no power
on earth will save you from the consequences."

"No?" he said slowly, raising his eyebrows.

"And it may interest you to know that my friend,
Mr. Faversham, is at this moment waiting for me not
a hundred yards from here."

"Indeed! He must be tired of waiting." He
rang the bell, and the Hindoo entered again.
"Deya, this gentleman's friend is waiting for him
outside on the cliff; kindly tell him that he need
not wait." Then he added a few words in a language
that I did not understand, and the servant left the
room. "An ideal servant," the old man said, with
an evil smile. "I trust your friend is not near the
edge of the cliff. It breaks away sometimes."

I knew then what he had said to the servant, and,
rising to my feet, struggled to burst my bonds. The
cords only cut into my flesh, and I sank back again
on to the chair.

"You devil!" I yelled at him, the blood rushing
to my head from my violent struggles.

"Pray be calm, Mr. Maxwell," he said; "let us
talk this matter over quietly. You have made an
unprovoked attack upon an old man, and have found
yourself too weak to overcome him. I bear you no
ill-will, but if you stand in my path you are nothing
to me—absolutely nothing. Again I ask you, is
there anything you would like to know?"

" I know everything," I replied sullenly. " I know
that you are Dacobra. I know that this girl is Alice
Borrodaile. I know that you lied to me when you
said you had broken down the barrier between life
and death. I know what you fear, and I know what
you intend to do. I know, too, that as long as I
have life I will try and prevent your doing it."

" Are you sure there is nothing you would like to
know ? " he repeated.

I thought for a moment, then recollected my
own work and the statue of Ormuzd and Ahriman.
There was something I wished to know about
that.

" When you promised me, Dacobra, that my
statue should be the greatest in the world, I suppose
it was an idle jest, and the words were as empty as
those in which you told me you had solved the
problem of life and death ? "

A dark flush spread over his face, and he stepped
forward as if to strike me. But he did not forget
himself so far as that.

" It is not wise of you to mock me, Mr. Maxwell,"
he said sternly, " now you know I have failed in the
work of my life. No, I did not lie to you. You
must have seen in my face that I thought I had
spoken the truth when I said I had succeeded. I
had succeeded up to a point. With your own eyes
you saw the piece of granite decay like a lump of
rotten cheese. But my success went no further. If
it had done so, I would have made your work the
greatest work in the world—for I would have given

it life. But I failed. While I could produce all the symptoms of animal decay in inanimate matter, there I stopped. I had discovered not the secret of life, but the secret of death. And if you know what the ceaseless work of sixty years devoted to a single object means you will know the agony of my soul during the last few days ! "

As he spoke he moved the fingers of his hands, as if he would like to tear the web of fate into a thousand pieces.

" I apologise," I said. " I believe that you thought you had succeeded. But why, in the first place, did you offer me so enormous a price for it ? You might have had something much less expensive to test your powers upon."

Dacobra smiled.

" Money," he replied, " is not much use to a man who knows that the day of his death is at hand. I wished to leave behind me some permanent memorial of Elaine. I selected you for the work because you happened to be in this neighbourhood, and also—if I might say so—because I knew no one more fitted to execute it."

" You flatter me," I said coldly.

This praise of my work was very distasteful, coming as it did from the lips of a man who was going to murder me.

" Not at all," he replied. " Can I give you any further information ? "

My mind reverted to the monkeys. I had some curiosity on that point—idle, it is true, a few minutes before one's death ; but still, an explanation might gain time.

"What do these monkeys mean ? " I asked. " How do they come here ? "

" They are the servants of the Priests," the old man replied, "and they come by perfectly natural means. Some have, perhaps, hidden themselves in ships ; some of them have allowed themselves to be captured, like the one which belonged to the tramp. They have all concentrated here from various parts and places ; and they are here to watch me. Their powers are almost human, and they are invaluable to their masters. These Priests, you must understand, have no supernatural powers to overcome natural obstacles, or I should not have fortified this castle. Yet their natural mental powers are so stupendous that they seem to work miracles. They do most of their physical work through the hands of these servants of theirs. The White Priests would give much for a key of this castle, and if one of these animals is about the place now, it will not leave until it has found some way of entrance for its master. That is why I fear them, and not merely because they bring back the memory of the past. But there can be very few of them left. The fire must have destroyed them in hundreds."

"You are fighting against great odds," I said thoughtfully.

" Will you not fight on my side, Mr. Maxwell ? " he replied gently, and almost in a tone of entreaty.

"Believe me, it is the only chance. Consent to let
me carry out my purpose."

For a moment I hesitated. Opposition seemed
to be useless, but when I have made a plan, I am
obstinate in my purpose. My determination only
grew more strong within me, though a voice
whispered to me that my struggles would be all
in vain.

"I will help you by taking the girl away from here
to-night," I said.

He rose to his feet, and the red light from the lamp
seemed to bathe his face in the fires of hell.

"No!" he screamed. "A thousand times, No!
She shall not leave me for an hour. When the
time comes we will be together. I have loved this
soul for more than sixty years. I have clung to this
soul as a man clings to his God. It has been with
me always. It is my religion, my life, the keystone
of my very existence. Do you think that in this
last hour I will lose my grasp of it for a single second?
No! not if all the devils in hell are coming to tear it
from me!"

He strode rapidly up and down the room, and
stopped before the portrait on the wall. And as I
watched his face and saw the change come over it, I
forgot the girl, I forgot Faversham, forgot even the
immediate terror of my own death. The cold mask
had dropped from his face, and I saw for the moment
into the awful depths of this man's soul, where sin
and love and passionate grief were tossed together
in one furious tumult. Then he sank down upon

his knees, and mumbled something in an unknown
tongue. Tears streamed down his old cheeks; his
hands were clenched; his whole body shook with
emotion. There was something unearthly in this
paroxysm of despair. His face might have been
that of a lost soul cast forth from all it loved into
the outer darkness.

Then suddenly he sprang to his feet; his eyes
flashed at me with fury; and he broke into a hoarse
laugh. The mask dropped once more over his face,
and he was a hard and indomitable man.

I gazed at him stupidly, with mingled feelings. I
could not exactly define my mental attitude towards
this extraordinary man. Hatred for his works of
devilry; admiration for his indomitable will and
courage; terror of the strange network of unknown
forces that were about his life; blind rage at my own
impotence; but through all a warm vein of pity for
one who had sacrificed, and would sacrifice everything, to keep a woman's soul from endless torment.
My lips were dry, and I could not speak; but I fixed
my eyes upon his face.

"Have you decided?" he said sternly. "Are you
with me or against me?"

"I am against you," I replied, "and unless Miss
Rawlins is out of this house to-night, and in safe
hands, and with the means of self-destruction taken
from her, I will fight you till the very last moment."

He did not answer, but looked at me thoughtfully,
as if weighing something in his mind. I heard the
clock tick on the mantelpiece, and looked at the

hands. It was just midnight. I knew my fate was being decided, but somehow or other I did not seem to take much interest in the decision. A terrific blast of wind came against the castle, and rattled the shutters outside. Dacobra took out his watch and looked at it.

"I will give you five minutes, Mr. Maxwell," he said, in a cold voice. "At the end of that time I must ask you for your final decision."

He walked over to the window, and, gripping my revolver in his hand, pulled up the sash and cast open the shutters. The sound of roaring wind and sea came rushing into the room, and a vase blew off a bracket with a crash. I caught sight of the sky, and saw the dark clouds being driven over the moon like smoke from a furnace.

"A storm!" he cried, closing the shutters—" a glorious storm! The *Silurian* is due at Glasgow to-morrow morning. She should be coming up the coast now. It is a dangerous coast at night."

"I do not take any interest in the *Silurian*," I replied coldly.

"A glorious storm," he continued, not heeding my interruption. "One that drives ships across the sea like paper boats, and tears them into shreds no bigger than a man's hand."

Another long roar of wind swept round the building, and a door banged in some distant room. There was a roll of thunder, and a flash of lightning gleamed through the eye-holes of the shutters.

"I will see it through to the end," he said,

turning sharply towards me. " Mr. Maxwell, I bear
you no ill-will." He looked at his watch. " Two
minutes more," he continued. " Do you see how
useless it is ? If I set you free and let Elaine go
with you, it would all be in vain. You could not
save her, and you would condemn the soul I love
to eternal unrest. There must be no chance of
your doing this. You understand me ?   No chance!
No chance whatever ! "

" I have made up my mind," I replied.

" I have no wish to harm you," he went on ; " you
are nothing to me ; but even if an insect is in my
path I must crush it.   I only ask that you will leave
this house, that you will be silent as to our intentions,
and that you will make no opposition to what I am
about to do."

" I refuse to be silent, and I refuse to withdraw my
opposition."

" You are aware that your silence is ensured, and
that your opposition is already overcome ? "

" I understand."

He looked at me almost, as it seemed, with pity.
But I knew that it would be as useless to try and
move him from his purpose as to try and cast the
towers of Balath into the sea.

" I am a desperate man," he continued, " fighting
for what is more to me than my own life, clutching
at this one escape with the grasp of a drowning
man ; and I am as strong as I am desperate.   Do
you hear the storm ? "

The rain was hissing against the window, and the

flashes of light seemed to shoot from the eye-holes
of the shutters like guns from the port-holes of a ship
The wind was like the steady roar of falling waters.

"Do you hear the storm?" he repeated. "Even
the elements fight for me to-night. Victory is in
my grasp."

"Not yet, Dacobra," I replied—"not yet."

He looked at his watch again.

"The time is up," he said; "give me your
answer!"

"I have given you my answer."

He came a step or two closer to me with the
revolver in his hand.

"So you would add this to the list of your other
crimes, Dacobra," I said.

"Would that I had committed them all in so
worthy a cause," he replied. "You do not know
Lionel Maxwell; you do not understand. Perhaps
you too have loved; but my love for this soul is
to the poor human love that men feel for the fair
body they worship as the light of ten thousand suns
is to one pale moon. There is nothing of earth in my
love. The casket that holds my jewel is nothing
to me. I loved the soul of Zuhrah as dearly when
it dwelt in the form of a snake as I do now, when it is
enshrined in the body of a fair woman. To keep
such a love with me for a few hours longer I would
risk all that is in heaven, or earth, or hell."

"You are too late. Look behind you, Dacobra."

He looked, and then saw, as I had seen, a small
white paw thrust through one of the holes in the

iron shutter, and feebly scratching the glass of
the window. He raised his revolver and fired.
He had spoken the truth when he said he was an
excellent shot. The ball shattered the pane, and
went clean through the hole, cutting off the paw of
the animal in its passage, so that it dropped down
between the shutter and the glass. He smiled and
turned to me again.

" I do not fear that," he said, " save that it is the
servant of its master ; let it go and pray for its
master on the sea."

Again he raised his revolver, and this time the
barrel was pointing at my heart. Then he seemed
to change his mind, for he lowered the weapon
sharply, and placed it in his pocket. Then, crossing
the room, he rang the bell, and in a minute the
Hindoo entered.

" Deya," he said, " this gentleman is anxious to
join his friend."

For a moment a ray of hope flashed through my
mind—but it was only for a moment. I saw the look
in Dacobra's eyes, and saw that my doom was sealed.

" Good-bye, Mr. Maxwell," he said, and motioned
to his servant.

The muscular Hindoo picked me up, and, though
I am a big man, he carried me towards the door like
a child. When he reached it, I strained my head
back and looked at Dacobra. His face was buried
in his hands.

" Good-bye, Dacobra," I said ; " I understand,
and—I pity you."

CHAPTER XVI

THE RIDE THROUGH THE NIGHT

THE man carried me into the passage leading to the postern door, and setting me down for a moment on the stone flags, turned the key in the lock. Then he turned the handle, and the wind drove the door in like the stroke of a battering-ram, shrieking down the passage, and rushing through into the innermost recesses of the house. A blinding torrent of mingled foam and rain struck me in the face like a whip. He picked me up again, and setting me down on a rock outside, tried to close the door. There was a flash of lightning, and for a moment I saw the great muscles stand out on his bare arms, as he put forth all his strength. Then there was darkness, and a crash, as the door closed. He locked it, and placed the key in the folds of his waistband.

At first my eyes could distinguish nothing, and I was deafened by the ceaseless roar of the wind and water. Then I saw breakers of white foam rolling through the blackness like long lines of a ghostly army, and I watched them rise up to their assault, and fall back again, broken and shattered into fragments. Deya picked me up again, and carried me

249

along the foot of the cliffs. The tide was going down, and there was just room to pass. After struggling along the narrow strip of shingle for some distance, he stopped and set me down against the wet cliff on a spot sheltered from the storm.

"Well, Sahib," he said, "death comes to all men."

"Yes, my friend," I replied lightly; "but could you not manage to put me down in a drier place?"

"Death comes to all men, and great is my master."

"Your master is a scoundrel," I replied, "and we hang such men in England. These sort of tricks are best confined to the East, if the conjuror does not wish to dangle at the end of a six-foot rope."

There came a flash of lightning, and I saw steel glittering in his hand. Drowning was evidently not to be my fate. I idly began to balance the one form of death against the other, and could not decide which would be preferable.

Then a wild desire for life rushed into my brain, and the stoic calm with which I had resolved to meet my death left me. I would appeal to this man's pity, to his cupidity, to his fear of justice, and to any spark of human feeling that was in him. I was rich; surely I could buy my life from a poor Hindoo. But there came another flash of lightning, and I saw his face—a fine, noble face, calm and impenetrable as death itself. I felt a peculiar sort of jealousy, and hardened my mind. I would not speak. I would show this man that I was his superior. I would not lower myself by grovelling before him. I set my teeth close together, and resolved to be silent.

"The Sahib is a brave man; yet life is sweet."

"Will you kindly proceed," I replied coldly. "You are paid to kill me, and not to bore me with your conversation."

For answer he stooped down and placed his left hand on my shoulder. I wondered where his fancy would lead him to stick the knife into me. The hand went softly down my arm till it reached my wrists. Then there was a quick movement, and the ropes fell apart, and I felt the blood rush into my numbed arms. Before I could raise them to see if I were really at liberty, there was another movement of the blade, and my legs were free. The man rose to his feet.

"Will the Sahib take my hand?" he said. "H's limbs are probably sore."

I was too dazed to reply, and, leaning on his arm, I rose and stood till the blood flowed more freely through my veins.

"What is the meaning of this?" I said at last.

"It may mean death to me."

"Your master has not changed his mind, then?"

"My master supposes the Sahib dead by now."

"Why have you disobeyed him?"

He came close to me, and put his lips to my ear. I expected a request for money, but I wronged him.

"There is one above the master," he whispered, "and your life will serve his cause. Hark!"

I listened, and above the hiss and roar of the waters I heard the sound of a gun. I looked out to sea, and caught the intermittent flash of a light, now clear, now hidden in a mist of foam. Then a rocket swept up into the darkness.

"The *Silurian*," he whispered. "He is there."

"Well," I cried, with a nervous laugh, "whoever is there is not in a pleasant position. It is more profitable to serve the living than the dead."

"It is better to serve those who cannot die," he answered.

I understood everything. Dacobra could not even command the services of his own faithful servant, when this secret and terrible power was at hand.

"And my friend?" I cried eagerly. "Did you spare him too?

"He awaits the Sahib at the top of the cliff. There seems to be a rope, and the Sahib can climb." And he vanished into the darkness without another word.

I started to follow him, hoping to be able to get back into the castle, with my limbs free, and burning for vengeance. But I was stiff, and before I had gone half-a-dozen paces I heard the postern door close with a crash. I turned back, and resolved to reach Faversham, if I could find him. I groped my way along the bottom of the cliff, feeling for the rope in the darkness. But before I touched it with my hands the wind drove it, wet and slippery, against my face. I gripped it tight and began to ascend.

It was almost a miracle that I reached the top. My limbs were still stiff and numb, and before I had got half-way my strength began to fail me. The wind swung me to and fro, and buffeted me against the rocks. The rain beat in my face, and the rope itself was so slippery that I could scarcely hold on to it. However, I set my teeth until I reached the edge of the cliff. Then I scrambled over and sank to the ground utterly exhausted. I had been climbing for twenty minutes ; most of the skin was off the palms of my hands ; my clothes were torn, and the water was running from all over me.

I called to Faversham. There was no answer. I could see nothing in the blackness, and no shouting could have been heard in that storm. I rose and scrambled forward a few paces, calling his name again and again. Then suddenly I ran against someone who was blundering in the opposite direction, and clutched hold of his arm to save myself from falling.

" Faversham ? " I cried.

" Yes ; is that you, Maxwell ? I thought you were never coming. Isn't this awful ? I have been in it since you left. My pipe won't burn, and I have emptied my flask. Heaven knows in what direction our horses lie What has happened ? "

" The worst," I said breathlessly. " I have only escaped with my life. I am half dead. Haven't you a drop in your flask ? "

" Not a drop."

" Well, we must get back, both of us, into the castle. Have you the key of that other door ? "

" No, of course not. I left it in the house. What use would it be ? "

" There is just a chance we might get over the palisades. I think we had better go back to Ardrachan and get it."

" What has happened ? "

" I will tell you when we get home. Nothing can be done now. If I do not get some brandy soon I shall faint. Give me your arm."

" Where are we ? " he said, as I leant heavily on his arm. " I have been wandering round and round. I could not stand still in this rain. I wonder I did not walk into the sea."

" I know the direction," I said. " Come along."

Then the whole sky seemed to be split apart by a chasm of light, and the surrounding sea and land were lit up for miles. The darkness closed in again ; but not before I had seen something small and white running in the direction of Ardrachan. It was not more than fifty yards off. I wondered why the animal was leaving Balath. Then I suddenly remembered Dacobra's words : " The White Priest would give much for a key of this castle." My fingers closed more tightly on Faversham's arm.

" Do you remember where you left the key ? " I said sharply.

" I do not know. I think it was in the studio. I could find it ; but it is of no use to us."

" It might be of use to someone else," I replied. " Can you remember where you put it ? "

" I think it was in the studio. Yes, I am sure it

was in the studio, on the small table by the window.
But I do not see that it would be of any more use
to another person than to us."

"It might be of use to a very small person," I
replied ; "one who could squeeze through the bars
of the palisade. Did you see that white monkey
just now? It was going towards Ardrachan.
Dacobra says they are almost human, and faithful
servants of their master. The White Priest wishes
to enter Balath to-morrow. Do you understand?"

"Good heavens!" he cried, "is it possible? But
the windows and door of the studio are sure to be
shut."

"There is just a chance that they are not," I said.
"It is quite likely the door is open, and the
animal might easily slip into the house. Quick,
Faversham! we must reach those horses and be at
Ardrachan in an hour. Come along, we must run.
I know the way. You've seen nothing of the *Fire
Fly*, I suppose?"

"I saw a rocket and heard a gun just now," he
replied ; "but it must have been a larger ship than
the *Fire Fly*."

"It was not the *Fire Fly*," I said. "But come
along, we must get to those horses."

I let go of his arm, and we set off across country
in one of the worst storms I have ever seen or ever
expect to see again. I shall never forget that
journey. How we slipped and fell on the wet grass ;
how we knocked our feet and ankles against granite
boulders ; how we stumbled on small loose stones ;

how we dashed blindly into hedges and fought our way through them, torn and bleeding; how we plunged through water up to our knees; and how above our heads the storm raged, and the rain beat against us, and the lightning played across the sky— the only gleam of light in the whole world of darkness. At last we stopped from sheer exhaustion.

" Where are we ? " Faversham cried breathlessly.

I peered vainly into the darkness all around.

" We ought to have struck the road by this time," I shouted. " I have tried to keep a straight line for it. Heaven knows where we are! Let us keep on. It is our only chance."

" Are we going in the right direction ? "

" I can swear to it," I replied. " Come along. We have not got as far as I thought. We must get those horses or—"

There was a brilliant flash of lightning, and a vista of bending trees and wet grass and glistening hedges crossed our sight for a thousandth part of a second. Faversham caught hold of my arm.

" What was that ? " he cried. " Did you see it ? "

" No," I replied sharply; " I want to see nothing but the lights of that inn."

" It was the monkey again," he cried—" a little white thing, hopping away as fast as it could go in the next field. I saw it through the gap in the hedge."

" How fast was it going ? " I said quickly. " Faster than we can run ? "

" About the same pace, I should think."

"Good!" I replied. "We shall do it yet if we can strike that infernal inn. It is obviously making for Ardrachan, and mark you, Faversham, we have to get there before it. If we can once get to the horses and the road, we shall do it."

We started off again at a run. My limbs were tired with slipping and falling, and the cord had hurt the tendons of one of my ankles, but I set my teeth and kept the pace up for ten minutes. Then suddenly I broke through a hedge; my feet sank into the water of a ditch, and I fell forward on the hard road. I gave a shout of joy, and, rising to my feet, pulled Faversham through, leaving half of one of his sleeves on the spikes of a blackthorn.

"Now then, Faversham," I cried, "let us do a spurt."

We started off down the smooth wet road, like runners on a cinder track. In a few minutes some lights showed through the trees, and shortly afterwards I was thundering at the door of the inn. It was opened quickly. The warm glow from within spread out into the tossing, heaving darkness.

"Come in, sirs, come in," the man said, clutching the door with both hands. "It is an awfu' night. Quick, sirs, or the house will be blown inside out."

We came into the warmth, and he shut the door. Then he looked at us and grinned. We were a sorry spectacle; covered with mud; water running from our clothes and hair; our hats gone, and our coats in ribbons.

"An' ye'll no' be going to Ardrachan to-night?"

"Our horses, quick, man! Our horses, quick!" I cried; "and let us have something hot while they are being saddled. It is a matter of life and death."

He looked at my white face and twitching lips, and saw that I meant what I said.

"I'll no' be losing time," he said, and slipped quickly from the room.

His wife poured us out two stiff doses of whisky, and filled the glasses with boiling water. We drank greedily, and once more life and warmth came into my body. By the time we had finished and paid our reckoning, the horses were at the door. We sprang into the saddles and were off into the darkness without a word. I turned my head back, and saw the old inn-keeper standing in the light and staring after us. Then the door crashed to, and I felt that we had fairly started on our race.

After toiling over fields and hedges on foot, it was pleasant to feel a good horse under one, and hear its hoofs beat on the firm road. But it is no easy matter riding full tilt in the darkness, with a great wind struggling to tear the rider from his seat, and the rain beating all sense of feeling out of his face. A man must trust a good deal to his horse to keep out of ditches, and it is merely a matter of luck whether, after all, he is not pitched into a hedge, and left there to listen to his horse's hoofs dying away in the distance. But I refused to draw rein. I told Faversham to keep behind me, if he found the pace too warm. It was only necessary for one of us to reach Ardrachan before the animal.

"If anything happens to me," I cried, "ride straight on. Go to the studio, and put the key in your pocket. Don't mind if I come to grief. Ride straight on."

I sprang ahead of him, for my horse was the better of the two and knew the road, and Faversham has not a very good seat in the saddle. As I dashed along, the tempest hissed in the trees, and I heard the crack and swish of falling branches. In the lightning flashes I could see the trees themselves bent down and curled like ostrich feathers.

Then a flash showed me a great fallen trunk right across the road, and I had to dismount and take the horse over it, for we could never have cleared it in the dark. I had then to wait for Faversham to come up, and warn him. I cursed the delay, but it could not be helped, and it was fortunate for us that the flash of lightning saved our necks.

Then we continued the race, and I began to wonder where the white monkey had gone to. I calculated that it must be well behind, for few animals could go the pace we were keeping up. I was convinced that we should win. The excitement had driven all other thoughts out of my head. I only thought of who would be the first to enter the studio. I spared neither myself nor the horse. Fortune was on my side. There were no more fallen trunks, and I dashed out from under the trees to where the long desolate heath spread on either side of the road. I drew rein for a few seconds, and listened for the sound of Faversham's

horse ; but either he was too far behind, or else
the howling wind drowned the clattering of the
hoofs.   Then I thought I heard the distant sound
of a gun.   The wind was blowing on shore, and would
carry the sound.   It was the *Silurian* in distress.

I dug the spurs into my horse, and we started
forward.   As we did so, there came a long crackling
blaze of light that crossed the whole sky.   The
heath was lit up, and showed as clearly as in the
daytime.   Then the darkness closed round more
heavily than before.   I spurred my horse again and
again, and lashed him with the whip, for the glare
had shown me something that I did not wish to
see—the little white monkey scampering along ahead,
a hundred yards to the left of the road.

"Curse the thing," I said to myself; "it has, of
course, gone straight across country, and saved at
least a mile."

But it could not make a short cut now; the road
was as straight as an arrow, and the house was about
two miles distant.   I was bound to pass the animal
in a level race.   We flew along like an arrow shot
from a bow.   There was no danger now from the
trees and hedges.   It was like a race-course, and my
horse seemed already to scent the warmth of his
stable.   I took him a little off the road, and we sped
so quickly over the turf that in a little over five
minutes we were cantering up the drive.   I flung
myself from the horse and rang the bell violently.
The door was opened, and I stood in the hall with
the water dripping from me.

"Close the door, John," I said, "and get someone to see to the horse;" but scarcely were the words out of my mouth when something brushed for a second against my legs and disappeared through the door into the darkness.

I rushed out into the drive, called the dog, and sent him into the shrubbery to search for it. But he found nothing, and remembering what I had passed on the way, I went back into the house and closed the door. Then I took a lamp from the hall table and went up into the studio. The window was shut, but I saw that it had been open, for the floor beneath it was wet with rain.

I searched everywhere for the key, but it was gone. I was too late. There were muddy footprints on the floor, and here and there a few specks and stains of blood. If any animal had been there, it was obviously not the one I had passed on the road, but another, which might have started hours before I met Faversham on the cliffs. I looked round the room. There was nothing to be seen. Then I shut the door of the studio and sank into a chair. As I did so, I heard something come hopping softly up the stairs, and there was a faint scratching on the panels of the door. I held my breath and listened, then I laughed nervously : the other animal was in the house ; it could not have been far behind me.

I had half a mind to open the door and kill it, but the strain and excitement had affected my nerves. A strange feeling of horror came over me, and I was afraid to look out of the well-lighted room into the

R

darkness. The scratching continued, and I could
hear the little feet pattering, and an occasional
thump of a tail. My nerves were certainly upset.
I rose, and giving the door a kick, locked it. There
was a scuttering, and then silence.

I resumed my seat for a minute or two. Then
I rose and lit the fire, and taking a cigar from the
mantelpiece, soothed my nerves with a smoke. Then
I took off my wet clothes and put on an old suit I
kept in the studio for working purposes. After that
I went to the cupboard, poured myself out a drink,
and sat down in front of the fire. The scratching at
the door began again, and it was followed by a feeble,
chattering noise of vexation. I could not shake off
the feeling of horror from my mind. I looked
nervously round the room, and wished Faversham
would come.

Then in the firelight, with the blue smoke curling
up from my cigar, I began to think of my friend and
all the hopelessness and pity of his love. Most
human love is the love of the body, with all the fair
graces and charms that belong to it, and such love
was his—the love of the dead Alice Borrodaile, whose
form still lived, though tenanted by another soul and
another life. The soul is unseen and unknown ; it is
hard for a man to love it. But the body he sees and
knows, and even if it is dead, he still cherishes its
memory. Faversham still loved this girl, and could
not dissociate her from the past. But after what I
had seen to-night, I knew that even if the girl lived,
he might beat out his heart in vain against the rocks

of love. It would be better for her to die. She
was bound for life and death to Dacobra, the
Hindoo.

And here, on the other hand, in Dacobra's case,
was the true love of a soul, mystic and incompre-
hensible, almost terrible in its intensity. He needed
no outward form to worship. It mattered not to him
where the soul dwelt. He saw through the dull
substance, clear and straight to the spirit within. So
long as it was near him, nothing else mattered, and
he was prepared to sacrifice everything to keep it by
his side. He had given his own soul into bondage to
purchase it. The lives of those who crossed his path
were unconsidered trifles, to be swept aside with a
smile. And he was prepared to make his last fight
to-morrow, and fight to the death.

Indeed, a strange pair of lovers for one poor
trembling girl! I knew Faversham well enough
now, and the strength of his determination. They
would fight to the end. But I did not doubt to
whom would be given the victory.

My meditations were interrupted by a loud
ringing at the hall door. Then Faversham's welcome voice came along the corridor. I did not open
the door, but I heard him ask John where I was,
and then there was the sound of his footsteps coming
up the stairs. As he reached the top, I heard him
stumble and utter a curse. Then he fumbled at the
door-handle and called out my name.

"The door is locked," I answered. "Is there
anything outside?"

" I cannot see," he said ; " it is too infernally dark ! Let me in."

" Go and change your wet things," I replied, " and then come back."

He went away, and in a few minutes returned and rapped on the door. I opened it, and he entered. His face was scarred and bruised, and as white as death. He limped a little.

" What is the matter ? " I said.

" I came a most awful cropper a mile from here. I have broken both your horse's knees, and am shaken to bits. Luckily I fell on something soft. Were you in time ? "

" No," I replied, " I was too late."

He flung himself into a chair, and stared at the hot coals in the grate.

" Too late ? " he repeated, in a low voice. " Impossible ! Were you delayed ? "

" There was another messenger," I said. " It came out of the house, and brushed past me as I opened the hall door. I passed the one we saw, but it has got into the house somehow, and has been scratching and chattering outside the door for the last twenty minutes. I confess to being a coward. I dared not kill it. I merely locked the door and waited for you. What is the time ? "

" Two o'clock by the clock in the hall. Have you got any tobacco ? "

I handed him my pouch. He filled his pipe and smoked in silence, still gazing steadily into the fire. I began to think he was dazed by the fall.

"Tell me everything," he said, after a while. "I know it is late, and I know we are both dead beat, but I should like to hear everything to-night."

In as few words as possible, I told him all I had seen and all that had happened to me. But he questioned me closely about details, and it was nearly three o'clock before I had finished. When at last I reached the end of the story, he rose to his feet with a look of such awful misery on his face that I think of it to this day.

"I will fight to the end," he cried hoarsely, gripping the mantelpiece with his hands. "Alice Borrodaile is dead, but I will fight to the end, if it is only for her dear memory. I am not beaten yet. I will fight for that girl, though she cannot love me. I will fight all the devils from hell, if I have to give my life for it."

"My dear old chap," I said, rising and laying my hand upon his arm, "I wish you had never come here. Is it not better to let this poor girl's fate run its course? It is inevitable."

"No!" he cried. "No! Shame on you, Maxwell! Have you no pity for her?"

"I will help you, Faversham," I said simply. "We can but do our best; but I am afraid we are not strong enough. Let us go to bed now; we shall want all our strength to-morrow."

"Yes," he replied slowly, "all our strength and all our courage. Look there!"

He gripped my arm and pointed to the window. Outside, on the window, hopping about and grimacing, was a little white monkey. We could see it clearly in the lamplight. It was patting the glass, and miserably trying to effect an entrance. Its white fur was soaking wet, and the wind and the rain beat upon it, as it shivered and wiped its head with its paws.

Faversham uttered an oath, and, picking up the poker from the grate, strode across to the window. But as he neared it, he suddenly stopped, and the poker fell from his nerveless hand. Then he came back to me with a look of horror on his face.

" Look !" he cried, catching hold of my arm ; " do you see it ?"

I looked, and for a moment saw nothing but the monkey. Then what seemed to be a white face slowly rose to the level of the window-sill. And as I looked again, it seemed not so much a face as a human skull. For a moment we both gazed in terror. Then we recovered ourselves and dashed towards the window. We opened it and looked out. There was nothing there but the blackness of the night. I hastily closed the window and drew down the blind.

" The master," Faversham whispered.

I looked at him in silence.

CHAPTER XVII

WHAT THE SEA GAVE TO THE SHORE

THE next morning was bright and sunny; the storm had blown itself out in the night, and the whole country looked fresh and sweet after the rain. I felt less despondent, and whistled cheerfully as I dressed. After all, our spirits are very dependent on the weather; no philosophy will prevail against a foggy day, and a man can face the darkest hour with hope if all the world is fair and sparkling. The news that awaited me on the breakfast table, however, was sufficiently depressing; there was a long letter from Alan Steyning, posted at some small port on the coast, and explaining why he had not arrived at the appointed time. The *Fire Fly* had encountered the storm before half the journey was accomplished, and had attempted to battle through it until her shaft broke; then she had to make for the nearest port under sail, and it would be quite impossible to take her to sea again for at least a month. Her boats had been carried away, her rudder smashed, and her decks and sides terribly strained. The people on the boat had had a narrow escape from death, and if they had not encountered a tug when their rudder went, a few miles from port, it is probable that all would have gone to the bottom.

"So much for that," I said, when I had read the letter out to Faversham.

"We must trust to ourselves," he replied gloomily. "After all, it is best to be independent in a crisis like this ; arrangements with other people are bound to go wrong."

After breakfast we went round to the stables, and despatched a groom on horseback to Balgowrie, with instructions to purchase two revolvers and some cartridges. Then we walked round the garden to the outside of the studio window. There were no footprints or marks to be seen on the window-ledge or on the flower-beds beneath ; but the rain had probably washed them away in the night. Faversham, however, discovered a small piece of white linen, about an inch in length, hanging to an old nail in the wall. He examined it carefully and put it in his waistcoat pocket.

It was impossible to make another attempt to enter Balath until the evening, and we resolved to take a walk along the cliffs. The exercise would do us good, and the keen air would freshen both our minds and bodies. We had also much to talk over, and it was just possible we might see something of the *Silurian*. She had evidently been in distress last night, and it was quite likely that she had been obliged to lay off the coast till daytime.

Yet I shuddered when I thought of the face I had seen at the window, and wondered if the White

Priest had been cast ashore by the sea. He could not have reached this part of the world in any other way. The *Silurian* would not reach Glasgow until that morning. But the glorious sunshine soon drove these gloomy thoughts from my brain. Life and hope were still strong within us as we made our way along the cliffs, some three miles from the house. The gale had died away into a fresh breeze. The sea was a magnificent sight; huge waves heaved and towered, and died away in foam, as far as the eye could reach. Now and then, as the sun caught their summits, a tiny rainbow flickered for a moment in the mist and spray, and their crests sparkled with the light of a thousand emeralds. Directly beneath our feet they rolled and thundered upon the cliffs, and the white froth poured through the sluices and channels of the rocks. I looked carefully over the tossing surface with a small telescope I had brought with me. There was no ship in sight.

"She has either gone down, or battled through it and steamed out to sea," I said. "Can you see anything?"

I handed him the glass, and he scanned the sea with an anxious face.

"No, I can see nothing," he replied, and gave me back the telescope.

We walked along the shore towards Balath, Faversham keeping close to the edge of the cliff, while I walked a few feet inland. Suddenly he stopped, and cautiously lying down, peered over the edge.

"Wreckage," he said ; "come and look."

I looked down on the rocks below, and close under the cliff lay a spar, splintered and torn into ribbons. A piece of rope was still hanging to it.

In a few minutes we came to a break in the cliffs, where the land sloped gently down into a little bay. We ran down the slope to the beach, and looked about to see what we could find. I caught sight of a broken piece of plank, evidently wrenched out of some shattered boat. There was a small flag painted on it. We came close up to it and bent over it eagerly. The flag was white with a green cross. I knew it well. I had travelled on the line myself from Persia. The *Silurian* was one of their fastest ships.

We hunted carefully, and it was not long before we found another small piece of the boat. This left no room for doubt in our minds. The letters SILU were painted on it. The rest was missing.

Faversham looked at it thoughtfully.

"It does not prove anything," he said, after a pause. "It is quite likely that the boat was washed overboard."

"You are right," I replied. "And most of this wreckage is from some tramp or small sailing ship ; it is certainly not from a liner."

Faversham picked up the piece of the boat and examined it carefully ; one of the copper rivets was still in the wood, and attached to this were a few threads of some cotton fabric ; he pulled them off and threw away the piece of the boat. Then he took a small white fragment from his waistcoat pocket and compared it with the threads in his hand.

" The same material," he said, holding out the two pieces towards me.

I examined them carefully. He was right. It was undoubtedly of the same material, a soft, unbleached cotton of a yellowish colour.

" Well," I said, " what then ? "

" That is how he came ashore," he replied—" in this boat. I expect the *Silurian* is safe in Glasgow. It must have been a pretty risky journey; the boat is nothing but matchwood now."

" There is not much risk, if a man cannot die," I replied. " Perhaps we shall find something else."

We groped about among the wreckage, and walked a quarter of a mile farther along the shore. We found other .pieces of the boat, and a mast with a fragment of sail still hanging on to it. Then Faversham, who was ahead of me, suddenly stooped down over a great piled-up mass of weed and cordage.

I came up to him, and saw that the heap had a distinct shape. It was long and rounded like a grave. We began to tear the wet tangle away at one end with our hands, until a stern brown face looked out at us with staring eyes. It was the face of Deya, the Hindoo.

We looked at it in horror. Faversham was the first to speak.

" This is murder," he said, in a low voice.

" There is no proof."

" It is murder, I tell you," he repeated ; and he

scraped away more of the weed till the whole body lay exposed to the sunshine.

We examined it for any signs of violence, but beyond a few bruises and scratches, such as the rocks might have inflicted, there was no mark to tell us how the man had met his death.

But I remembered Deya's words after he had cut my bonds. Dacobra had discovered the faithlessness of his servant, and had thought it best to remove all opposition. Doubtless he had many methods of death at his fingers' ends, and the fact that the body bore no traces of violence did not alter my opinion in the least.

"This might have been our fate, Faversham," I said quietly, "if it had not been for this dead man, who saved us. Dacobra is keeping his word; he is fighting to the end."

I looked at the body and felt that this man had sacrificed his life for us, though probably only the fear of one greater than his master had stayed his hand. Poor Deya! he had discovered too late that his master was still powerful, and that the Unknown was not at hand to save him.

We drew the corpse out of the dripping tangle of seaweed, and laid it on the bank of smooth, firm sand. Then as I caught hold of the long scarlet sash that was wound about the man's waist, I felt something small and hard in the folds, and drew it out. It was a key, and when I turned it over and examined it, I laughed and looked along the shore towards Balath.

"There is a joint in every armour, Faversham," I said, with a smile.

"What is that key?" he asked quickly.

"I saw the Hindoo place it in his sash last night, under circumstances that it would be hard to forget. It is the key of the postern door."

"Are you sure?" he said. "Are you sure, Maxwell?"

"I am positive," I replied. "I saw him place it there."

"Thank God!" he said fervently. "Little did Dacobra think that a dead man would be an instrument of vengeance in our hands."

"He may have discovered its loss and secured the door in other ways," I replied.

"It is a chance, Maxwell, a chance! Let me only get face to face with him. If I had only been in your place last night! But I will kill him—I will kill him before to-morrow."

Faversham's mind had been unbalanced of late, and as I looked at his passionate face and twitching lips, I saw that it would be impossible to keep his hands from Dacobra's throat.

I was not altogether sorry, though I knew that the old man's life was in many respects the nobler of the two.

"What shall we do with this?" he went on, pointing to the body.

"Give information to the police at Balgowrie," I replied.

We drew the body a little higher up on the beach

so that the tide could not reach it, and unwinding the scarlet sash, I placed it reverently over the face, securing the ends with two large stones. Then we turned away and made for home.

When we got back to Ardrachan, we despatched another man to Balgowrie with a letter to the inspector of police, and then we had luncheon.

About 2.30 in the afternoon the groom came back with two revolvers; one was a Colt and the other a Webley; both were second hand. He explained that there was no gun shop in the town, but that he had purchased them at a pawnbroker's. We looked at them a little doubtfully, but they seemed good, serviceable weapons, and we spent the afternoon up to sunset practising with them.

We dined very early—six o'clock—and made such preparations as we had to make before dinner. Directly afterwards we rode to the inn, left our horses, and at eight o'clock we stood on the beach together beneath the walls of Balath. We were two desperate men, armed, and driven to the last resources of violence—one fighting for all he held dearest in the world, and the other for his own dim ideas of right and wrong and for the love of his friend. Yet, as I stood there, I thought it would be perhaps kinder to shoot Faversham through the head than to help him in his errand. It would go hard with Dacobra that night if we gained an entrance, but perhaps harder for Fox Faversham if the girl were saved.

Stretching away from our feet, the sea glittered

like black steel in the moonlight, and the white path across it to the horizon seemed to mark out a course for us away from this accursed place. Above our heads the cliffs and castle walls towered gloomy and black against the sky. We looked up at the drawing-room window. All was in blackness. Then, as we stared at the dull iron shutters, a faint glow came from the eye-holes, and in a few seconds a sharp gleam of yellow light. Evidently the lamp had just been lighted.

We stole quickly along the beach to the postern door, avoiding the shingle and creeping from rock to rock. Before we left home Faversham had very sensibly suggested that we should wear shoes with rubber soles. He said they would give us a better foothold for climbing, and would be perfectly noiseless in the house.

I took a feather and a small bottle of oil from my pocket, and carefully oiled the lock.

"Now for our last card, Faversham," I whispered, taking the key from my pocket.

"May it prove the ace of trumps," he replied, watching my movements intently.

I inserted the key in the lock and turned it round. To my surprise it met with no resistance. I turned it several times, but there was no result. There was no click, nor any welcome music of grating wards. I looked at Faversham. He was deathly pale in the moonlight. I stared at him with parted lips and questioning eyes. Then I took the key out of the lock and looked at it. He snatched it from my hand, and as he peered at it eagerly, I saw a gradual look of rage and despair come over his face.

"Look here," he whispered hoarsely, and pointed to the handle of the key. I looked and saw a faint red stain upon the steel. "Blood," he continued, with a laugh — "blood from my own hand. I remember the key well now. I did not look at it when you found it this morning. It is the key of the door in the courtyard; the one I brought back with me from Balath—you remember how I cut my hand—the one that was stolen from the studio last night."

"The game is up then, Faversham," I said gravely.

"There is a door for this key," he replied. "We will go in that way."

"It will take at least an hour from where we are. At any rate, we shall not be able to get over the palisade."

"There is the window."

"It will not be opened again for me to-night," I answered.

He clenched his hands, and I saw the blood running down his lip where he had bitten it.

"I will effect an entrance," he murmured, in a low voice, "if I have to wrench down the door," and catching hold of the iron ring that formed the handle, he threw the strength of his whole body against the solid mass of oak and iron. There was no resistance but the weight of the massive door itself, and it swung so sharply back that he was only just in time to save it from clanging against the stone wall of the passage.

He stood in the entrance, breathless, with a smile of triumph on his face. I sprang to his side and looked at the dark and narrow staircase.

"What does it all mean, Maxwell?" he asked.

"It means victory," I replied, with a laugh.

Then I saw the smile die from his face, and he clutched me by the arm.

"It means that we are too late," he whispered, "and that someone has been in before us."

For a moment I looked at Faversham, in silence. He seemed to have broken down entirely, and paused irresolutely upon the threshold. I stepped past him, and laid my hand upon his arm.

"Come along, Faversham," I said; "follow me, and quietly; I have been this way before. Keep your left hand on the wall and your right on your revolver. You may want it."

I pulled him in after me, and as I closed the door, the last ray of moonlight disappeared and we were in absolute darkness.

I felt my way along the wall to the foot of the stairs. There was not a sound in the house—nothing but impenetrable blackness and silence. Our rubber shoes made no noise on the stone floor, and I could only hear my heart beating like a sledge-hammer, and Faversham breathing between his teeth behind me. I kept my left hand on the wall, and put my right in front of me, moving cautiously up the steps, for I could not remember how many there

s

were, and I did not know when I might strike against the door at the top. The ascent seemed endless, but at last my fingers touched solid wood in front of us, and I stopped. Still there was no sound. The whole place was as silent as a tomb. Faversham stopped behind me, and I felt carefully for the handle of the door. It opened easily, but still into nothing but darkness. To the left, however, I caught a glimmer of light, such as might come through a keyhole, and we moved towards it.

Then suddenly the silence was broken by the report of a pistol fired close at hand. It was followed by another report, then another, and two more in quick succession. Then there was silence, and the smell of gunpowder drifted down the passage into the entrance.

We rushed forward, and I crashed against a door. In a moment I had found the handle and flung the door open. It opened into the drawing-room, and through the drifting clouds of smoke a strange sight lay before our eyes.

CHAPTER XVIII

THE MASTER

WITH his back to the iron shutters and a revolver clutched in his right hand, stood Dacobra. His face was a sickly yellow, and the veins stood out on his wrinkled forehead. His whole attitude was one of tension and terror. I could see the muscles of his neck and hands quiver like tightly strung cords, and he was staring fixedly at a point on the wall opposite him.

I looked to see if there was anything there, but I saw nothing except five little holes in the wall, and they could all have been covered by the rim of a tumbler. They were about four feet off the floor. In another part of the room stood Elaine Rawlins, her beautiful face white as death, and her dark eyes filled with the shadow of some great terror. As we entered, she moved closer to Dacobra's side, and laid her hand upon his arm.

For a few seconds the old man did not seem to notice us, for his eyes were fixed upon the five little holes in the wall. Then he smiled and raised his eyebrows unpleasantly.

"Good evening, gentlemen," he said quietly. "This is an unexpected pleasure."

"Good evening!" Faversham replied, drawing his revolver from his pocket and examining the chambers.

"May I ask—" Dacobra began; but I broke in upon his utterance.

"We have come to thank you for last night, Dacobra," I said, "and also on other business, the nature of which you may perhaps guess. Your door was kindly left open for us, and we took the liberty of walking in."

He moved a step or two towards us, and his lower jaw dropped.

"Left open?" he cried—"the postern door left open? It has not been opened since last night. Then it was not the fancy of my brain? He—"

"Perhaps we come at an inopportune time?" I said politely. "You are expecting someone else?"

"A truce to your fooling!" he cried, snarling like a dog. "I am an unarmed man," and he flung the empty revolver he had taken from me the night before into a corner. "I am unarmed, but I will destroy you both if you are trifling with me. Was the door left open, or do you jest?"

"It was certainly open," Faversham replied, "and I am not trifling with anyone to-night, Dacobra. I have come to take away Miss Rawlins to some place of safety. If I meet with any opposition on your part, I intend to shoot you. Is that plain speaking enough for you?"

Dacobra laughed and turned to the girl.

" What do you wish, Elaine ? " he said. " Would you like to go, or to stay with me ? "

" I will stay with you," she replied, in a clear voice, and looked up into his eyes with so tender an expression of love and devotion that Faversham winced as if a blow had been struck between his eyes.

" You have your answer, Mr. Faversham."

" I require no answer," he replied sternly. " I asked no question, and I ask no one's leave for what I do to-night."

His fingers moved nervously on the butt of his revolver, and his eyes burned with the fire of madness. I laid one hand on his arm, but he shook me off and strode slowly across the room towards the girl.

As he came near to her, I saw Dacobra whisper in her ear. Then he took her face in his hands, and kissed her reverently on the forehead. Faversham stopped and fixed his eyes on the girl's left hand. It was closed, as if she held something, and as he watched she raised it a little from her side. Then she hesitated, and looked at Dacobra. He pulled out his watch.

" It is ten minutes to nine," he said, in a low voice, and then he spoke some words which I could not catch, but his lips seemed to form the word " Good-bye ! "

I knew now what the girl held in her clenched fingers, and stepped quickly forward. She raised her hand to her mouth, but before she touched

her lips Faversham sprang upon her like a flash
of light, and struck her hand aside. Something
small and white fell to the floor, and she gave a
sharp cry of pain. Faversham, in his haste, had
struck with all his force, and the blow must have
been a cruel one.

Dacobra's face grew white with rage, and he made
as though he would spring at Faversham. Then he
turned sharply round and walked across the room
with clenched hands. Elaine drew herself up
proudly, and her eyes flashed. I knew that Faversham would have rather died than have hurt a hair
on her head. He seized hold of one of her hands
and pressed it gently to his lips. She drew it
sharply from his fingers, but I could see the look
of pity in her eyes.

" Forgive me ! " he cried, " forgive me—but it must
not come to that ! "

" You mean well," she answered slowly, as though
it were an effort ; " but this is not worthy of you, Mr.
Faversham. You once said you loved me. If you
still love me, give me the means of death. It is the
only release. I am not afraid to die."

" No, no ! " he cried hoarsely, " I will save you ! I
love you, Elaine ; whoever you are, I love you ! "

" Men have shot those they loved best before
now," she replied, " to save them from worse than
death ! "

" I will save you, and you shall live ! " he cried,
" and no power on earth shall harm you while I have
a hand to lift in your defence ! "

"Fine words!" she said, with a smile.

A look of pain crossed his face.

"No; forgive me," she continued; "I did not mean to sneer at you. I am grateful to you, Mr. Faversham, but I know that in this matter you are powerless. If you have any pity for me, any love, any spark of manliness in you, give me that poison that is on the floor."

For answer, he picked it up and rose to his feet. She held out her hand, and for a moment I thought he was going to restore it to her. I had never seen her look so beautiful before. Her face was almost unearthly in its loveliness, and her eyes seemed to draw out Faversham's very soul as she looked at him. I saw him wrestling for his will against the fascination of her beauty; his lips were parted and his face drawn with agony; the whole contest lasted but a few seconds. Then suddenly he turned his back upon her, and walking to the fire-place, threw the poison into the heart of the flames.

"You coward!" she cried, as he returned to her side and looked her in the face. "You pitiful coward!"

Then she stopped, for she read that in his blood-shot eyes which frightened her—all the passionate desire of his heart, all the determination and longing of weeks breaking forth in one burst of madness.

He seized her by the wrist and drew her to him. I moved forward to interfere, but he cried out to me to open the door, and picked her up bodily in his arms. She did not resist, and her head lay back on his shoulder as if she had fainted. Then Dacobra, who had been busying himself at an escritoire at the far side of the room, and had apparently taken no notice of what was going on, turned round and walked towards us. I noticed that he had a small cardboard box in his hand, and taking out my revolver, I held it so that he could not mistake my intentions.

"Stop, Mr. Faversham," he cried ; "and you need not threaten me, Mr. Maxwell. Let me tell you, for the last time, that you gain nothing by these means." He took out his watch and looked at it. "It is now a matter of minutes. Let me implore you both to fight on my side to-night ; it is the only chance."

"We have our own methods, Dacobra," I replied, " and no confidence in yours. No, stay there ! "

He had moved, and I menaced him with my revolver.

"At least," he said, with a look of agony on his face—" at least, you will let me say good-bye. Remember what this means to me. I am powerless, but I will not leave her side till I have touched her hand again."

"Don't let him come near," cried Faversham. "He will kill her, as he would have killed her before."

"Nonsense, Faversham ! " I said.

I was moved to pity by the sight of the man's face ; it had grown ten years older since last night.

We could hardly refuse a request like this, but it was necessary to be careful.

"Hold out your hands," I said, "and come closer to me."

He did so, and I gave a sharp glance at them to see if he had anything concealed in his palm. His right hand was empty, but in the left lay a small cardboard box.

"What is in that box?" I said.

"You can look," he replied, and I took it from his hand and opened it. It contained nothing but a dead butterfly. It seemed brown and uninteresting, and its wings were closed. "Nothing very deadly, you see," he said, with a smile. "I was merely turning out one of the drawers, and it chanced to be in my hand."

"Put it in your pocket," I said.

I thought, perhaps, some subtle poison might be concealed in its body. He placed it in his waistcoat pocket, and held out his empty hands. I took hold of them and examined them carefully.

"That will do, thank you," I said; "you can say good-bye to her."

He moved to the side of the girl, who still seemed to be unconscious in Faversham's arms, and took hold of her hand. I watched him like a lynx, and half interposed my arm between his other hand and her body. It was not unlikely that he had a weapon concealed about him.

For a moment there was absolute silence. Then I heard a sound behind me like the patter of a small foot, then a click, and then a thud. I was standing with my back to the door and turned sharply round. For the tenth part of a second I saw a flash of white in the darkness of the passage, and I heard the sound of something pattering softly down the corridor. I rushed out into the darkness and listened. There was nothing to be seen or heard, and I came back into the room.

"Did you see anything, Faversham?" I cried.

"Nothing," he replied. "What is it?"

"Nothing of any importance," I said, and I looked at Dacobra.

He was gazing intently at the girl's face, and did not move. He did not seem to have heard or seen anything.

"Good-bye, Elaine," he said, "good-bye," and he pressed his lips to her fingers for a minute.

She opened her eyes and struggled feebly in Faversham's arms. The old man slipped his left hand into his waistcoat pocket, and drawing out his watch, looked at the time. Then he replaced it, and kept his fingers in his pocket for a few seconds. His right hand was still holding the girl's wrist, as if he were feeling her pulse.

Then suddenly she ceased to struggle, and a deep sigh escaped her lips. Her head sank gradually on Faversham's shoulder. Dacobra kissed her hand once again with reverence, and walked to the other side of the room into the shadow of a distant corner. I looked at the girl's face, and started back with a cry of horror. It was drawn and changed, and perfectly white, like marble; the jaw had dropped slightly; the eyelids were open, and the eyes staring horribly at nothing.

" Look at her, Faversham! Look at her face! "

He had not noticed the change, for her head was upon his shoulder. He glanced quickly at her, and at once carried her to the sofa. Then he laid one hand on her heart, and the other on her pulse at her wrist. For half a minute he stayed thus. Then he rose to his feet with a look of horror.

" She is dead! " he cried hoarsely. " Her heart is perfectly still! "

" Yes," said a voice from the other side of the room. " She is dead," and Dacobra advanced into the light, holding the small cardboard box in his hand. " Yes, she is dead," he repeated, crossing over to the couch, " but the life is still here. I can crush it between my finger and thumb."

We did not answer him, and in the silence I heard the faint rustling of wings within the box. This was the first manifestation we had witnessed of the powers which we half doubted. He had outwitted us. We had forgotten these powers in the excitement of a purely physical contest. Faversham made a step towards him, and levelled his revolver at his head.

" Give her back her life," he cried, " or I will kill you like a dog."

Dacobra smiled.

" Do you think I care for my life? " he answered quietly.

We were silent. We knew he cared nothing, now

that she was dead.   He held the box firmly in his hand, and even if he were killed he would probably crush the life within it in the agonies of death. Besides, what would it matter if he failed to do this. He alone could restore life to the girl, and his death would remove our last chance.   Faversham lowered his hand, and I scowled in silence.   We were defeated.

" Swear to me," Dacobra said, laying one hand on Elaine's forehead—" swear to me that you will fight on my side to-night, and that you will make no attempt to take her from me, and I will give her back her life."

We hesitated, and I wondered why he did not let the life go from her there and then.   But I did not reckon on the natural man, which instinctively clings to existence until it is torn from him. ·

Dacobra took out his watch.

" In less than two minutes it will be out of my power to take or restore this life.   The sands in the glass are nearly run out."

I looked at Faversham, and read his answer in his eyes.

" I swear," he said, " by all I hold most sacred, to fight on your side to-night."

I repeated the same words ; it was useless to do otherwise ; the man had us in his power.

He laid his hand again on the girl's forehead, and gradually a faint flush came into her cheeks, and her bosom moved slightly ; then she opened her eyes and heaved a deep sigh ; but she closed them again, and had all the appearance of one wrapped in a peaceful sleep.

" Now, what is to be done ? " Faversham exclaimed quickly.

Dacobra did not answer, and appeared to be listening for something.

" Did you hear it ? " he said. " The sound of the sea ! "

I went across the room to the door, and looked down the passage. All was silent, and my eyes peered into the darkness in vain for the sight of something. Then I heard a low murmur come through the stone corridors, as if the postern door had been opened. It died away again, and I thought I heard a faint shuffling sound. It came nearer and nearer, and then I heard a series of clicks, such as boots would make on a stone floor.

" Lock the door ! " cried Dacobra ; but a strange paralysis seemed to have seized my brain for the moment, and I could not move.

Then I recovered myself, banged the door to with a crash, and put my hand down to the key to turn it. It was not there.

" The key is gone ! " I cried, " yet I could swear that it was there when we entered the room."

Then I remembered the faint sound I had heard, and the flash of white I had seen a few minutes ago. We had been outwitted. Dacobra clenched his hands in wrath, and crossed the room to the dark shadow of a corner. I heard a faint scratching on the pane, and a moment later the handle of the door turned.

I threw all my weight against the solid oak, but it began to move slowly and persistently forward. There appeared to be no violence exerted; only a slow, steady pressure that moved me back inch by inch. I set my teeth and beckoned to Faversham, but he was standing by the side of Elaine with his revolver pointed at the widening crack. I drew back suddenly and retreated a yard or two into the room. The door ceased to move, and through the opening hopped a little white monkey, but there did not seem to be anything else in the darkness. Faversham covered it, but I called out to him to save his cartridges. The animal came into the room and looked round timidly; then it ran suddenly under the sofa, as if frightened. Dacobra still sat in the shadow of the corner, and Faversham and I both gripped our revolvers in our hands, and watched the half-open door.

Then I saw a hand come slowly round the edge of the doorway—a small, white, skinny hand, feeling the wood-work up and down as though uncertain whether it had found what it wanted. Then the figure of a small man, clothed in some white costume, appeared in the entrance, and then the other hand felt the other side of the doorway. I gazed at the face in horror. It was the face of a man, who, judging from his shrivelled and wrinkled appearance, might have seen centuries pass over his head. It was white as the whiteness of leprosy, and absolutely hairless; it was more like a skull than anything else. The eyeballs were colourless, and seemed as if they were covered

with some sort of scale. They were evidently sightless, for the thing shuffled forward inch by inch, and
felt its way along the wall like a blind man. I
shuddered. I was not exactly afraid, but the sight
was so unlike anything I had ever seen before. I felt
that I could not touch this creature; it seemed so
loathsome. Dacobra was cowering in the shadow,
and his eyes were turned from it. We were all three
silent. I saw Faversham's hand steal quietly to his
pocket as the White Priest moved slowly towards the
sofa with groping hands, passing from chair to chair
with some unerring instinct. Then the silence was
broken with a cry, and Dacobra sprang from the
corner and stood between the couch and the
advancing figure.

The White Priest stopped. For a moment the
spell seemed to be lifted from me, and I stepped to
Dacobra's side.

"What do you want?" I said sternly. "Who are
you? Why are you here? This is England, and no
one can enter another's house without the owner's
consent."

To my surprise the answer came in perfect English,
but the voice was like some echo from a distant hill.

"Young man," he said, "it is you who should not
be here. As for your questions, I want that which is
my own. I am one who is able to take it. I am
here because what I want is here, and I enter where
I will. Dacobra, we meet again," and stretching out
his skinny hand, he laid it upon the sleeve of Dacobra's
coat.

The latter shrank back imperceptibly, but his courage returned to him.

"We meet again, my lord," he said.

"Yet I was old when thou wert young, Dacobra."

"And I am old and thou art eternal," Dacobra replied mechanically, as if chanting some response.

"I am here to take my own."

"To take thine own," he repeated.

"To take the price."

"The price I give willingly."

"Yet not so willingly that which thou hast bought."

Dacobra was silent. I watched the agony on his face, and in spite of all the injury he had tried to do me, I swore a vow to myself to stand by him to the last. I realised now his love for the soul of this woman, and how it was that he had stopped short at nothing—not even murder—to keep it by his side. I wondered that he did not seize the wretched little object before him, and crush the life out of it; but then I remembered the strength that had been exerted to open the door.

"You are silent, Dacobra," the Priest continued; "yet I can read your answer. I need no eyes to read your thoughts. For sixty-three years, Dacobra, for sixty-three years. You made the bargain. What do you desire?"

"Peace, my lord, peace—not for myself, but for this soul which I love."

"There is no peace," was the stern reply—"no peace for those who have given themselves to us.

We have no power to compel the gift; but the gift that is given we keep for ever."

Faversham laughed.

"Let those take who have the power," he said lightly, taking his revolver from his pocket and tapping the barrel affectionately, "and let those keep who can."

A faint smile passed over the inscrutable white face of the Priest.

"Another?" he said. "Is this a feast, Dacobra, that you have gathered your friends together?"

"They are not my friends, my lord," Dacobra answered, "and if it had not been for their folly, we should have escaped you to-night."

"Is that the truth, Dacobra?"

"That is the truth, my lord," he answered, "for I should have slain her and let this soul pass forth into the night, where even you could not have followed it."

Again a smile appeared on the white, wrinkled countenance.

"Did you love her so much, Dacobra?"

"Aye, my lord, so much that I put off her death till it was too late. Yet they are on my side to-night."

"They are on your side to-night?" echoed the little voice. "You are honoured," and he once more spread his hands in front of him and moved towards the sofa.

I divined his intention, and catching hold of his arm, tried to swing him back. The force I exerted

T

was terrific, and I thought I should have dashed him against the opposite wall ; but the arm felt like the arm of a marble statue, and the little figure did not sway an inch. I am a fairly strong man, and I strained every muscle in my body, but with absolutely no result. Then quick as lightning I loosed my grip on his arm and whipped out my revolver. But there was a quicker hand than mine. There was a flash and a report, and a cloud of smoke drifted across the room. When it had passed, I saw the White Priest standing by the side of the girl with his hand upon her forehead, Faversham with the smoking revolver in his hand still pointed at the Priest, and on the wall a small hole about four feet from the ground.

Both our revolvers were pointed at the loathsome object by the couch. Our fingers were on the triggers, but we both paused, for we were looking at Elaine's face. It was white and drawn, and the jaw seemed to have dropped a little. And then something that glittered on the Priest's arm seemed to catch our eyes : Two bright jewels, and a glistening coil that moved and began to unwind itself. I caught hold of Faversham's arm.

"We are too late!" I cried hoarsely. "It is all over."

"Not yet," Faversham replied, in a low voice.

Only Dacobra was silent, but his face was like the face of a wild beast driven into a corner. His upper lip was drawn slightly back, and his yellow teeth protruded like fangs. There was a slight foam at the corners of his mouth; his fingers were curved like talons; his eyes were red with fury and despair, and I doubted if even his fear would keep him from springing at his master's throat.

The White Priest moved towards the door, holding out one of his hands to find the way. Again we saw the glitter of the snake's eyes and the movement of its thin body, and I think the same thought struck all three of us like a flash. Dacobra sprang forward and clutched at the reptile, but the Priest laid hold of his arm, and swinging him round, hurled him against the wall with such force that he fell in a heap on the floor. He lay there for a second motionless; then he raised himself painfully to his feet, and staggering to the door, leant against it and gasped for breath. The Priest moved towards him.

" Fire ! " Faversham cried to me. " Fire, and kill it ! The soul shall at least be free. Kill the snake ! "

It was our last chance. We knew the girl was lost to us, for the dead body was lying before our eyes, and I knew no power of ours could force the white devil to restore her life. We knew he was resistless, eternal, indestructible ; and we saw that he was within a few feet of the door, bearing out that sweet soul and life into the eternal night of his devilries, to be tossed on from century to century in unrest. But at least we could save it from that.

I fired at the jewelled eyes and missed. The White Priest drew the reptile into the folds of his garment. Again we fired—once—twice—thrice

again, straight at the spot where the skinny hand
was thrust into the white robe. The bullets cut the
linen into shreds, and passing clean through the
creature's body, drove out little spurts of plaster
from the wall behind. He moved quickly in front
of Dacobra and smiled. I had two shots left in my
revolver ; Faversham had one in his. We paused,
for we saw we must kill Dacobra if we fired again.
He was crouching against the door, and glaring at
us. Faversham looked at me, as if asking some
question, and slipped five more cartridges into his
weapon. I refilled mine. And still the White Priest
smiled.

Dacobra crouched down as if to spring. But some
unseen hand seemed to have pinned him to the door.
He struggled and shrieked like a madman, raising
his hands above his head and clutching at the air.

The White Priest moved a foot nearer to him.

"Fire!" the old man shrieked. "Fire, you accursed
fools! Fire! Can't you fire! Kill it! Kill us
both! Quick! it will be too late! Fire, you
fools! Do you think I shall live an hour after it
has gone? Kill it! Kill us both! For the sake
of your love, your religion, your honour, your God,
fire! I implore you, fire!" and he pressed his hands
before his eyes.

We raised our weapons, but hesitated for a
moment as the White Priest drew his arm from
under his robe, and felt the snake's body with his
fingers. Then we saw that one of the bullets had
almost cut it in half. He turned to us.

"Let there be peace," he said. "I will restore the maiden her life."

We all three stood in silence. He groped his way back to the couch, and laid his hand on the girl's head.

In a few seconds the snake uncoiled itself, and dropped lifeless to the floor. We had not been a moment too soon. A faint flush came into the girl's face. She opened her eyes for a few seconds, then she sighed and closed them again.

The Priest seated himself by her side.

"Let there be peace," he said harshly, "and let us talk this matter over."

Faversham and I walked away from the door, and sat down about a couple of yards from the couch.

Dacobra crawled slowly across the room into a corner, and leant his arm upon a strange piece of furniture, which I had noticed several times before when I had been in the room. It was an old German cask of black oak, beautifully polished and mounted with silver. It appeared to serve no purpose, and to be merely an ornamental curiosity.

"We have conquered!" Faversham cried exultingly. "We have conquered! He's beaten, and he owns it."

"I think we have put an end to his tricks," I said sternly, with my finger still on the trigger of my revolver.

"No," the Priest said quietly, "the end has not come yet." Then he called out a single word in some language I did not understand.

In reply there was a faint shuffling and scraping

under the couch, and a moment later a small white
monkey crawled out into the light, blinked its eyes,
and scrambled up on to the Priest's knee. I had
forgotten that it was in the room, and at once made
up my mind to kill it at the first opportunity.

The Priest caressed it gently with his hands, and
it waved its tail. We watched him in silence, but
alert to stop any fresh movement in the game. Then
suddenly the animal gave a fearful screech, and I saw
that the bony fingers had tightened round its throat
till they seemed to be completely buried in white fur ;
then there was a faint gurgling noise ; then silence.
The Priest continued to caress the head, but I noticed
that the body was very limp and absolutely motionless.
The animal was evidently dead.

I at once perceived his object. He thought to try
and carry away the girl's life and soul in this form, but
it would be easier to kill the monkey than the snake.
I laughed aloud.

"Dacobra !" said the Priest, in a low voice.

The old man was still standing in the corner, leaning his head on his hands ; but when his name was
called, he came slowly forward, and I saw that he was
clutching something tightly in his hand. At the same
time I noticed a very faint smell which I seemed to
recognise, but I could not quite remember what it
reminded me of.

"Dacobra," the Priest repeated, "the time has
come."

"It has come, my master," he answered wearily.

"Dacobra," the Priest said, "it is farewell."

The old man pulled himself together and crossed the room, as if in a dream. He reached the couch, and falling on his knees beside it, took one of the girl's hands in his own and kissed it tenderly.

"Let her wake!" he moaned. "Let her soul wake into her eyes and look at me."

But the girl still slept. Dacobra caressed her forehead, and, smoothing back the dark ruffled hair, looked with agony at the closed eyelids, as if he would force them asunder.

The wind was rising again, and it moaned round the house and rattled the shutters. I heard a door bang in some distant corridor. We neither of us spoke, but we watched Dacobra. The expression on his face was terrible, as he gazed into those closed eyes. Then he turned on his knees to the Priest and clasped his hands.

"Is it farewell, my master?"

"Yes, Dacobra, it is farewell. It is the hour for the price to be paid."

"I pay it gladly, if she will but look at me. For pity's sake, great master, let her look at me!"

The Priest stretched out his white hand—it looked like a hand of bleached bone—and felt along the couch till he reached the girl's face. He passed his fingers gently over her eyelids, and she opened them. Dacobra bent forward and looked into the open eyes, as if he would draw the very soul out of their depths.

"Good-bye," the old man said hoarsely; "good-bye, my child. I could have given you freedom, if they had not stayed my hand. But though we spend our eternity in bondage, at least we shall be together."

The girl did not speak. She looked into his eyes and did not seem to notice that there was anyone else in the room but him. Then she raised her hands and drew his face closer to her own. I do not know what he saw in her eyes, but his features were suddenly lit up with the sunshine of a great joy, and he kissed her on the lips. As he did so, she closed her eyes again.

Dacobra rose from his knees, and crossing over to where I stood, put his lips to my ear.

"When the end comes," he whispered, "set fire to the place. It will burn well."

Then he walked across the room to where the picture hung on the wall.

"I leave her to you," he said, turning to Faversham; "you will save her."

Then he buried his face in his hands. If I had not guessed what he held in his fingers, I should have thought that he was praying. He stayed in the same position for quite a minute. Then he put up both of his hands and touched that other face—the face of the girl he had loved sixty-three years ago on the wild slopes of the Kohrud Mountains, and whose soul was still near him in this hour.

We watched him intently, wondering if we could save him. Then suddenly his body swayed forward, his fingers seemed to curve and dig into the picture, and he sank to the floor, rending and tearing the canvas into pieces as he fell.

But directly his body touched the ground and he began to writhe in the agonies of death, the White Priest passed by us like a flash of light, and, stooping over him, laid his hand on one of the twitching arms. The body suddenly stiffened and lay quite still. Death had been quick, but we knew that it had not been quick enough ; for as the Priest rose, something white sprang from his arms and hopped away into a dark corner. We rushed across the room and looked for it, hoping to kill it, and show this last mercy to the dead man. However, it was in vain. The animal had either gone out of the door, or had effectually concealed itself. But, wherever it was, we knew that there too was the soul and the life of Dacobra.

CHAPTER XIX

HOW DEATH WROUGHT VICTORY

WE turned from the lifeless body and looked at the Priest sitting by the couch. His face was calm and impassive as a mask of bone. I threw myself down in a chair, and, burying my face in my hands, ran a dozen schemes over in my mind for the rescue of the girl, and cast them one by one aside as useless. Force had only produced a deadlock, and though neither side could claim the victory, it seemed unlikely that we should retain our advantage for long. It only remained to resort to cunning, and in this respect the accumulated wisdom of centuries might well prevail.

The Priest's sightless eyes were fixed steadfastly on us, and for quite five minutes no one spoke. Fox Faversham was still standing and looking at the body of Dacobra. He was very pale, and his fingers were playing with the butt of his revolver. Then he suddenly turned round to me and smiled.

" Well, Faversham ? " I said.

He crossed over to me and sat down. He had apparently solved the problem, for he looked quite cheerful.

"What are you going to do, you devil?" he said sharply, turning to the White Priest.

"I am going to take my own," was the quiet reply.

"We have stopped you once," Faversham said grimly, "and we shall stop you again."

"I can wait my time."

"You must have plenty of time on your hands," Faversham replied. "Look here, Sir Priest, you will never leave this room with the life of that girl. You have had a taste of what we can do. And as sure as there is a God above you and your little devilries, we will destroy the life you hold, rather than let it pass into your hands again," and as he spoke, his face grew hard and set, as if with some fixed resolution.

The old Priest looked at him with his sightless eyes, but did not speak.

"You know that we are two resolute men," Faversham continued, rising from his seat, "and I should advise you to come to terms with us."

"You saw Dacobra die," the Priest said meaningly.

"His life was in your power," I replied. "He gave it of his own free will sixty-three years ago; but you have no power over us, and you know it, or you would never have let us live for five seconds after we first thwarted you. You are right, Faversham; the game is in our hands."

"What are your terms?" the Priest said, laying his hand gently on the girl's wrist.

"That you give up all claim to this life," I replied.

"Yes," said the Priest, "and what do you give me in return?"

"We will not prevent you from leaving this house, or from returning to your own country," I answered.

The old man's face wrinkled with laughter.

"Have you nothing better to offer than that?" he said, moving his head towards Faversham.

"Yes," Faversham replied slowly; "I have something better to offer than that."

He rose, and walking over to the other side of the couch, looked steadfastly at the girl's face. The Priest's sightless eyes followed him, and one skinny hand stretched across the couch and touched the sleeve of his right arm.

"Yes," Faversham repeated, looking the old man full in the face, "I have something better to offer than that. Will you take it?"

"If it is worth the taking," the Priest replied, and the wrinkled hand seemed to close more tightly on Faversham's arm.

I noticed that my friend's fingers had once or twice moved slightly towards the pocket which held his revolver, and saw plainly by the tightening of the muscles on the Priest's hand, that a quiet force was being exerted to hold them back.

"It will be as useful for your purposes," Faversham said, in a low voice; then he whispered some words which I could not catch.

"Come, Faversham," I said, "there must be no secrets in this matter."

He did not look at me, but kept his eyes anxiously fixed on the Priest. The wrinkled face was still inscrutable, but I saw the hand close more firmly on

Faversham's wrist, and a twinge of pain crossed the latter's face.

"Well," Faversham said sharply, "will you take it?"

"You realise what it means?"

"Yes, yes; I know what it means. Will you take it?"

"I will take it," the Priest said quietly.

"And she will be absolutely free?"

"She shall be absolutely free."

"How shall I know that?" Faversham said.

"I will swear it to you," the Priest replied.

Faversham laughed. "And you will take the price now?" he said.

"I will take it now."

"It is a bargain," said Faversham.

I could stand it no longer. I walked over to him, and catching him by the shoulder, swung his face round to mine and looked into his eyes. I read the truth there in a flash.

"No, Faversham," I cried. "A thousand times, no! You shall not do it. What is her life to you? The woman you love is dead."

"Yes," he broke in sharply, "the woman I love is dead, but I love her still, and I— My dear old chap, don't look at me like that; it will be rather a joke."

"Don't be a fool, Faversham," I said. "There is no jesting with this sort of thing."

"A conjuring trick, my dear fellow," he replied. "You don't think I am afraid of this—this charlatan."

"You are mad, Faversham!" I cried. "Come away!" and I caught him by the arm and pulled him to his feet. "Come away," I repeated. "Come to the other side of the room. Let us talk things over quietly."

He raised his hand to my chest and gave me a push which sent me staggering backwards.

"Leave me alone, Maxwell," he said sternly; "I am not a child. I am ready," he said, turning to the Priest and looking at him intently.

But, as he looked, I saw a sudden change come over his expression. He did not move or speak for quite two minutes, and seemed to be turning over something in his mind. I moved a step nearer to him and gripped him tightly by the arm.

"An end to this fooling, Faversham," I said; "or must I stop you by force?"

For answer, he whispered into the Priest's ear, and the bony fingers loosed their hold on his wrist. Then his hand went quickly to his side, and in another second I was looking down the muzzle of his revolver. I stepped sharply back. His brain was undoubtedly turned.

The Priest chuckled to himself and rubbed his hands together quietly. He was evidently amused at the strife that had arisen beteween his antagonists. But the look on Faversham's face suddenly changed, and I saw a faint smile at the corners of his mouth. Then like a flash he flung himself across the girl's body, and fired his revolver three times into her left side. She was dead in a second. His threats

towards me had been simply a ruse. The priest
was defeated

I was struck dumb and immovable with horror.
I had not dreamt of anything like this. But
Faversham rose to his feet with a smile of triumph,
and his eyes glittered like the eyes of a madman.

"A murderer!" he cried. "A murderer! I could
not trust him. I offered my soul for hers, and would
have given it, if I could have trusted him. But I
could not trust him. At the last moment I read his
face and saw the truth. He would have enslaved us
both. As it is, we are both free."

The pistol spoke again, and he lurched heavily
forward.

As he fell, his arm caught the standard lamp and
hurled it with a crash to the ground. A hot flame
leaped up and singed my eyebrows. I sprang back
and saw little rivers of fire run along the carpet
and blue flashes of flame flicker up the curtains.
In less than a minute the whole room was in a
blaze. I could not make out what had happened.
The mere breaking of a lamp could not possibly
have produced so sudden a conflagration. Then
I remembered the faint smell I had perceived
ever since Dacobra had crossed the room a few
minutes before he died. I put my hand to part of
the floor that was not yet alight. It was quite
damp; and, raising my hand to my nostrils, I learnt
the truth. The carpet was soaked with petroleum.
In the excitement of the last few minutes we had
noticed nothing, except the main object upon which

our minds had been centred, and I had given no second thought to the faint, sickly odour which pervaded the atmosphere.

But there was no time to think of the cause. The whole place had instantly become a furnace. Something white and furry dashed blindly against me, shrieking with pain, and I saw through the smoke that one side of it was black and burnt. I backed to the wall, and, coughing and gasping for breath, felt swiftly along it for the door. I stumbled over a chair, crashed into a cabinet, and fell to the ground. I was on my feet in a second, and felt my senses going. I could not breathe. Then a rush of air swept through the room and carried the fumes and smoke along with it; the door had evidently been opened. And in the clearing atmosphere I saw a dim figure crawl from the ground, and, flinging itself upon the burning couch, catch something in its arms.

I dashed in the direction of the current with my arm before my face, and came crashing against the wall. I stretched out my right hand, clutching for something to draw me out of this awful hell. There was nothing but wall—wall—wall! It was a burning tomb! I sank to my knees and crawled like a crab to the right, my nails cutting ridges in the wall-paper as I went. Then my right hand slipped over the edge into space. I was saved! I sprang to my feet and dashed through the opening, only to fall back stunned and bruised on to the floor. It was not the door—only the recess by the window. For a second or two I lay motionless, the hot smoke choking the life out of me. Then I stretched out my hand and touched a face, and my fingers caught in some long hair. It was Elaine. I raised myself up and moved my hand until I touched another face.

Then, for one moment, God gave me sense to think of others than myself. The girl was dead, with three bullets in her heart. But I remembered that Faversham had had sufficient life in him to crawl a few feet nearer the couch. It was possible that he was not mortally wounded, and I resolved to save him if I had strength to do it. It was a tremendous task. I doubted if I should even escape with my own life. I was weakened and blinded with smoke, and Faversham was a big man. However, I laid one hand on the collar of his coat, and dragged him from the side of the couch.

Then a flash of knowledge came into my dizzy brain. I remembered that the door was almost opposite the recess by the window. The centre of the room was a flaming furnace, but I had to face it. With every muscle in my body strained to its utmost, I held my breath and dashed into the heart of the flames, dragging my burden after me, and sweeping burning furniture out from my path. My very hair blazed on my head ; the skin seemed to shrivel up on my face, and the agony was terrible. In about five seconds—it seemed a week—my hand caught on the opening of the door, and swinging out into the passage, I stumbled along it, found the handle of another door, and drew in a long breath of cooler air. Then I stooped, and lifting Faversham's limp body in my arms, descended the stone staircase. The smoke poured after me in volumes, and the sparks swept past me into the darkness. Then at last, shaken and trembling, I reached the bottom, and stretching out my hand, struck the cold iron of the postern. door. I found the handle, and wrenching the door open with all my strength, passed through it and saw the stars of heaven. I was on the beach, and the cool air was on my face.

I laid Faversham on the stones, and shutting my eyes, tried to think. For a few moments I could think of nothing but that the whole world was burning, that the ground was hot beneath my feet, and the heavens a lurid furnace of smoke and flame. I sank on the stones and buried my face in my hands.

Then I began to collect my thoughts. I heard the splashing of the waves on the beach, and the grating of the pebbles as they were driven backwards and forwards by the tide. The wind carried a shower of spray over me. The moon was shining on the sea in the distance ; but close to the shore the waters were as black as night. I looked up and saw a vast pall of smoke wreathing and whirling above my head, and the sparks dancing away in the darkness. I remembered then ! All that was left of Elaine and Dacobra was in that hell of smoke and flame ! The best thing for both of them had happened. They were dead, and the fire had hidden the story of their death.

Then I looked at my feet and saw the motionless body of Fox Faversham. I knelt beside him and laid my hand on his heart. It still beat, though feebly; and I could see in the moonlight that the blood was trickling from his blackened face. It was as I had thought possible; the flesh was torn away from his scalp, but the bullet had glanced off, and failed to penetrate his brain.

I rose to my feet, and not till then did I realise what I had been through. One of my sleeves dropped from my coat—a mere charred rag. My hands were raw and bleeding, and every part of my body seemed to be racked with scorching pains. I tried to move towards the sea to get some water to revive Faversham, but my limbs seemed powerless. Then something dropped from my pocket with a clang on the pebbles. It was my revolver. The pocket had been completely burnt through. The dim idea came into my brain that I ought to conceal all traces of this night's work. I stopped and picked up the weapon from the pebbles, and exerting all my strength, flung it as far as I could into the sea. Then I tried to call for help, but my tongue was parched, and my throat dried up with the smoke.

Then, as in a dream, I heard the shouts of voices on the top of the cliff, and saw lanterns dancing above my head like will-o'-the-wisps. Then the roar of the sea seemed to rise and swell in my ears like thunder, and all was darkness.

CHAPTER XX

THE END

IT was six weeks before I was convalescent, and even then poor Faversham was not able to leave his bed. We had both been terribly burned, but he had the additional disadvantage of a wound in the head, and the anguish of his mind must have severely retarded his progress. The doctor had refused to allow either of us to be examined by the police ; but when I was sufficiently well to give evidence, an inquest was held on such poor fragments as they recovered from the ruins.

The story I told was simple enough. It was the truth, if not the entire truth. An overturned lamp ; a barrel of petroleum, for some unexplained reason kept in the room ; a few quick flames ; a general blaze ; and then, in less than a minute, a furnace in which nothing could have lived !

And so Elaine and Dacobra passed out of our lives—the former, young, beautiful, and I think the noblest woman in her perfect trust and self-sacrifice that it has ever been my fortune to meet ; the latter, old and wrinkled, with the curse of a thousand crimes on his soul, and with but one virtue to set against them ; yet both bound together in life and death by a strange and mystic bond, the nature of which lies beyond the explanation of human mind and human science.

I only relate that which I have seen with my eyes. I have set forth in plain language the simple facts; but I have neither the power nor the inclination to offer any satisfactory explanation of them.

It is enough that the tragedy left its mark on both our lives. Faversham was never the same man again, though I think he realised that the best thing had happened. After that day his youth left him, and he never knew that calm resignation into which he had schooled himself after the first death of Alice Borrodaile. But he plunged like a man into his work, and I think the world has gained by the depth of his sorrow, and that he has left behind him a name which will always be remembered.

Such poor ashes as were recovered from the ruins received a Christian burial in the churchyard at Balath.

We placed a plain granite column, hewn from the rocks which faced the sea, to mark the place where they lay. But three years afterwards the lightning struck it and broke it into two pieces ; and so I believe it remains till this day—a witness of the hand of God. Yet I do not doubt that one of those souls, at any rate, has found rest.

And yet one thing more. The statue on which I had bestowed so much skill and labour was never destined to add to the reputation of its creator. The

night before my departure for London—I had
decided to leave Ardrachan for good—I was
awakened from a troubled sleep by a voice calling
my name.   Then, as I sat up in bed with a start, I
heard a distant crash and a thud.   The noise seemed
to come from the studio, and though a strange fear
haunted me, I felt I must find out what was the
matter.   I got up, lighted a candle, and putting on a
pair of trousers, slipped a loaded revolver into my
pocket and went out on to the landing.   I proceeded
softly along the passage leading to the studio, and
stopped to listen outside the door.   Nothing stirred
within, and with a beating heart I unlocked the door
and pushed it open.   Then I saw what had happened.
The statue of Elaine Rawlins was shattered into
pieces on the floor.   I glanced sharply round the
room ; there was no one there.   I examined the
windows ; they were closed.   I lit two or three more
candles, and looked more carefully ; there was no
sign of any living thing.   There was absolute silence,
and the dust of several weeks lay undisturbed over
everything.   There was no footprint nor a sign that
anyone beside myself had entered the room since I
last was in it.   But on the floor lay the greatest work
I had yet accomplished, dashed into fifty pieces.

I stooped down and looked at the fragments.   To
my surprise I saw that they were slightly stained and
discoloured, as though the weather had rotted the
stone.   I took a piece in my hand, and as I looked at
it, I gave a cry of surprise, for it crumbled away
in my fingers like a lump of dried mud.   It was

absolutely decayed. Then I remembered Dacobra's words: "I have not discovered the secret of life, but the secret of death."

I crossed the room to the window and looked out into the garden. A long avenue of trees stretched away from the house on this side, and down the avenue moved the dark shadow of a small cloud crossing the moon. But I looked at the face of the moon and saw that it was shining clearly in a cloudless sky. But closer the shadow came, and still closer, till the darkness touched the lawn beneath the window-sill. Then, for one brief moment, a terrible face was pressed against the glass, close to mine. It was the face of Deva Dacobra, and I saw in the fierce anguish of his eyes that his soul had found no rest.

THE END

www.ingramcontent.com/pod-product-compliance
Lightning Source LLC
Chambersburg PA
CBHW030934260626
47169CB00002B/471